AFTER THE WINTER

AFTER THE WINTER

Guadalupe Nettel

Translated by Rosalind Harvey

COFFEE HOUSE PRESS

Minneapolis

2018

First published in Spanish as *Después del invierno* by Editorial Anagrama,
Barcelona, Spain, in 2014. First published in English by
MacLehose Press, Great Britain, in 2018.

Coffee House Press books are available to the trade through our primary distributor, Consortium Book Sales & Distribution, cbsd.com or (800) 283-3572. For personal orders, catalogs, or other information, write to info@coffeehousepress.org.

Coffee House Press is a nonprofit literary publishing house. Support from private foundations, corporate giving programs, government programs, and generous individuals helps make the publication of our books possible. We gratefully acknowledge their support in detail in the back of this book.

LIBRARY OF CONGRESS CATALOGING-IN-PUBLICATION DATA

Names: Nettel, Guadalupe, 1973– author. | Harvey, Rosalind, 1982– translator.
Title: After the winter / Guadalupe Nettel ; translated by Rosalind Harvey.
Other titles: Después del invierno. English
Description: First U.S. edition. | Minneapolis : Coffee House Press, 2018.
Identifiers: LCCN 2018004536 | ISBN 9781566895255 (trade pbk.)
Classification: LCC PQ7298.424.E76 D4713 2018 | DDC 863/.7—dc23
LC record available at https://lccn.loc.gov/2018004536

ACKNOWLEDGMENTS

Lines from the poem "Ed è subito sera" are from *Tutte le poesie* by Salvatore
Quasimodo, © 1942. Published by Arnoldo Mondadori Editore, S.p.A.

Excerpt from *Trilce* by César Vallejo was translated by Clayton Eshleman,
© 1992. Published by Wesleyan University Press. Used by permission.

PRINTED IN THE UNITED STATES OF AMERICA
25 24 23 22 21 20 19 18   1 2 3 4 5 6 7 8

To Ian, in memoriam.
And to my father, who has fought so hard.

CONTENTS

I

II

Et de longs corbillards, sans tambours ni musique,
Défilent lentement dans mon âme; l'Espoir,
Vaincu, pleure, et l'Angoisse atroce, despotique,
Sur mon crâne incliné plante son drapeau noir.

CHARLES BAUDELAIRE

When people are about to die, all they want to do is fuck.

ROBERTO BOLAÑO

AFTER THE WINTER

I

CLAUDIO

My apartment is on 87th Street on the Upper West Side in New York City. It is a stone corridor very much like a prison cell. I have no plants. All living things inspire in me an inexplicable horror, just as some people feel when they come across a nest of spiders. I find living things threatening; you have to take care of them or they die. In short, they take up time and attention, and I am not prepared to give those away to anyone. Although I do at times manage to enjoy it here, this city, if you let it, can end up being maddening. In order to protect myself from the chaos, I have imposed on my daily life a very strict set of habits and restrictions. Among them is the absolute privacy of my lair. Since I moved in, no feet other than mine have crossed the threshold of this apartment. The very idea that someone else might walk upon this floor can unhinge me. I am not always proud of the way I am. There are days when I yearn for a family, a discreet and silent wife, a child, preferably a mute one. The week I arrived I spoke to the other residents in the building—most of them immigrants—to make the rules clear. I requested, politely, with a hint of a threat, that they abstain from making the slightest noise after 9:00 p.m., the time I usually come home from work. So far, my request has been respected. In the two years I have lived here, no one has ever held a party in the building. But it also means that I am obligated to assume certain responsibilities. I have forced myself, for instance, to develop the habit of listening to music only through headphones, and to whisper into the mouthpiece if I use the telephone (whose ringer I have turned down, as with the answering machine's). Once a day, at an almost imperceptible volume, I check my messages—very few, as it happens. Most of the time they are from Ruth, even though I have asked her several times never to call and instead to wait until I do so.

I bought this apartment for a good reason: the price. The first time I viewed it and the woman from the real estate agency uttered the amount, I felt a tingling in my stomach: at last I would be able to own something in Manhattan. My fear of embarrassment—ever vigilant—prevented me from rubbing my hands together, and the joy I felt finally settled in the region of my intestines. I like nothing better than acquiring new things at a low price. Only once the transaction was complete did I realize, with some disappointment, that there was no view of the street. The two windows must have measured all of twelve square inches, and they both looked out onto a wall.

I find thinking about the apartment disagreeable and yet it happens all the time. The same thing occurs with this girlfriend who insinuated herself into my life without my being able to stop her. Ruth is as careful and as obstinate as a reptile, capable of vanishing whenever my boot is about to squash her into the ground, and also of waiting until I want to see her. As soon as I settle down, she comes slithering back to me, smooth and slippery. To call her intelligent would be an exaggeration. Her skill, in my humble opinion, has more to do with her survival instinct. There are animals that have adapted to live in the desert and she belongs in this category. How else to justify her sticking with me in spite of my character? Ruth is fifteen years older than I am. Her eyes always look as if she were about to cry and this gives them a certain allure. Her silent suffering beatifies her. Her wrinkles, commonly known as crow's feet, give her an air like that of an Orthodox icon. This martyrdom makes up for her objective absence of beauty. Once a week, usually on Fridays, we go out for dinner or to see a movie. I sleep at her house and we screw until dawn, which allows me to polish my sword and satisfy my weekly needs. I will not deny my girlfriend's virtues. She is attractive and refined. Walking around with her is almost an ostentation, like walking arm in arm with a store window: Lagerfeld purse, Chanel eyeglasses. In sum, she has money and style. It goes without saying that a woman like this, in the city where I live, is a key that opens every door, an *Eleguá* who opens all paths. What I do not forgive her for is that she is so very female. Increasing the frequency of our encounters would be impossible. I have explained to her more than once that I would not be able to endure spending any more time with her. Ruth says she understands but nonetheless continues to insist. "That is just what women are like," I say to myself, essentially resigned to sharing my life with a lesser being.

Every morning, I open my eyes before the alarm clock set for six goes off and, without knowing exactly when, I am already looking out the window as if I had never done anything else. I can barely make out the gray wall on the other side, since the glass is protected by a kind of grill. I suppose a child used to live here, or a person with suicidal tendencies. I usually sleep in the fetal position on my right side, so that when I wake up, the first thing I see is this window, through which the light enters but no images, save for the cracks in the wall which, by now, I know by heart. On the other side of the glass, the city gives off its incessant murmur. For a moment I imagine this wall does not exist and that from my window I can see people walking quickly by, heading for their offices or business meetings like worms writhing around in a glass tank. Then I am glad that chance placed a barrier between my body and the chaos out there, so that when I wake I feel clean, remote, protected. Few people escape this uniform mass whose clamor reaches my ears, few people are autonomous, sensitive, independent, and really capable of thinking like I am. I have come to know a few of them in the course of my life through the books they have written. There is Theodor Adorno, for instance, with whom I identify a great deal. Ordinary individuals are deficient, and it is not worth establishing any kind of contact with them, except out of convenience. Every morning, as soon as the menacing noise of the world penetrates my window, the perennial questions arise: how to protect myself from contagion? How to avoid blending in, becoming corrupted? I believe that, if I have achieved this so far, it is thanks to a set of habits without which I would not be able to leave my apartment. Every day I execute a routine I established many years ago and on which my existence hinges. "Execute" is one of my favorite verbs. For example: when I get out of bed, I place the soles of both my feet on the floor. This allows me to feel firm and unswerving. I go straight into the shower and wake my body up with a stream of cold water. I dry myself, always taking care to use the rough side of the towel, and rub my skin until it turns red in order to stimulate the circulation of the blood. Sometimes, without meaning to, I glance over at the mirror—a gesture that makes me lose a few precious seconds—and am reminded with horror that my chest, just like my arms and legs, is covered in hair. I am unable to resign myself to the large quantity of animality human beings possess. "Instincts, impulses, physical needs are all worthy of our contempt," I think to myself as I sit down to defecate in the toilet, strategically placed where it is impossible to see myself reflected anywhere. I never throw toilet paper into the toilet bowl—just the thought that it might become clogged horrifies me. Every morning I press the flusher with my finger and hold it down until I am sure the waste has been lost forever in the antiseptic whirlpool of water, dyed blue from the disinfectant I pour into it.

I ingest my sustenance quickly, standing up by the other window, which, as I said before, also looks out onto a wall. This window faces a building, and occasionally I see one of my neighbors come out to water the potted plants on their balcony, wearing an idiotic smile. Whenever this happens I choose to hold off on breakfast rather than run the risk of having to respond to some greeting. The slightest contact could be irreversible. If I allow politeness to be interpreted as a friendly gesture, the neighbors might start to introduce themselves with all kinds of excuses or, worse still, ask me for a favor. This is a shame, because politeness is something that is in theory a fine thing. I like it when people I do not know behave nicely toward me. Whenever this happens, I enjoy it very much and would like to be able to reciprocate. Unfortunately, not everyone responds in the same way. Politeness can also serve as a gateway to intimacy and, needless to say, there is no shortage of opportunists in the world.

CECILIA

At different periods in my life, graves have protected me. When I was a girl, my mother began a secret relationship with a married man and would leave me at my paternal grandmother's house so she could be with him. In Oaxaca, or at least in my family, it was not well regarded for children to go to nursery school before starting primary. It was seen as preferable for a mother to leave her four-year-old daughter in the hands of her in-laws, in the morning and the afternoon, if she could not or did not wish to take care of her herself. My grandmother's house was an old villa with an inner courtyard and a fountain. Some of the rooms were home to my father's younger brothers, who had not yet married. As well as my grandmother and the servants, my uncles showered me with affection, so I did not feel my mother's absences too keenly. The images I have from this period are very hazy and yet there are things I recall perfectly. I know, for instance, that the kitchen was large and had a wood-burning stove. I also know that, every morning, my grandmother would send the housemaid to buy fresh unpasteurized milk from the market for me to drink and that, if it boiled over on the stove, she would scold her loudly. In a yard out the back where I was forbidden from going, my grandmother kept chickens. One morning I found that the door leading to it from the kitchen was open, and I slipped out to explore freely. I walked around for a while, indifferent to the shouts of my family as they searched anxiously for me inside the house. I did not want to go back yet, so I hid behind the trunk of a cherry tree from where I could see a small mound of earth with a cross on top. Even at that young age I understood that it was a grave. I had seen them before on the roadside and, from a distance, when we drove past a cemetery in the car. What I never managed to find out, despite my insistence, was to whom these remains belonged. My grandmother never relented when I asked her for an explanation and, as tends to happen when things are banned, eventually the grave became an obsession.

At the end of that year, my mother left us to go to a city in the north with her lover. Papá and I moved in with Grandmother for good. I grew up with the stigma of this abandonment. Some people teased me about it; others were overly protective. To shield myself from people's judgments and pity, I sought refuge in my schoolbooks and at the local cinema, one of the few in the city at that time. As the years went by, I gradually gained access to the forbidden patio and the cherry tree and would spend hours under it, staring at the little mound of earth. Secretly, I decided to consider it my mother's grave. When I needed to cry or to be alone, I would seek out this place where the chickens strutted about freely. There I would sit, to read, or to write in my diary. I began to notice other graves, the ones in the cemetery or in churchyards. On the Day of the Dead on November 2, I asked my father to take me to the municipal cemetery and gradually we got into the habit of going there together. It is easy to be passionate about graveyards when you are yet to suffer the death of anyone yourself. After Mamá left, I never lost another relative or any of the close friends on whom my equilibrium depended. Death had an impact on other people and, at times, allowed me to see it up close, but did not once meddle with me, at least during my childhood and teenage years. I must have been eight years old the first time I went to a wake. That evening, my neighbors put a black ribbon on the door of their house and, as is the custom in villages and small towns, left the door open for anyone who wished to come and pay their respects. I went into the house and walked around the living room without anyone noticing me. The deceased was an old man—the waning patriarch of the family—and had been ill with Alzheimer's for several years. It was enough just being there for me to understand that, despite the immense sadness they felt, his passing had brought relief and liberation to the house. The scent of the candles, the resin, and the chrysanthemums arranged on the wreath seeped forever into my memory. Some years later, on their way back from a holiday, two twins who had been in my class in the first year of secondary school died in a car accident. When she announced it, the headmistress asked us to hold a minute's silence. I remember the shock we all felt for more than a week, a mixture of pity and fear for ourselves: life had become more fragile and the world more menacing than it had seemed up to then. At around this time, the painter Francisco Toledo donated his personal library to the city, creating a reading room inside an ancient monastic building—which nonetheless felt strangely comforting—situated a few blocks away from my house. The place became my refuge. There I discovered the major Latin American writers, but also many more translated from other languages, above all from the French. I devoured Balzac and Chateaubriand, Théophile Gautier, Lautréamont, Huysmans and Guy de Maupassant. I liked fantasy stories and novels, especially if they were set in a cemetery somewhere.

At around the age of fifteen, I met a group of kids who used to hang around in the Plaza de la Constitución. The clothes they wore distinguished them from the rest of the city's inhabitants: dark, tatty garments with skull designs, heavy work boots, and black leather jackets. At first glance, I had nothing in common with these people, other than that their favorite place to meet up was the San Miguel cemetery. I seized the first chance I had to show them that I knew all their hangout spots. The penchant these kids had for all things funereal reminded me of my best-loved authors. I began to talk to them about these writers, telling them tales of apparitions and phantoms, and ended up becoming a member of their group. It was they who introduced me to Tim Burton, Philip K. Dick (whose novels I adored right from the beginning), and other authors such as Lobsang Rampa, whom I never quite got into. My father did not look kindly on these friendships. He was worried they would introduce me to certain areas of literature, to drugs and, of course, to sex, which he considered improper if not practiced within an institutional context such as matrimony or prostitution. He seemed not to realize that I was painfully shy, and that my loyalty towards him far exceeded any curiosity or desire to break away. Erotic awakening—common at such ages—took place in my life like a tornado one watches from afar. My attitude could be considered anything but provocative, and by no means sexy. The only things that interested me about this group were the walks among the tombstones in the late afternoon and the swapping of stories that made your hair stand on end. It was in this same period, however, that I gradually began to lose interest in everything, including books and my new friends. If I had spoken little before, now I took refuge in a general muteness and apathy that alarmed my family even more than my eccentric friends did. Instead of waiting until the end of adolescence, my father, consumed with worry, chose instead to consult a psychiatrist. The doctor suggested I take a cocktail of serotonin and lithium for a few months, to stabilize my brain chemistry. And so I began the recommended treatment, but my situation grew considerably worse: not only did I continue to be excessively reserved, but I also started falling asleep all over the place. As the doctor himself said, the pills had a contradictory effect on me, and so he decided to send me for some lab tests that, fortunately for me, my father did not ever take too seriously. We never returned to his consulting room. They left me as I was, *au naturel*. Oaxaca is full of demented people who wander the streets or pester passersby. One mute young girl, as long as she was chaste and virtuous, could not bring the family into too much disrepute. Unlike many of my classmates' parents, my father never minded that I chose to study humanities—quite the opposite. It was he himself who signed me up for French literature at the University of Oaxaca, and when I graduated with a top-class degree, he helped me to find a scholarship to study in Paris. Changing environments so abruptly was not easy. Until that point I had lived protected by my family and my teachers. Everything I knew about life I had learned in books, not on the streets, not even with the goths or out in the courtyard of the university.

RUTH

I became Ruth's lover convinced that in terms of love I was handicapped. At first, my attraction to her was minimal. I was seduced in large part by her elegance, her expensive shoes and perfume. I met her one evening at my friend Beatriz's house, a Swedish woman who had immigrated to New York at the same time that I had, and who shows in a couple of SoHo galleries. Beatriz has a loft in Brooklyn, decorated with furniture from the '70s she has collected from the garage sales she often goes to. Perhaps I could sense that night that something was going to happen, or perhaps I felt particularly alone and this propelled me to open up to the kind of lowlife I do not tend to mingle with. In general, artists seem to me to be frivolous people who are interested only in comparing the size of their egos. Over dinner they talked without letup about their projects and how they had managed to achieve critical acclaim. Among the guests was Ruth, a fifty-something woman who just sat listening in a corner of the living room. Next to her, an old painted hag dressed in garish colors and wearing a pair of yellow spectacles was describing the recent Willy Cansino exhibition as a smash hit that was going to put every Latino artist in Chelsea in the shade. I found Ruth's silence pleasing, and could only interpret it as a compassionate gesture: she was more adult and serene than the rest of the crowd, to the point where I felt moved to sit next to her in the corner. More than anything, I felt like sitting in silence at her side, resting in her calm, and this is what I did. As soon as the woman in the glittery glasses moved a few paces away to pour herself another glass of whiskey, I shamelessly took her place. I smiled at Ruth with genuine warmth, and no power on earth, not even that of my friend Beatriz, could make me move from that spot all night. That was the start of our affair. In her face, preserved by the magic of cosmetics, I discovered a fascinating weariness. I guessed—and I do not believe I was wrong—that she was a woman without energy. Her presence was so light that at no point was she going to represent a threat to me. I looked at her without saying a word for more than a quarter of an hour, and then, with no preamble or introduction, I assured her that a mouth like hers deserved my undivided attention, that with a mouth like that beside me I could spend my whole life prostrate. Ruth's lips are large and full, but it was not this, nor the crimson color they were stained with that night, that inspired my comment; rather it was her emphatic way of being silent. I asked for her telephone number. The following week, I forget whether it was a Saturday or a Sunday, I invited her to see a French movie, *Conte d'automne* by Éric Rohmer, in which nothing happens, as in all my favorite movies. There was little to talk about as we left the theater, but I took the opportunity to dazzle her with my French, a language she had learned at school and remembered very little of. It was Ruth who chose the Tribeca bar where we had the only drink of the evening, an excellent wine at forty-five dollars a glass. I liked the restraint with which Ruth consumed alcoholic drinks. The women I have met in this city either avoid alcohol completely or abandon themselves unreservedly to it, which, most of the time, leads to some pretty embarrassing scenes. She, on the other hand, would always drink a single glass, two at the most, but never more, and this attitude seemed to me a clear demonstration of her good judgment. She insisted on paying, and this act of generosity not only convinced me of the goodness of her heart but also managed to make me feel seduced, wrapped in that protective aura rich women have, which over time I have grown accustomed to. Two weeks later I called her again, enough time to cause her a little anxiety and longing. The month of April tends to put me in a romantic, seductive mood, and with Ruth I employed my most effective technique: switching between indifference and interest, warmth and contempt, which usually brings women to their knees. Nonetheless, this impassive female remained calm and resigned. Apparently it was all the same to her whether I harbored an urgent need to kiss her or saw her as vapid and frivolous. Her affability intrigued me.

Then one afternoon, Ruth called me at the office. I had stayed late, still editing a history textbook for secondary school students, and was the only employee left on the 43rd floor. Relieved, I answered her call with the knowledge that no one would be able to overhear us. When there are people around, I find it almost impossible to pronounce a single sentence on the telephone without feeling that everyone at the publishing house is hanging on my every word. Reveling in the utter solitude of the office, I stationed myself in front of the main window up there. The city emitted its nocturnal murmur. At my feet lay the lights of Manhattan. I felt exalted looking out onto the view of Penn Station, whose architecture I know by heart, as if, instead of talking on the telephone to a woman I hardly knew, I were whispering into the city's ear, this impersonal city I love precisely for the freedom it grants me. I told her the details of my day, where I had eaten lunch and the people who had joined me, the book I was editing. I told her about the gym

I go to every evening and described the pleasure I felt when I increased the speed of the treadmill.

"When are we going to see each other?" Ruth said, and her husky voice brought me back to reality. New York might lie before me, but there was someone on the other end of the telephone. I nearly hung up. "Would you like to come for dinner tonight?" the voice asked. "My children aren't staying over and we'll be able to relax." The word "children" resounded in my ears. I was surprised at the ease with which it was said, as if it were the most natural thing in the world. This woman who, up until that moment had seemed to me translucent, tremulous as a piece of tissue paper on which you could just trace, not write or paint, had all at once acquired an unexpected dimension. For the first time I considered the possibility that she had a history, a family, a life.

"You didn't tell me you had children."

"I'm telling you now," she said, serene as ever.

I arrived in Tribeca with a three-dollar wine that my tactful hostess put away in the cupboard, discreetly replacing it with one of better quality. She still has that other bottle, next to the Saint-Émilions and Château de Lugagnacs in her wine rack, like a precious souvenir of that first visit.

I screwed Ruth for the first time in the kitchen of her apartment. She had stood up on tiptoe to look for one spice or another in the cupboard. I lifted up her silk skirt and made love to her like no one had ever done in her life, because she had never been with a Latino before, never mind one of those men they only make on the island where I was born. At her fifty-odd years of age, Ruth cried out like a cat when my cock hammered into her ovaries. We ended up in her bed between peach-colored sheets and I slept there with her that night. In the morning, I left without a sound and showed up to work smelling of alcohol and a long, late night. Not one of my coworkers made a comment. They know me well enough to know that I cannot bear tactlessness. I did want to tell somebody about my fling, however, even though I knew there was no one in the office it was worth my confiding in. And so at lunchtime I decided to call Mario, my closest friend, who knows every aspect of me, from the time we were children in El Cerro right up until the most recent episodes in my life, which at that moment he could not even imagine. More than a year had passed since our last conversation and neither of us had attempted to get in touch.

When I had finished telling him the story, with an excitable, almost romantic air, Mario stayed silent, a gesture I considered a sign of respect on his part. He probably wanted to bask for a few more moments in the atmosphere of my story.

"Poor woman," he said at last, in a low voice. "What terrible thing can she have done to deserve you?"

He was serious.

When I put down the telephone, the reason Mario and I had grown distant became clear to me. The courtesy that existed between us had been crushed beneath a relentless sincerity. Once more I saw the image of Ruth bent over her kitchen counter, half undressed by my furious caresses. I saw again her look of abandon, of someone who delights in offering herself to another, even though I was a stranger, her blond hair spread out around the sink, the freckles on her shoulders. That slender body that lets itself be grabbed with a feigned innocence, resembling that of an unsuspecting fifteen-year-old girl. I felt sick, although I do not know exactly why. I did not call her again for a month.

PARIS

Idyllic Paris, the Paris of films that conventional tourists hope to find on their trip, begins in May and lasts, with a bit of luck, until the start of September. In those months the whole city seems determined to grant an amnesty, to call a cease-fire in its hysteria, its frenzy. There is a smell of flowers, the Parisians hum to themselves in the streets, waiters and newspaper sellers adopt an amiable attitude, and good humor spreads through the air like a benign cloud. I arrived here to live in this season and spent the first few months enveloped in a picture-postcard atmosphere. At my twenty-five years of age, I viewed happy people with a certain amount of suspicion. I was of the opinion that intelligent people, those with the necessary valor for facing up to reality, could do nothing but go through life with a heavy heart. All this spring-like joy seemed to me not just phony, but disappointing. I had left my country to escape the omnipresent sound of Oaxaca's organ-grinders. I found the constant clamor of Mexico oppressive. The notion I had of Paris was not this city where dozens of couples of all ages kissed each other in parks and on the platforms of the métro, but of a rainy place where people read Cioran and La Rochefoucauld while, their lips pursed and preoccupied, they sipped coffee with no milk and no sugar. Like many of the foreigners who end up staying forever, I arrived in Paris with the intention or, rather, the pretext of studying a postgraduate degree. The French government had given me a grant and I was enrolled on a diploma of advanced studies, a *diplôme d'études approfondies* or DEA, in literature at the Institute of Latin American Studies. It was June, when exams took place, and most of the professors were uncontactable, my own included. I had no friends in the city. Of the four million people in Paris, I knew not a single one. All I had were two names written in my diary: David Dumoulin and Nicole Loeffler. These distant friends of my father and my aunts and uncles were all the contacts I had. Although I thought about it several times, I failed to overcome my shyness and embarrassment to call them and ask them to put me up. Instead, I decided to lodge at a student hostel located on rue Saint-Jacques, where I shared a room with a young Romanian woman who spoke no language but her own.

One afternoon, as I waited in line at the university to pay my enrollment fees, I struck up a conversation with a girl called Haydée. It was a long queue and, as we moved forward, she had time to tell me, at dizzying speed, something of her life. She explained she had been studying for a degree in visual anthropology for four years and wanted to write her thesis on Caribbean Santería practices. When my turn came and I told her about my situation, she insisted I come and stay with her. Although I barely knew her, I much preferred Haydée to the Romanian girl. At least we could communicate with each other. And so that same afternoon I left my room in the hostel in the rue Saint-Jacques and arrived at my new friend's apartment, situated on the sixth floor of an old building in the 17th arrondissement. In Paris, floor space is very important. People tend to talk about floor measurements as the primary characteristic of their homes, rather than the direction they face or the number of rooms. The apartment where Haydée and her partner lived was fifty-three square meters, divided up in the following way: an open-plan kitchen with a breakfast bar that served as a dining table; a living room; one small room, and another tiny one; a bathroom; and a balcony. Haydée was an affectionate person with a cheerful disposition. From the day I turned up with my five suitcases, she treated me with an exaggerated friendliness that at first I found disconcerting, but which I later identified as a demonstration of Latino solidarity. When I got to her place, I felt that the best way to show my gratitude was by invading her life as little as possible, making my presence only as obvious as was necessary and, of course, contributing money towards my expenses within the house. The first few days I tried to eat breakfast and dinner at different times from her and her partner, but they would have none of it: before every meal, they would knock at my bedroom door to let me know it was time to come and sit at the table. Little by little, through the simple fact of living there, I became part of the couple's daily life. Just what I, out of consideration, had resolved to avoid.

Haydée's boyfriend was an art student. His name was Rajeev, and he had been born in India. The two of them occupied the bigger room and offered me the smaller one. Unlike his girlfriend, Rajeev hardly ever went out to parties. He had finished all his classes and was trying to write his thesis. Every morning, at around six, he would emerge from their bedroom, have a shower, and immediately settle himself down on the living-room rug to practice some kind of breathing ritual. When he had finished, he would put on a CD of sitar music and make himself a vanilla tea that he left boiling for several minutes, in which time the smell impregnated the entire house. Then he opened his laptop at the breakfast bar and would sit there writing until half past nine, the time Haydée usually got up.

The main time all three of us spent together at home was at breakfast. We would drink Rajeev's concentrated tea and eat baguettes with jam, while Haydée told us about her nightly round of the city's bars. If it was a market day, Rajeev would go shopping while Haydée was in the shower and getting ready. When he came back, he cooked. The trips to the market, the post office, and the library were the only times he left the house. At around two, Haydée left the apartment and we did not see her again until last thing in the evening. This 53-square-meter apartment was a good place to touch down in the French capital and to familiarize myself with its people and their customs. Outside, the city seemed strange and somehow menacing to me. I spent most of my time dealing with bureaucratic matters, at the police *préfecture* and at the university. Although my days were generally spent pleasantly, in the middle of the night anxiety and uncertainty saw me tossing and turning beneath the sheets. I could hear Rajeev's breathing, much calmer than in the morning, and sounds in the street, which back then I found terrifying, and the purr of the building's lift. Haydée and I were very different and it is likely that we hit it off precisely for this reason. Despite her generosity in offering me a place to live, ours was not spontaneous friendship. It took us several weeks to figure each other out, but once we had, an unwavering affection grew up between us that remains to this day. I remember that one afternoon, when I had come home exhausted after having spent the day dealing with immigration paperwork and was getting ready to have a siesta, she asked if she could come into my room. I thought she needed to look for something in the desk in there, or in her university files, and that, when she saw me sleeping, she would leave pretty fast. But once she was in the room she sat down on the edge of the bed with the clear intention of staying to chat. Try as I might, I just could not fathom her. Her voice was hypnotic and I had to make a huge effort to keep my eyes open. Who can silence a Cuban woman who wants to talk? I have yet to meet anyone who has managed it. The conversation that afternoon marked the start of a custom. Unless I had first locked the door, she would come into my room whenever she felt like it to tell me about any silly little thing going round in her head. Some of these conversations were interesting, others not at all. In the end I grew used to her badly timed visits, and even came to be genuinely interested in her daily stories.

All the time I lived in her house, Haydée applied herself to observing me. She would scrutinize my clothes and my shoes as if my way of dressing were a code to be cracked. After a few days, she summoned up the courage to voice her doubts and asked me, with evident impatience: "Are those five suitcases of yours all full of rags like those?" I was not so much offended as surprised by her chutzpah. She immediately offered to take me to a couple of shops near the Alésia métro station, where I would find something that would "stop me looking like a high school student." I agreed so as not to displease her, but made sure she never followed through on her promise. Unlike her, I did not attribute so much importance to clothes. Trousers, to me, are not and have never been anything more than a piece of fabric, not a message we send to society. But she was very insistent about such things.

"The first thing you need to do," she told me one day, with characteristic tact, "is buy yourself a bike to get rid of those extra kilos you're carrying."

I soon realized that this obsession with the body was not a personal feature of Haydée's, but rather a typically French mindset. The ads in the métro were forever hammering home the importance of preserving one's figure—not to mention the magazines displayed at the newsstands. The entire city seemed to be focused on the cultivation of beauty as a matter of life or death. Haydée's bathroom, for instance, was an eloquent reflection of the way that advertisements had taken over a section of her brain. You only had to open the cabinet in there to find a whole stack of products, most of them designed to help you lose weight. Vichy, Galénic, Decléor; all the brands that can be found in the city's pharmacies were represented on her shelves, where there was no space left for one more bottle. Every time I toweled off my chubby thighs in the same spot as she slathered her body with these luxurious concoctions, I wondered with genuine curiosity if they really worked, and whether it was worth spending a fortune on them.

Despite what you might think, Haydée was not a frivolous woman. She followed the news in the papers and had opinions on politics and art. Beneath that shock of impenetrable curly hair, she harbored an endless string of unanswerable questions she loved to mull over out loud. With a Cuban father and a Moroccan-Jewish mother, French nationality but a very Hispanic surname, Haydée Cisneros felt implicated in the majority of the polemics that have a habit of getting whipped up in this city. I have never seen anyone so ready to be offended. She could not discuss the embargo, the conflict in the *banlieues*, the war in Israel, without feeling somehow involved. While everyone else defended Castro, she assumed the exile and persecution of intellectuals and gay people as something personal. If anyone criticized him, on the other hand, she would hold up the fruits and importance of the revolution in terms of increased levels of health and education, which, compared to the rest of Latin America, were undeniable.

One day, after thinking long and hard about it, I decided to take her advice and buy a bicycle in a shop in Saint-Michel, but I could not work out how to get home on it. With a great deal of effort I managed to pick it up and get it onto the RER overground train. At the time, nothing scared me more than getting lost, and so for the first few months I never went out on the bike alone. To get at least some use out of it, I started going with Haydée to the library at the Pompidou Centre, where she would stay for a maximum of two hours at a time, studying for her exams. The rest of the afternoon we would spend in a café-bar on rue Vieille du Temple, called Le Progrès, which she had nicknamed "The Communist." She went there every day to meet up with her classmates from the institute, and anyone else who was looking for her. I soon grew used to the hours she kept and her way of life, so different from the one I would have had if I had never met her.

In the time I spent in her house, Haydée took me to some of the nightclubs in Paris. Places like Le Nouveau Casino, La Locomotive, the 9 Billiards, the Satellit Café, nearly all of them situated on the Rive Droite. We always turned up in the small hours of the morning, never before 2:00 a.m., when most bars shut their doors. My favorite place was called Le Batofar. It was a boat moored on the Seine, near the Bibliothèque Nationale, where they played jazz, reggae, and Latin tunes. The best parties I went to that summer were held there, fancy dress parties where exoticism and a sense of humor were the most prized attributes of any outfit. There were cross-dressing boys, others dressed like the Jackson Five with bell bottoms and Afro wigs, and women with banana skirts like Josephine Baker. No matter where we went, the routine was more or less the same: after waiting for a while—between twenty minutes and an hour—in a queue, we went through to the cloakroom where we left the heavy bag Haydée used to take with her everywhere, full of videotapes, makeup, changes of clothes, and even a bottle or two. Once we had got in, we would walk around the edge of the main room, saying hello to everyone we knew. This was how Haydée got the lie of the land. Once this phase was over, and as soon as they put on one of her favorite tunes, she would take her bow on the dance floor.

When Haydée danced, you could not take your eyes off her. Next to her, I was absolutely invisible; worse than that, I was just one more of her many accessories, like a pageboy or a little pet. I could easily have slipped away from this woman, disappeared into the sea of humanity that laughed and smoked like an autonomous mass, lived my own version of the party in which I had the starring role; and yet, without ever being able to explain why, I never gave myself that freedom. Each night, I stayed next to Haydée and her diminutive skirts, privately criticizing myself for not having more rhythm, for not trying to meet people, for not enjoying the music, and it was in this condition that I traipsed along at her side through the various nightclubs of Paris.

Haydée's other friends, the ones she met up with on Vieille du Temple or who showed up halfway through the night in the clubs and at the house parties, were as scrawny as she was. Some of them were still students, or else they worked in cinema or the theater, or made cultural programs for television, and, although they were never short of topics of conversation, nothing interested them so much as the new drugs for preventing fluid retention. When did I become so obsessed with my appearance? When did I abandon my healthy indifference to my physique and start contributing with my very own malaise towards this collective psychosis? The bicycle and the lifestyle Haydée introduced me to over five weeks, in which there was no time for eating dinner, made me lose weight almost without realizing. My trousers hung looser than ever on me and my face began to look more angular in the mirror and yet, rather than be happy with this, the change induced a strange sense of greed in me; no longer was I content simply to be less fat: I now wanted to belong to the privileged ranks of the skinny. I did not care that my bones were big and that my "Oaxacan constitution," as Haydée called it, had been robust since childhood. There had to be something I could do. Anyone interested in such matters knows that the first thing one must cut out of one's diet when one wishes to lose weight is alcohol, and yet you should have seen how those girls could drink! You only had to watch them for one night. Almost every time I went out with her, Haydée had several different cocktails, without stopping to count either the number of glasses or the euros she was spending, until rapidly she reached a peak of alcoholic euphoria and no one, not even me, was able to stop her racing towards total intoxication, which generally reached the point of no return at around 4:30 in the morning. Fortunately, at the late-night venues we went to, they used to serve a foul rum that not even she was capable of drinking, so that after dancing for a couple of hours she was able to recover her composure and set off for home on the night bus, whose routes and timetables she knew by heart. Once or twice when we got home we found Rajeev, already halfway through his prana yoga and other morning purification rituals. I still do not understand what it was that enabled those two to be together, apart from the fact that they hardly ever saw each other. Romantic relationships are a mystery and I suppose my lack of experience in this area turned theirs into an even greater one in my eyes.

By the time the summer was over I knew half the dives in Paris. According to Haydée, those holidays were particularly full-on for her, never mind how intense I had found them! My friend ended up with a hernia in her liver and a large hole in her bank account. Both things prevented her from going out for several months. Not surprisingly, being shut up like this did not agree with her. Her irritation was constant, as were the arguments with poor Rajeev, accustomed to being lord and master of this hushed 53-square-meter kingdom. I said to myself that the time had come to move.

By now, Haydée's neighborhood was more familiar to me than any other and so the first thing that occurred to me was to answer some of the adverts pinned to the door of the local bakery that said: *Studio à louer, 12m carrés*. I visited at least five. Most of these studios were old servants' quarters with no bathroom or kitchen. The twelve square meters were in fact nine. To get to the communal shower, you often had to go down one floor or walk along a long corridor exposed to the elements. The only studio with a bathroom I found was an attic room with a low, sloping ceiling, which the landlady showed to me with inexplicable pride. The much-coveted toilet was in the kitchen, between the stove and the fridge, with nothing to separate it from them aside from a flimsy curtain rail. The landlady suggested I hang up a piece of fabric or some blinds in case I ever had guests round. I could not bring myself to live in any of these holes. Before trying my luck in any of the student residences (by now, the start of September, the rooms would all be filled in any case), I decided to make use of one of the contacts I had arrived in France with. First I called Nicole Loeffler. A friend of my father's had given me her number insisting she owned a whole building. With any luck I might be able to rent one of her apartments.

Madame Loeffler was aware of my arrival. Our mutual friend had contacted her as soon as I had left Mexico and she had been waiting for two months for me to get in touch with her. She told me that one of her properties would be available from October 29.

It was a thirty-square-meter *deux pièces*, in good condition and with a bathroom. All I hoped was that the price did not exceed my paltry budget. Mme. Loeffler received me at her house as if I were a distant relative. She served me tea and little almond cakes. I hadn't eaten a thing all day and was worried she would hear the rumbles of pleasure in my stomach as I gulped down her delicious *financiers:* if I could not afford to eat, I would be even less likely to be able to afford the rent. This, at least, is what would have gone through the mind of any suspicious old French person. Madame Loeffler, however, who in her childhood had known exile and war, never put my economic solvency into any doubt whatsoever. She did not ask me for any kind of guarantor, nor for a deposit. When we had finished our tea, she took me to see the *deux pièces*, which she was prepared to let to me for as low a price as necessary. And so we walked together up the rue du Chemin Vert until we got to the boulevard de Ménilmontant, where the building was to be found. It was early autumn, and the trees were still covered with green and orange leaves. This was the first thing I saw that afternoon, when I looked out through the window. Beyond the curtain of leaves, the vast cemetery spread out. This vista seemed not just an enormous stroke of luck, but a sign, too. There could not be an apartment more suited to my character in the whole of Paris. All of its defects ceased to be important. It did not bother me, for instance, that the place had nothing but a dilapidated old heater with which to survive the winter.

By the time I moved in, in November, the leaves I had seen on my first visit had disappeared completely. The taxi driver put down my five suitcases and, as Haydée set them down in the doorway to the building, I looked up the entrance code in my diary. I was so happy to finally have a space of my own! I loved that building from the very first moment, despite the smell of damp, the parquet floor that creaked as soon as you stepped on it, and the chilly wind that blew in through the communal windows. We had to make three trips to get all my belongings up, because the stairs were steeper than usual in a nineteenth-century building.

"Oh, my God!" Haydée said, looking out at the tranquil landscape of gravestones, the only thing visible from my window. "With a view like that you're going to get depressed on me before winter's even begun."

I tried to explain that I did not find graves upsetting. I preferred my neighbors to be inordinately quiet rather than the opposite. The room came with a bed pushed right up against the wall, a small desk, a bookcase, and a disused fireplace with a huge mirror hanging above it over the mantelpiece. I furnished the rest of the place—which Haydée and I optimistically dubbed the living room—with two Moroccan rugs I bought around the corner and a couple of poufs. The bathroom was the size of a cupboard: the shower, sink, and toilet, behind a folding screen like an accordion. Both Haydée and I used it several times that day, not like animals trying to mark out their territory, but because of the cold that afternoon.

INITIATION

Aside from its absence of windows, my apartment is a mausoleum that bestows an epic dimension on the important moments of my existence: the books that have shaped me, a few letters, some photographs and, more than anything, my records, without which life would be colorless and bland. With my headphones on, immersed in an all but perfect silence, I surrender myself to the music of Keith Jarrett, and then sometimes a feeling might appear, a subtle, unobtrusive sensation, like when a ray of sunlight filters through to my neatly made bed, radiating heat and light for a few minutes onto the quilt and the floor. These are fleeting moments, when a part of me, usually buried, awakes as if by enchantment to tenderness, gentleness. My lungs swell, opening and closing with the notes of the piano. I feel fragile, like when I was a child. And then back they come to me, the stinking, pot-holed streets of Old Havana, the sticky heat I never quite managed to get used to, my brothers and sisters sticking their dirty little hands into the pot in the kitchen bubbling away full of *malanga*, that ever-present tuber whose vile odor wafts throughout the house, forcing me out into the yard where my neighbors play. Jarrett notwithstanding, I can never bear these memories for very long. That kind of life—rough, miserable—pains me.

I first began to hate at the age of five, when Facundo Martínez and his family showed up at our communal house. Until then, this big old house with its one floor and an inner courtyard had been exclusively ours; that is, it had belonged to my parents, my brothers and sisters, and my aunts, uncles, and cousins. We lived on one side of the patio and my uncle, aunts, and cousins on the other, in a harmonious, balanced existence. I can still remember the morning the moving truck pulled up outside the front door. A militiaman arrived with a piece of paper and a smile, to inform us that the Martínez family had been assigned half the lot. Only then did I realize that my house, the house where I had been born and spent the first five years of my life, was not quite mine, but belonged to the Revolution, and that the Revolution could send whoever it felt like to live in it. We—that is, my uncles and aunts and my parents and their respective families—became a single family, the Ruvalcabas, and as such we were entitled to half the house. It made no difference that there were fifteen of us, and only eight of them. At that moment, the house became a chessboard: they were black, we were white. I saw all this at the age of five with the timeless gaze of someone watching his world collapse, and yet no one said a thing. My mother received the militiaman wearing her housecoat and apron, and the same resigned smile he was giving her. She waved pleasantly to Facundo's mother and started showing her around, while my siblings and I helped our cousins take their things from the front part of the house and move them into what was now our one shared room. She showed her the kitchen, and the backyard where she and my aunt would wash our clothes by hand and where, ever since, Facundo's underwear would forever be swaying out on the clothesline, like a flag symbolically marking his territory. Hidden behind a pillar on the patio, I watched without blinking as the Martínez family moved in, and still without blinking, I saw them take possession of my uncle and aunt's rooms with their brightly colored furniture and their religious statues. From that moment on, Our Lady of Charity of El Cobre and San Lázaro stared balefully down at us whenever we went out to play on her side of the yard. When they had finished unloading all the boxes and bags, two feet exactly the same length as mine but much wider appeared by the pillar where I had hidden myself. I looked up and saw a boy with frizzy, straw-like hair. We exchanged not a word, but in that long look of recognition it became clear that the pillar was in his territory, that is, the part of the inner courtyard closest to his domain, and that, by hiding behind it, I had immediately become an intruder. Facundo held out his hand to me, as we had seen his father greet mine and, with the same humiliation, I took it, knowing that we would grow up together and also that I would detest him for the rest of my life. But it was one of those certainties that later on you cease to be aware of, in the same way you get used to sounds from the street. In time, you no longer hear the garbage truck early in the morning, or the purr of the water pump. I lived alongside Facundo every single day of my childhood. I saw him get home from school at the same time that I did and, at night, turn off the light in his room so many times that in the end I stopped thinking about him and my hatred, just as you do not think of your liver, even though it is there, working away, until one day it bursts open, letting you savor the unmistakable taste of bile.

As I said before, time passes slowly at that age, and in a few months I had forgotten that the other side of the house had been occupied by the invading enemy. The Martínezes ceased to inspire hostility in me and became simply our neighbors; that is, one more element of daily life. Facundo and I were the same age, but we led an existence that, at least back then, seemed very different to me. While to me the streets of our neighborhood, El Cerro—where I just happened mistakenly to have been born—were hostile territory, inhabited by unknown beings with a delinquent air about them, to Facundo they were no more than an extension of the playground. Every afternoon, while I worked hard to stay in school (the Colegio Felipe Poey, where I had been enrolled thanks to a distant relative who worked for the Central Committee), he went out to the park to play baseball with the other kids from the block. Despite this, we did occasionally walk home together, and I would sometimes accept an invitation into their dining room, full of candles and little statues of saints, to have an after-school snack: bread with oil and garlic that his mother would prepare for us, or the guava cake, which was our favorite. As food grew scarcer, the slices of guava grew so thin and translucent that you could see right through them like a photographic slide. On Saturday mornings, Facundo's cousin Regla would come to help with the chores. Regla was a sixteen-year-old black girl, whose ass mirrored the shape and hardness of a coconut. Her soft skin and her movements created an electric tension in this house inhabited almost exclusively by males. Facundo, who was not yet ten years old, was the only one who seemed immune to his cousin's spell. His age, however, did not stop him from noticing the anguish the girl caused in me, and he took pleasure in stirring it up whenever he could. He would find any pretext to invite me to his house whenever Regla was engaged in her domestic tasks. My heart would beat faster just looking at that little dark-skinned girl ironing clothes or bending over to get something from a low shelf in the kitchen. Facundo seemed to enjoy my desire. When the afternoon drew to a close and Regla went to wash up, he would lead me out toward the back of the house and to a hole that he had made himself in the partition wall, through which it was possible to watch her in exchange for a one-peso coin.

"Does she give you a hard-on?" he would ask, with the air of someone in the know.

And the truth is that—clothed or naked—Regla provoked an urgent need in me. As soon as she emerged from the shower wrapped in her immaculate towel, impossible to forget, I ran to that same bathroom where she had been naked to masturbate. I do not know what would have happened if one day Facundo had for some reason denied me the spectacle of Regla; our story would likely be very different, just as my life would be different if his family had not transformed our home into just another communal house in that deplorable neighborhood. You might say that this childhood friend played the role of initiator into the pleasures of voyeurism, a shameful activity it took me a long time to shake off. There are some mental deviances that are as easily transmitted as venereal diseases.

Mario, of whom I see less and less, appeared during this formative period and it is perhaps for this reason that he continues to be such an important figure in my life. Although he was a year older than me, he and Facundo had met at school and he sometimes played with us in the yard. Mario enjoyed the company of books as much as I did and, since they were not plentiful in his house, he would scheme and swindle his way around the cities' libraries in order to get his hands on them. When he found out that the part of the house belonging to my family was full of novels and books of poetry, he began visiting us assiduously, not bothering to say hello to the family living on the other side of the house. I remember him clearly, perched on a chair as he inspected the dusty bookshelves in my house. With him I struck up the very first intellectual friendship I can recall. He liked the plays of Lorca and Ionesco, but would as happily read Sophocles if I recommended it.

Together we read Hesse, Borges, and Cortázar, and when there were no more books by these writers left on my shelves he found a way to obtain other titles from the National Library, taking them out using a fake membership card from the UNEAC, the Cuban National Union of Writers and Artists. Mario was curiously blond for someone who lived in El Cerro, and looked much older than his fourteen years. He used to go to writers' parties in apartments in El Vedado as if it were the most normal thing in the world, and hung around with a few of the rich little kids from my school. While I settled for keeping my place at school, studying like a lunatic, he had a close relationship with my classmates I could never even dream of. A few times I saw him go by in a car heading down Calle 23. He wore white most of the time. His shirts were always spotless. Not only was he successful with the girls from El Vedado; they actively pursued him. At my house, a few blocks from his own, Mario would take off his mask; he dropped the public persona, witty and good at dancing, that people knew and relaxed back into the simple, everyday habits of our own social class. In his whole life I do not believe anyone came to know him as well as I did. Instead of white suits, in my house he wore the gray slacks he had inherited from his father or his school uniform. The one thing he never let slide was his elegance and cleanliness. Since deodorant was hard to get ahold of at the time, he washed at least twice a day, leaving his armpits coated in soap when he did so. He always had a little stalk of parsley in his mouth to prevent bad breath and indigestion. In a climate where everyone sweats, where one's skin becomes sticky with humidity, where the stench of body odor turns the air into a dense, asphyxiating mass, I was grateful to my friend for reminding me that some human beings can be pleasant if they take pains.

Unfortunately for me, Mario went to live in Cienfuegos for two years, leaving me in a bottomless solitude. I remember that two days before he left, he showed up at my front door in a car. It must have been around midday on a Sunday. He had on his characteristic white outfit and in his hand he carried an open bottle of Havana Club. At the wheel was a guy wearing dark glasses and a short-sleeved plaid shirt.

"Get in!" he said. "I'm taking you to celebrate."

I obeyed without telling anyone. I did not ask where we were going. Mario's friend drove us to the UNEAC, where Alejandro Robles was launching his book *Ornithological Fictions*. We sat down for a few minutes at one of the tables on the patio. Someone brought us a couple of mojitos. When the event started, Mario asked me to come with him to the library, the biggest I had ever seen in my life, and handed me his membership card:

"This is for you, brother. Take good care of it."

"Are you sure?" I said, surprised.

"Of course I am. You can get more out of this shit than I can in Cienfuegos. Almost every book allowed on the island is here. When you've finished those, start looking for the banned ones, if they don't find you first, that is."

I took his advice. From that evening on, I treated the reading room in the library of the UNEAC like a home away from home. I did not even bother taking the books out, I would just put a bookmark in and come back the next day to finish them. Those two years were key in my education. The more time I spent in the library, the more devoted I became to Regla's showers. I would have paid anything to watch her several times a week, but she only came on Saturdays. The rest of the time I had to make do with my memories.

"Don't wait for her to come out of the bathroom!" Facundo insisted. "Do it whenever you feel like it. No one knows we're here."

And so, driven by the urgency the girl aroused in me, I would put my hand down my pants until it was covered with the paste of my semen. At first, Facundo remained as impassive as before, but age pardons no one and he too ended up joining the Saturday afternoon jerking-off session, although far less modestly: rather than put his hand through his fly, as I did, he would take out his cock, a thick, heavy member like one of his feet, and, in the silence of the incipient night, would ejaculate, ostentatiously spattering the patio tiles or the wall through which we watched Regla undress.

At times, while the notes of the piano echo around my stone corridor, a protective barrier rises up between me and these images. This barrier has allowed me to survive all these years, in the knowledge that my father is ill and alone in the province of Cienfuegos; that my brothers and sisters still live in that same house where we spent our childhood, although now with the families they have formed. The record ends, and everything goes back to normal. God bless the barrier that keeps me dry, impervious to emotions.

A few weeks went by without my receiving any sign from Ruth. Not a single telephone call, not a single e-mail inviting me to the movies or to have dinner in her Tribeca loft; nothing. For the first couple of weeks I was relieved not once to hear her smoker's voice. Nothing seemed to betray the fact we had met each other. I did not even have the impression she was thinking about me and holding back. She simply vanished. As ever, the only messages on the answering machine were from a coworker trying to verify some detail or other about proofs, or a family acquaintance recently arrived from Havana with news of my mother, but from Ruth not a word.

As the years go by, the news from Cuba seems increasingly like one big fiction to me. My mother's voice on the telephone sounds like an ageing radio announcer reading out an old soap opera, the daily life of characters who become steadily more blurry and lost in oblivion. What the hell do I care that Aunt Carmen has dyed her hair red, or that Robertico, her son, has dumped his fourteen-year-old girlfriend? I don't even remember many of the friends she attributes to me, and whose news she relates while my money trickles away on the AOL phone card. I cannot describe how badly I want to hang up the telephone. If I do not, then it is because among all the faded names and faces that flash in my memory as my mother talks away endlessly, the only clear images are the ones of her, of her dedication and devotion, of the times I was ill as a child and she did not leave my side; the countless occasions she made my siblings leave the bedroom—where all six of us slept—so that I could read in peace and quiet. Thanks to her, to her certainty that of all the good-for-nothings she had given birth to, I was the only one who would excel, I managed to read the classics and the Russians, Pablo Neruda and César Vallejo, Walter Benjamin and Marcuse. On more than one occasion, with the money she made washing other people's clothes, my mother even went to the La Moderna Poesía bookstore to buy me books—awful ones, usually—such as Nicolás Guillén's Communist poems, or *With These Same Hands* by Fernández Retamar, recommended to her by a bookseller. In this unreadable book, I could not help but see the hours my mother had spent washing faded shirts. Every one of the pages bore out the hope that she had placed in me, her one worthy child, her golden boy, her vindication, her lifeboat. Later on, Mario told me that Retamar gave the manuscript of *With These Same Hands* to José Lezama Lima to get his opinion on the collection. A few weeks later he went to see Lezama and asked him what he thought. Lezama, displaying his characteristic exquisitely refined irony, replied: "*With These Same Hands* that you wrote it with, destroy it." I never found out if that anecdote was true or if it was one of my friend's frequent inventions.

By around the third week, Ruth's absence went from being a relief to an amusing and curious mystery. What could have happened to the old thing? I found it unthinkable that she would have chosen to distance herself after having had such a good time with me between her peach-colored sheets. Was she ill? Could she be traveling? Had she met somebody else? In time, my initial rejection of her slowly turned into well-intentioned curiosity. If I went into a Starbucks and saw a woman who reminded me of her—even though I knew perfectly well that she would never set foot in a place like that—I would think of her house, of how well I had eaten there, and say to myself: "I wonder how the dear old thing is." Before a month was up, I called her to find out.

"Where have you been hiding?" I said, with genuine interest.

"I haven't gone anywhere. You said you'd call me, and I was waiting for you."

And then I remembered: before leaving her house I had fired off the usual phrase, the one I use with all my lovers: "I have a lot of work right now—I'll call you when I'm not so busy." Incredibly, a woman—this woman—had understood right away, with no need for any prior rebuke.

And so it was that I fell back into Ruth's clutches. That evening, we met for dinner in Les Lucioles, a classic French restaurant, a little conservative for her tastes, perfect for mine. I cannot bear the brightly colored lights and the '70s-style decor that has become all the rage in the bars in her neighborhood. That period is over and no one hated it more than I did. You could not buy bell-bottoms in Cuba, but people would sew a triangle of fabric into their jeans, almost always in a different color, to turn them into elephant legs. They would also glue pieces of wood onto the soles of their shoes to turn them into heavy, flamboyant platforms. These attempts at slavishly following a fashion that had nothing to do with us seemed ridiculous to me, and quite a few people ended up in jail simply for insisting on wearing their hair long. In any case, all that weird paraphernalia came back into fashion a few years ago here, both the clothes and the decor, and Ruth in particular is very fond of it. The restaurant she picked to please me was as austere as a postwar Parisian *brasserie* might have been, my favorite period from the twentieth century. Although it was a Friday, the place was practically empty, perhaps due to the prohibitive prices. Ruth ordered a salad of fresh vegetables—I remember because the pale color of the carrots caught my eye and I asked the waiter why they looked like that.

"We import these carrots from France," he told me, as if this were an answer, this short, plain little man who looked as if he had lived off vegetables like this his entire life. But this did not bother the old thing. My *confit de canard*, meanwhile, was delicious. Even though I offered, Ruth refused to let me share it with her, another of the kindly gestures she invariably displayed with me, such as the discreet way she had of paying the bill. When we left I felt exultant, almost overfull, and so I suggested we go back to her house on foot. I like walking the streets of Tribeca. The solitude of the sidewalks contrasts with the faint light issuing from the windows of the buildings. Although there were no cars, we waited for the traffic lights to change. I remember that, despite her usual ways, Ruth was a little tipsy that night. We had drunk two bottles of Nuits-Saint-Georges with dinner, but instead of talking loudly or laughing loudly, like most American women—or Cuban ones, for that matter—in similar situations, she maintained her lovely silence. Only occasionally did she stumble a little on her high heels, with a nonchalant abandon that turned me on. When we reached the corner of the street, my hand went to one of her butt cheeks. The light had changed to red and she stopped immediately, letting me give it a squeeze. It was absurd to wait for the lights to turn green before crossing the street. If we had not done so, perhaps we would have avoided what happened next: before either of us realized, a scruffy individual wrapped in a threadbare coat that I remember as gray and Ruth as green came up to us brandishing a sharp, pointed object, somewhere between a knife and a screwdriver.

"You give me just the money. Do quick motherfucker!" he said, in a strong Dominican accent, pointing the curious tool at me. I immediately put my hand in my pocket to take out my wallet to give to the man.

"Don't move!" Ruth ordered me, preventing me from doing so. In her voice there was not an ounce of nervousness.

The man came over to us then. His bulging eyes displayed an ancestral rage. It seemed as if Ruth's reaction had increased his fury and, with a bear-like growl, he came at us. But before he could reach us, something made him trip and, before we knew it, he was down on the ground. That something had been Ruth's foot, purposefully extended close to the ground. The sangfroid I had always considered part of her beauty now took on an epic dimension. Immediately afterward, without losing her customary insouciance, the old thing hailed a taxi coming down the street. We climbed into it as two shipwrecked sailors climb aboard a lifeboat.

As in Baudelaire's poem, music is for me at times like a ship that transports me to nonexistent places. For instance, I sometimes fall prey to a foolish train of thought in which I have an impeccable life, different from the one I lead, without its shortfalls and its imperfections. I would like, for instance, for my stone corridor to be the size of a real house. I could remain locked up in there for years, walking through it in silence, with the same lack of urgency with which I move around this apartment. There would be room for my books on the shelves and, rather than being stacked on top of each other, they would be able to breathe with satisfaction and dignity. In a bigger place, the newspapers piled up on the floor could occupy a special room, an archive, a library. I would not have to worry about the neighbors, because there would be nothing surrounding me except for a cool, wooded garden where I could listen to my records without having to use headphones. In this ideal world, a perfect woman would also exist; that is, a woman very similar to me, a sensible, lucid, cultured being with whom it would be possible to fall in love. Like me, she would know how to appreciate silence, order, and cleanliness. She would not frequent the frivolous stores where Ruth buys her clothes, nor would she invite me to the restaurants where we eat to make up for the deficiencies in our relationship. Being with her would be enough. I almost know this woman; I know precisely the sensation caused by her proximity, her scent, the feel of her hair, the tender atmosphere that exists between us. How familiar her presence seems to me, a presence I can only tap into by way of certain musical notes, certain chords, or when I am asleep. I do not know if I find it more painful to think of the past or of this life so far removed from me and from my possibilities. Even though I try to freeze the image, it never lasts very long. The ideal woman always turns into a face I know, and therefore an ominous one. It is pointless to say that I consider this dream as impossible as the one of the house in the forest. In the past, I have lived with enough members of the female sex to understand that not only are they inferior, but their emotional instability can drive us to death. Frankly, I would say that, to me, the experience of love exists only in a utopian, imagined fashion, such as when we pause to dream of a memory.

Certain images from my youth send me back to this sublime feeling: for example, the evening I met Susana, or the trip we took together to Varadero five years later, two weeks during which we were almost permanently dazzled by each other. Susana was perhaps the most beautiful woman I have been with in my entire life, her skin almost mineral, a nubile expression in her intensely blue eyes, a woman devoted to me, lost in and given over to me entirely. The daughter of a well-to-do Spanish family living in Cuba for generations, she had no trouble entering or leaving this rotten island I felt chained to, and yet she decided to settle there forever in order to stay with me. The day I saw her for the first time, Mario and I had cycled over to El Vedado, where the prettiest girls in all Havana could be found. Both Mario and I like white, well-fed flesh, but he, being blond, prefers to look at dark-skinned girls, and I at those with fair hair and blue eyes. Most of the time we went to El Vedado at night. We had formed part of a group of mainly foreign kids, seduced by Mario's natural charm, his unique way of dancing *casino* or *guaguancó* at parties, but also by my intelligent conversation. I cannot dance, and do not even attempt to. I am not made for vulgar pastimes. That evening, the heat had died down a little and it was as if our bicycles were moving on their own, carrying us down the street without the slightest effort on our part. We stopped to have an ice cream at Coppelia, the two of us dirty, bathed in sweat. Then we saw Susana, and stopped in front of her like two men contemplating a ghost. Although we were used to talking to chicks, to chatting them up, ensnaring them with our tongues (my finest tool), on that day Mario and I were rendered mute in bewilderment. Susana was too beautiful to be real; she did not have that fire in her eyes that characterizes women from this island, the provocative smile, the impudence. Her eyes had a kind of resignation in them, like an animal contemplating the butcher's knife an inch from its neck. I suppose that back then neither of us had seen anything like it. Now, after many years, not only do we recognize it, but we know how to contend with that certainty that colors the gaze of our acquaintances whenever a doctor, or an Ifá priest, announces some fateful diagnosis. Her hair still damp from a recent shower—the scent of the soap was hanging in the air—Susana sat and ate her ice cream at a table in the back. When she eventually looked up and saw us, she too seemed surprised. Surely, never in all her life—which at that moment consisted of sixteen years—had she seen two such dirty, disagreeable idiots.

The rule was tacit and unbreakable: Susana was blond, ergo she belonged to me. Mario would have to sit on the sidelines, and so he got in line for ice cream to leave the path clear for me while I fell on the gazelle's neck. However, intimidated by her beauty and discouraged by my own appearance, I could think of nothing to do except move away from her and join Mario at the end of the line. We waited our turns in silence, and then ate our ice creams in silence, too. When he'd finished, Mario crumpled up his napkin as he always did, throwing it into the trash can with the precision of a basketball player. He turned to me and smiled, affectionately:

"You're such a jackass," he said.

The subject did not come up again until a week later, but I did not stop thinking about the girl from Coppelia for one minute.

MÉNILMONTANT

Autumn went by in the blink of an eye. Every day, the news did nothing but report on the snow falling throughout the country. According to statistics, the temperature was lower now than it had been for thirty years and the radio was there repeatedly to remind us of this fact. From my windows, I watched intrigued at how the leaves struggled to stay on the branches of the trees before their inevitable fall. Gradually I had come to get a feel for the curious location of my building. The boulevard de Ménilmontant separates not only the neighborhood of the living and that of the dead, but also two very different districts. It is a kind of border. In the 11th arrondissement, there are restaurants, greengrocers, cash-and-carry stores, and a huge number of bars. The 20th, meanwhile, is a poorer, much more working-class neighborhood. For a long time it represented the limits of the city, and for this reason has always harbored deprived people of all kinds.

I enjoyed walking down the street in the morning, when the city's hubbub had not yet reached its usual decibel level. On the metal shutters I passed I could see signs of businesses that had closed several years back. I peered curiously at the windows of the religious shops displaying their ritual fringes, their festive candelabras. Nearby was the kosher butcher's and, just around the corner, its halal equivalent. The atmosphere was so peaceful then, so familiar, that it was hard to imagine the relatives of these same people waging a bloody war not too many miles away.

I found the locals peaceable, but I could not say that they were friendly. When they saw me come into one of their shops, they could see straight away that I was not a member of any of the neighboring communities, the ones that made up their regular clientele. They allowed me to poke around the shelves filled with products whose labels you read from right to left, without expecting anything of me. This attitude, polite yet indifferent, suited me, although it made me feel somewhat isolated, too. There was such a concentrated mix in this neighborhood that no one was surprised anymore by my Latin American features. In Belleville, no one asked me which corner of the planet I had come from.

To someone who has never lived in Paris, the conditions I found myself in, with an apartment, a grant, and a plan to get my postgrad degree, might seem like enough to survive happily, at least for a while. Anyone who has spent a reasonable amount of time here, however, knows that it is not an easy city to adapt to. French people from other cities criticize the sullenness of its inhabitants, considering them a scourge that spoils the beauty of their capital. What is certain is that it is enough to stay here a couple of months to start being permeated by this grumpy, antisocial apathy. You do not even need to speak to anyone to be infected with it. The slightest dealings with Parisians—on the métro, on the stairs in your apartment building, in the bakery—are enough to make you start feeling the symptoms. Perhaps not even that. Perhaps all you have to do is breathe the musty air of the river or sample the tap water, which I drank without filtering it, in order to feel the inexplicable malaise so characteristic of Paris. Little by little, my enthusiasm dwindled until it disappeared completely. My main preoccupation was resisting the cold of winter, the frozen wind that battered my face, and the constant rain, quiet and stubborn, like a rat that has made itself right at home, impossible to drive out.

Haydée had guessed correctly: my five suitcases were full of rags. I had arrived from Latin America laden down with warm clothing that had belonged to my parents. Old clothes, some of them moth-eaten, good quality but not well chosen enough to be considered vintage. When I got dressed, I followed no style except that of avoiding the cold at all costs. I recall especially clearly a '70s-style wool coat, far too big for me, which became my second skin. My father had bought it to keep warm on a trip to Rome and kept it for years in the hope that someday his daughter or one of his nephews or nieces would travel to Europe and wear it again. There was one morning in particular when I did not manage to get to the institute. I had wasted more than forty minutes waiting for the métro, which on that day was running a poor service, when I decided to hail a cab on the corner of chemin Vert and Ménilmontant. Beneath my father's coat, I was wearing two sweaters and a knitted scarf, but I was still shivering with cold, and just as I was seriously considering going home, a taxi appeared. I flagged it down, anxious to find a warm seat. I shut the door and rubbed my hands together as I told the driver the name of the institute. Before moving off, the driver took a long look at me in his rearview mirror. It had been months since anyone had displayed the slightest bit of interest in me and so I was surprised by the way he was observing me. I had not yet decided whether to feel flattered or offended, when the driver snapped at me in his marked Parisian accent: "You can't get into my taxi with a coat like that, mademoiselle. You'll get my car all covered in fur. If you want me to take you anywhere you're going to have to put it in the boot." In time, I would come to see comments like this one as the spines a mutant hedgehog sprouts in an overly hostile and dangerous environment, but, as a recent arrival, I was convinced that such arrogant behavior was directed at me personally. And so when the cab stopped at the lights, I seized my chance and slipped out of the car without a word. I returned to my lair and spent the rest of the morning under the duvet.

Contrary to what I had imagined, the Institute of Latin American Studies was not a hospitable place. Almost all the students went home as soon as classes were over, and the restaurant was not full of smiling young people like the cafés frequented by Haydée— whom, incidentally, I almost never saw anymore. The seminars consisted of some fifteen people, if that. My classmates, spoiled and pedantic, made not the slightest bit of effort to get to know each other. Like a specter whom nobody notices, I would walk through the building's corridors, amazed at the silence and the solitude within its walls. In the evenings after class, I thought of nothing but leaving as quickly as possible. In order to reach my house I had to cross the whole city and change twice on the métro. I did not like being underground, but just looking at the bus lines on a map made me feel dizzy. In any case, it was unpleasant waiting in the cold. The Parisians had changed a lot since the summer. The people who had waved hello to each other and struck up conversations at ten o'clock at night in the month of June were the same ones who now pushed me brusquely towards the entrance to the métro, and woe betide anyone who dared to complain or say anything! This, I had absolutely no doubt, this was the elusive Paris I had dreamed of for so long, and yet, in spite of all my efforts, I just could not figure out how to deal with its inhabitants, its gestures, or its codes. Instead of being embraced like one who deserved it, I was being made a casualty of the city's resounding rejection. It was as if it had been decided, in some invisible courtroom, that I was not worthy of living there.

Among the first things I noticed in this wintry place was the number of people who seemed to belong to a parallel, independent reality, individuals who held heated conversations with themselves or with hypothetical interlocutors, who address passengers on the métro only to insult them for the sheer pleasure of insulting or else for some unknown reason. These disturbed people—whom I would not presume to classify as psychopaths—all seemed strangely similar to me, victims of some kind of psychological epidemic. The symptoms manifested themselves mainly in visibly impoverished individuals who, after lashing out at one or two bystanders, would get onto a bus or into a carriage on the métro and ask the passengers for financial help; but they might also show up as waiters, as the stallholders at the newsstands, or as telephone operators. Far too often, the métro would stop because of what the intercom explained was an "*accident de passager,*" a euphemism coyly employed so as not to articulate the death of one of those people who had jumped in front of a train. I watched all this without understanding the reasons, with the distant, bemused attitude with which one analyzes foreign customs. These people scared me. Where did they come from? And how, above all, could there be so many of them? But the others scared me, too, the ones who displayed an air of superiority and scorn towards those who seemed to have come unhinged or, as the French put it, gone off the rails.

What the hell did I expect from life? The question began to creep along like a menacing shadow, eroding the fragile equilibrium of my days. It stalked me as soon as I woke up, ruining the start to the day. It showed up again at breakfast time, or later, when I was having a shower to clear my head. It was there on the bus on the way to the institute, too, or when I opened the door to my class-room. If I had had a convincing answer, perhaps I would have focused my efforts on fulfilling this objective. But I had no pointers, not even an intuition. The truth, now that I can see it clearly, is that I expected nothing. For the first few months I had devoted all my time and effort to adapting to the city, but once I had resolved this problem I found myself faced with a huge number of dead hours. My small grant gave me enough to live on and I had no reason to try to earn more money. People save when they are chasing after some precise objective, such as buying a house or going on holiday, when they have children or parents to look after, while others save for the pleasure of accumulating wealth. Not one of these circumstances matched mine, however. Living in the present already felt to me like a heroic feat; thinking of the future was enough to make me feel I was suffocating.

In the evenings after leaving the institute, I could spend hours in a café, watching the pedestrians walk past, the students dressed in garish colors carrying out surveys in the touristy areas like Odéon or place Saint-Michel. Everyone was in a hurry. The urgent pace of people's footsteps, so different from my own, which most of the time lacked a precise destination, intrigued me. All of them undoubtedly had some objective in life, and I would end up asking myself what I had done to find myself outside this system. It was as if everyone around me possessed some information no one had passed on to me, or as if at some point in their lives someone had revealed to them a secret that I, for whatever reason, was ignorant of. It was as simple as this: they were clear about what they were doing in the world, and I was not. They were the protagonists of some thrilling or stupid story—as any life can be—while I was the spectator of a film whose beginning I could no longer remember.

It was not as if I had an irresistible need to know what that thing was that made other people's lives so interesting. There was not the slightest chink in my boredom to let in a glimmer of curiosity, or even the enthusiasm that arises when there is a chance to escape tedium.

By December, my life had been reduced to a ghostly state, reports of which reached no one, aside from the lady on the till at the supermarket, the man at the newsstand, which I walked past every day without stopping to buy a paper, and the woman in the bakery, who saw me come into her shop two or three times a week, wrapped in a dark gray coat the color of the sky in the city. I could not care less about what was happening in the world. Less and less frequently as the days went on, Haydée would call me to find out how I was. I told her I was concentrating on my studies. I could tell from her tone of voice that she hated this reply—the poor thing had enough on her plate, what with Rajeev's introspective nature—but this did not bother me. More than once, she tried to convince me to go with her to some party or other, but I never said yes. I was not in the mood to talk to anyone, let alone to go out boozing, giving in to bad habits with people I barely knew who talked only about dieting and irritated the hell out of me. I did not want to see anyone.

The situation got worse in the holidays. If I barely socialized before, my contact with others dwindled to nothing once classes finished at the institute. I spent my time waiting for December 21, the date that marked the start of winter, real winter, the prelude to which was this lacerating cold that could already be felt. Since I had no money, I hardly ever went out. I spent hours staring out of the window, half listening to the news on the radio. Any other activity felt like far too much of an effort. The wind whipped endlessly against the glass, inducing a kind of mental exhaustion. The rickety shutters let in the cold and all I had to protect myself was the old electric heater. I tried to wash myself only as much as necessary so as to avoid suffocating in my own odors, and when I went downstairs to buy anything I did so with my father's coat on top of my pajamas and a woolen hat I wore to hide my scruffy hair. Heat necessitates cleanliness just as the cold forces one to conserve one's bodily temperature at any price, no matter if we have to get used to our own stench or inflict it on those who come near us. The only times I went out into the street each week were to go either to the bank or the supermarket. This lifestyle, normal for any French student, seemed to me extraordinary. I never would have imagined I would end up living in such conditions, shamelessly living in a state of what in my country is known as "European filth." My apartment was a faithful reflection of my mood: covered in bits of paper, with socks strewn all across the floor. The radio, which I rarely paid any attention to, was on twenty-four hours a day, giving out a soothing background noise. I ate when I felt like it, and did not change my clothes or wash the dishes stacked up in the sink, and yet, never before had I lived with such integrity. All my previous years I had been forced to maintain a certain level of order for someone: my father, my grandmother, the friends I had lived with. Now, for the first time in my life, I lived alone and I did not plan to conform to any social rules at all.

As I said before, the only thing I noticed during this period was what I could see from my window: the boulevard with its cars, the family scenes, or the drunkards' squabbles. I liked the shabby look of the neighborhood, which made me feel at home. Unsurprisingly, the cemetery became right from the start my main source of distraction and of education. Rather than explore it on foot, something I did on very few occasions, I preferred to look at it from a distance.

On Saturdays or Sundays I would sit by the window to drink coffee and watch the funerals. In general, the ceremonies were as entertaining as the society pages of any newspaper. From my apartment I would watch as the Parisian bourgeoisie paraded past, showing off their luxury cars, clothes, jewels, sunglasses, and the odd hat. The discretion displayed by each family varied considerably. Some were extravagant, some exhibitionist, some frugal and austere, and there were Catholics, Jews, Muslims, and evangelicals. Some conducted the event with grandiloquent speeches, others enlisted every single florist on the block, or else the thing would take place so rapidly, almost surreptitiously, that the only outside observer of suffering was me, and perhaps, from their window, another neighbor who also had a liking for this kind of spectacle. This is how I discovered that each funeral has its own personality and style. People die, leaving their name inscribed on a tombstone, and their lives cease to run in a straight line. The body disappears, and with it its routine, its needs, and yet a myriad of traces do remain. The emotions that have evolved for years continue to float in the air: rage, frustration, and helplessness and tenderness, too. All of these things are like hard, mineral claws discernible beyond the gravestones. It is no accident that the graves are so different from one another. Not even the niches are the same. They are tarnished unevenly. One will have grease stains by the epitaph; on another moss will be growing; on a third the marble will look more polished, intact. Death has its ironies, too: the things one would rather banish are what remain, while what one would like to preserve is fast forgotten.

TRIBECA

The old thing goes out of her way to please me. I found it incredibly easy to get used to her world. Maybe it was the softness of her pillows, the big armchair in her living room where I enjoy reading the newspaper, or the quality of the wine she always has in the house, but in an unexpected, totally different way from what has happened to me before with other women, in her loft I feel comfortable and taken care of, and for many months this was enough for me to continue seeing her. On weekends, her children tend to go to the country with their father, and then there is nothing to stop me from enjoying this apartment like a king who, after a long day's hunting, returns to his castle.

Ruth likes to buy food in the delicatessens of Tribeca, which are like toy stores for wealthy women. Each portion of food comes in a little golden box or wrapped in waxed paper of various colors. On Saturday mornings, she lets me read the newspaper at my leisure and returns at lunchtime with all kinds of delicacies. My favorites are the Polish hors d'oeuvres, but Kutsher's is closed on Saturdays and Ruth does not always have time to pass that way on a Friday morning. And so, to make up for this, she brings home a selection of French cheeses and a bottle of wine instead. She spreads a spotless tablecloth over the table, lays out four crystal glasses, and we sit down to eat in silence: this woman knows perfectly well that I cannot bear needless chatter and she makes sure not to speak more than is necessary. While we eat, she voices at most a couple of questions about the bread or the kind of tea I feel like drinking. To reward her, I throw her the occasional affectionate glance. After we have finished, when there is nothing left on my plate but a few crumbs of strudel, Ruth clears the table, trying not to make any noise with the glasses and cutlery. I contemplate her out of the corner of my eye while I smoke a slightly dry Popular. A coworker brought a couple of packs of these cigarettes back from Cuba for me more than six months ago and, since then, I have smoked just one a week, generally on a Saturday. After eating, we go into her room for a long siesta that almost always culminates in violent sex.

One of the rules I set for myself with women is to not ask them anything about their lives prior to me. This keeps them, in their turn, separate from me. In short, discretion erects a barrier of distance as necessary in my eyes as the most basic hygiene. Nevertheless, one Saturday evening, as I was drinking my coffee in the armchair, I started to take a closer look at the shelves in the old thing's loft. Strange as it might seem, I noticed a series of details I had never before seen in the place that, by then, I had been frequenting for several months. I was curious to know where some of the masks that hang from the walls had come from, or the story of the silver candelabra that stands on the bookcase. She had finished clearing the table and begun to tidy up a few brochures that had been scattered for ages on the floor around the fireplace. This little corner is also where nearly all the books in her apartment are kept, many of them bound in leather, the old-fashioned way, like my grandparents' books, which my parents kept in their library. Oddly enough, I had never studied the titles of these volumes. Since my first visit I had considered them part of the furniture, like the objects decorating the shelves or the occasional tables. I had only analyzed the books on textile design that Ruth kept close to her in the bedroom, along with a few fashion magazines, including every single edition of *Vogue*. She could, it is true, claim her profession was an excuse for keeping such a huge quantity of junk in her bedroom. At first I had wondered whether, if she had had a different job, Ruth would have accumulated magazines like that, as lots of women in New York do, for the simple love of fashion, but the fact is she did not exactly speak passionately about subjects related to her work as a designer. It was unusual for her to open one of those enormous catalogs to show me some new design or to ask my opinion about an item of clothing. That night, while Ruth busied herself in the kitchen, I left the high-backed chair where every Saturday I read the newspaper from cover to cover, and went over to the library. When I read the titles I discovered, to my great surprise, that they were essays on philosophy and religion. Quite a few were in German, others in Hebrew, and a small number were in medieval Spanish. Among them I recognized an old edition of the *Zohar*, translated into English, and the *Guide for the Perplexed* by Maimonides. I opened a page at random. I felt only admiration for this cultural wealth from which Ruth is descended and which, at the same time, was forbidden to her, like a family secret no one had shared with her. I amused myself by looking at the photographs on the shelves, which showed a bearded man, probably Ruth's father, wearing a black hat. I do not know if it was because of his attire, but I got the impression that he belonged to a very remote era and not to the generation immediately preceding Ruth's. I said to myself that her father was actually a contemporary of my grandfather. Another photograph showed two children, Ruth and her husband's, a boy and a girl who both looked like her. A small painting, which I had not spotted before either, drew my attention toward the back wall. Something in it seemed familiar. Perhaps I had seen it somewhere before or knew the style of the artist.

"Whose are all these books?" I said.

"They were my father's. I rescued them when they took him to the nursing home."

"And what do you want with them?" I interrogated her a little mockingly. "Do you plan to read them someday?"

"No. I just have them as part of the decor of the house."

I wondered if there was a touch of irony to her answer, but immediately dismissed the possibility. It did not fit with her docile, good-natured character.

"I grew up surrounded by books like these. The smell of the pages makes me feel at home."

"Is there any coffee left in the kitchen?" I inquired, returning to my seat with difficulty. Yet again, we had eaten too much.

"Don't you move," she scolded me, as mildly as ever. "I'll bring you some right away."

But evidently there was no coffee left in the pot, because I heard Ruth open the fridge and turn on the machine again. Then the telephone rang, and she amused herself chatting for the time the coffee took to be made.

She came back to the living room with the coffee cups and a packet of cookies.

"That was Isaac." Although I had seldom heard it, I recognized her ex-husband's name. "He said the kids spent the afternoon at the lake yesterday and now they both have colds. What a weird thing to do, with it being so cold out! They'll have to miss school."

"It was hot yesterday," I reminded her, trying to calm her down. "The weird thing is that they got sick. Who's this painting by?"

"Which one? The little one on the back wall? That's a Mark Rothko. He was a friend of my father's and he gave it to him."

"What did your family do?" I said, intrigued. She must have found it strange that after so many months I was suddenly interested in her past. In all honesty, I found it strange, too.

"My mother trained as an architect, but she never practiced; people say I inherited her talent for design. And my father was a professor of Jewish philosophy at Columbia. Isaac was a pupil of his."

I was suddenly overwhelmed by a feeling of vertigo. I was drawing near to a depthless abyss or, at least, to a series of explanations similar to the ones that would unravel if I were ever to try to describe Santería customs to her, and so I chose instead to change the subject. I have never really accepted the American idea of the melting pot, still less when it comes to religion. I had made a mistake by asking so many questions. It was better to accept this and to try to find a way of preventing her from asking questions about my background. And so I put my hand up her skirt and pulled her toward me by her panties. I sat her on my lap and stroked her hair for a long time, tenderly, as you might with a young girl whom sooner or later you will end up taking advantage of. The old thing learned very quickly what kind of behavior turns me on. She knows that, at first, during what is generally called "foreplay," I like her to seem genuinely frightened by my body, to struggle or try to run away. It does not matter if in order to escape she has to bite me or dig her cat-like nails into my skin. But once I have her under my abdomen, once her legs are open beneath my furious groin, she must remain motionless, not even breathing if possible, until the point of orgasm, when I do allow her some release. The way that we screw frequently resembles rape. Unlike other women I have been with, she reacts to violence, whether physical or verbal, in a deliciously submissive way and this is another of the traits that make me feel so at ease by her side. More than once I have accidentally torn her silk panties or left a bruise on her delicate, fragile skin. Far from being irritated, she finds these displays of desire flattering. You might say that we are good lovers if it were not for the fact that when we have finished, I am flooded with an inexplicable sensation of disgust. Something in that shriveled body lying there on the mattress, the hair loose, spread out on the sheets, inspires it. At first I used the excuse of having eaten too much. After a few months, however, I decided to put hypocrisy aside and accept the reality of the situation, no matter how complex it might be.

This time the sex was particularly good and lasted the whole afternoon. I took a shower and left her house clean and relaxed. In the street I was met by the cool late September air. New York in all its splendor, with its dry leaves and auburn shrubs, like a woman surrendering herself in her mature years, in the knowledge that winter will soon dry her up.

Going back to my place after spending one or two days away brings me an indescribable sense of tranquility. Even though no one is waiting for me—or perhaps for this very reason—I feel cocooned in the lair I have constructed. I am not just talking about my few pieces of furniture, my books and my records, my newspaper clippings; even the lack of light in my apartment, the humidity and the temperature are familiar and therapeutic to me. Every day when I come home from work, I take off my shoes and put them in the place I have set aside for them, the closet in the hall. I put on my slippers and monitor any changes that might have occurred during my absence: I look through the mail, pick up the newspaper that has been left under the door, open the windows to let in the fresh air. Before I sit down to rest in my blue armchair, especially if I have been away for several days, I like to take the broom and the feather duster and get rid of any dust that might have gathered in my little stone corridor. I also scrub the bathroom and, if I consider it necessary, clean the windows, even though the only thing visible through them is the wall on the other side. Once this task is finished, I can settle down to listen to music, read, or fantasize about all kinds of appealing things until I fall asleep.

I realize that in New York, my apartment has come to discharge the functions normally fulfilled by your family or your mother in the earliest stages of your life. Here—and I give thanks to God for this—I have neither relatives nor friends I am overly close to. I have managed to preserve my privacy to the extent that I still feel at ease. Nonetheless, I have a need like any human being to possess a territory of my own, a refuge where I feel protected. This territory is my apartment, and my way of showing gratitude for its existence consists of taking the utmost care of it, the way you care for a loved one. Cleaning it, tidying it, giving it a structure, practicing in it a series of routines of good behavior. Protecting it from any intruders is my way of honoring my sanctuary and of turning it (I like the image immensely) into the mausoleum where I would like to be buried for all eternity.

NEIGHBORS

The day had started off rainy again and it continued that way for the entire morning. It was almost noon. The bakery would shut in ten minutes, as would the rest of the shops. The Parisians would stay at home all Sunday to read the newspaper, grumble to themselves, or watch television. I was hungry, but I could not decide whether to go out or stay in. The cold horrified me, the dome of low clouds that had taken over the world. If I managed to get to the bakery before it closed, I would get a telling-off for showing up so late. In her shrill, irritated voice, the woman who worked there would ask me yet again if people in Peru had no concept of normal business hours. She would say "Peru" despite the fact that I had explained to her countless times that I was Mexican. It was not because she was trying to be sarcastic or unpleasant, as I had at first suspected, but rather because, to her, Peru and Mexico were basically the same thing. Far from seeing it as an insult, I was reassured that people did not know how to locate either my city or the country I came from on a map. I had an urgent need to consume a croissant, but did not feel up to confronting the bad temper of the woman in the shop. As I considered what to do, I began watching the threads of a spider's web that, unbeknownst to me, had appeared in the entrance to the kitchen. Before I could make up my mind, I heard a knock at the door. Something bad must be happening for someone to bang that hard at it. I peeped through the spyhole into the corridor and saw the face of my neighbor from the apartment to the right. We knew each other by sight, and had said a few rushed hellos to each other on the stairs. In general he seemed a pleasant man, attractive even, but that morning his expression was very different. He looked annoyed and determined to voice a complaint. "Seriously?" I thought. I was denying myself bread so as not to have to face these people's neuroses, and now this.

"Is there something wrong?" I said defensively as I opened the door. I was wearing my own annoyed expression.

"The radio," he replied, like someone giving a password.

I was silent for a few seconds, trying to understand what he was referring to, but it was useless.

"It's been on in your room for more than five days and you haven't even got the decency to turn the volume down at night."

His reply surprised me. By that point, the presence of the radio had become a background noise I never thought about.

"If it annoys you that much I can turn it off," I said, to put an end to the matter.

I wondered if I should ask him in, mainly to stop the other inhabitants of the building from hearing our dispute, but I held back: my apartment was a state. As I was wavering, he pushed open the door himself with an exasperated gesture, went over to my room where the apparatus was, pressed a button, and immediately let out a sigh of relief. It was as if he'd just had a shard of glass removed from the sole of his foot. The expression that had been on his face vanished immediately.

"Listen," he said, rapping on the wall with his knuckles, producing a hollow sound. "These walls are like cardboard. My bed is right on the other side of this one. I can hear *everything* that happens on the other side. Come and see what I mean."

The way he pronounced the word "everything" made me smile. I thought that in my room at least, *nothing* ever happened. I did not have parties or bring friends back. I did not have a boyfriend either, or indulge in orgies or long, noisy sessions of masturbation. The only thing I had was a miserable radio and it appeared that this annoyed him. On the other hand, if the wall was as thin as he was making out, he did not exactly have an enviable private life, either. In short, my neighbor was as wretched as I was, and perhaps out of solidarity, I agreed to follow him instead of telling him to go to hell. And so I put on my slippers, closed my door, and followed him into his apartment.

I was immediately struck by the difference between our two living spaces. A model of order and cleanliness, my neighbor's apartment was the polar opposite of mine, not just for its elegance and spaciousness, but also because it faced west, in contrast with my own little broom cupboard, which faced north. The midday sun shone directly in through his windows. The sun! I had forgotten about this joy for several weeks. Another notable difference was the fact that his apartment contained a large number of plants, large and small, of various species and textures, while in my house I had none. A little larger than mine, his living room took the form of an inviting library. The dining room, situated towards the back near the kitchenette, reminded me of one in a doll's house. The windows were clean, too, and when I looked through them, the view was not of the monotonous landscape of the cemetery but of a little tree-lined cul-de-sac. From the dining room you could see the boulevard de Ménilmontant and, over on the other side, the expanse of the cemetery, although this did not dominate the view as it did from my own apartment. Being there, it was easy to tell that, years back, his apartment and mine had once formed a single space until Madame Loeffler had chosen to divide it in two so as to double her income. In that primordial period, his bedroom and mine had formed a single room divided exactly in half by the fireplace, which did not work, whose chimney we shared just as two Siamese twins share a spinal cord. Our bedrooms, however, were totally different. In his, the bed was made and not a single item of clothing was out of place. On the bedside table were piled the books which the sound of my radio had prevented him from reading.

To make conversation I asked him if he had chosen to live on this street or if, like me, had ended up in this building by chance. He answered without hesitation that it had been a choice and that he adored cemeteries. Tom—this was how he had introduced himself—invited me to look at the photographs hanging on the walls. They were pictures of graves in different places around the world that he had taken on his travels, almost all of them in black and white, although a few were in brilliant color. I recognized the Old Jewish Cemetery in Prague and the one in Fez, photos of which I had seen in the library in Oaxaca. Despite it being right opposite, Père-Lachaise appeared in several of them. Realizing that we shared this fascination suddenly endeared him to me. More than once in the months after we met he asked for my permission to look at the Père-Lachaise from my apartment, not the weekend funerals I observed with morbid curiosity, but the cemetery stripped bare, without tourists or visitors, in its moments of greatest desolation, which were generally during holidays or early in the morning. As I looked in amazement at his photographs I said to myself, without admitting that my admiration was of another kind, that we could without doubt be friends.

There was no longer irritation in his eyes. Tom observed me without surprise, as one observes an everyday object, a window that gives over to a familiar landscape, something that merits no judgment of any sort, except perhaps contemplation. A clear gaze in an attractive face. I felt strangely safe at his side, until he opened his mouth again.

"You know what? Neither of us ended up here by chance. It was our neighbors who live opposite."

"You mean the dead people?" I said, incredulously.

"Yes. They're the ones who decide who lives near them."

I felt afraid. Not of the dead, but of him. It was one thing to be fascinated by cemeteries, and another very different thing to believe in the existence of spirits or their supposed influence over us. I decided not to ask anything more, and, pretending I had some pressing matter to attend to, went back to my apartment convinced that my neighbor belonged to that legion of crackpots who stalked the streets and the city's underground system.

Back in my apartment, I immediately resented the silence of the radio, which, as I said before, was my only company, but I could not switch it on again: it would have been a slap in the face and by that point I knew very well that it was not worth provoking these mad Parisians. It must have been around four o'clock, and through the windows the sky was starting to grow dark, obscuring every evening as it did the graves in the cemetery. The silence brought on a sense of disquiet and unease. I remembered that on the shelves in my room two borrowed novels awaited me that I still had not started. I opened one of them, but could not concentrate. More than once, I found myself looking over at the lifeless radio. It was incredible how addicted I had become to the device. For a few seconds I thought about switching it on at a very low volume, then considered moving it to a different place. I could put it on a kitchen shelf for instance, far from the ears and ill will of my neighbor, but something inside me refused to carry on fueling this dependency.

Outside, winter had reached its nadir and we were at minus 8°C. I left the house as little as possible. For the most part I stayed home, trying to read. The sounds from the street and the stairs distracted me constantly. Ever since I had turned off the radio, I found any eruption of sound surprising and, above all, very annoying. I could spend hours listening to these sounds I had never noticed before. For example, I began to listen to the car horns and tires outside on the boulevard, but also to the people who lived in the building moving around, coughing, making calls. I realized it was possible to decipher their lives through the sounds. In a couple of weeks I even came to identify their different footsteps and the way they each closed their doors. Some of these noises I found consoling, among them the voice of a woman who lived on the third floor and who spoke on the telephone at around eight o'clock every night, in a language unknown to me, and similar to how I imagined Croatian would sound. Other noises, meanwhile, managed to shatter my nerves, such as the stilettoed footsteps of the woman on the fifth floor, who would come home late, drunk and tottering. But I detested her less than the coffee machine on the fourth floor, which whistled every morning, interrupting my sleep. Of all these noises, the most evident and inescapable were those that came from next door, from Tom's apartment, that is. Not just because it was the closest, but because, since my visit to his house, I had got into the habit of imagining everything he did. It was an embarrassing habit, in truth, which revealed to me the full extent of my idleness, and yet I indulged in it with less and less resistance as time went on. Sometimes, in an attempt to defend myself, I would reason that he was the one who, by depriving me of my radio, had caused this sort of compulsive espionage of which he was unknowingly a victim. Perhaps another, saner person might have taken advantage of the absence of background noise to read, to listen to music, or to ring up her friends. I could have finally accepted Haydée's invitation to go and visit her in her apartment on rue de Lévis for a change of scene, but instead I chose to make an inventory of my neighbor's activities.

A couple of weeks was enough for me to work out and memorize Tom's daily routine. I knew, for instance, that he woke up at 6:45 a.m. and that, while the electric kettle was boiling in his kitchen, he shuffled around from one end of his apartment to the other. At 9:30 he took a shower—the first of the day—which fired up the noisiest boiler in the whole building. Before getting under the water, he urinated at length. Every other day he shaved with a manual razor, tapping it three times on the edge of the sink after each stroke. In the evening when he came back from work, he would throw his keys into a glass bowl and make himself a cup of tea. The excess of caffeine must have been the reason for his frequent trips to the bathroom, which continued even through the night. The fact is that it was impossible not to imagine him standing up, in front of the toilet, as the liquid poured forth in great quantities.

Two hours after arriving home, Tom would begin to cook, and then it was not only the opening and closing of his cupboards but also the heavenly smells of the dishes he made that became unmistakable. I would have given anything to try them. The way he climbed the stairs was particularly intriguing and made him instantly identifiable. He walked with a slow pace unusual for a man of his age, a pace that betrayed a great fatigue more than apathy. He generally reached the fourth floor exhausted and out of breath.

Once I had his movements sussed out, the habit of listening through the walls intensified: with the help of my alarm clock, I began measuring the time that passed between one event and another. Thus I discovered that, after eating dinner, he took exactly eighteen minutes to clear the kitchen and wash the dishes. The intervals between each trip to the toilet were three-quarters of an hour. His morning shower took a little under seven minutes; the occasional baths he took, around thirty. Just as I had thought, my neighbor's romantic life was a real desert. The only female voice that could be heard in his house was that of an aunt who regularly left long messages on the answerphone, shouting in Italian that he should wrap up warm now that it was cold, or recommending he drink eucalyptus tea. How old could Tom be? He dressed and acted like a man of thirty, but the expression on his face and the look in his eyes made him appear much older. Perhaps he had lived a lot, as they say, or had drunk until he'd damaged his skin and his liver—who could say? Very few times—two, to be precise—I heard someone visiting him. On both occasions it was a male friend who had come by to have a cup of tea and talk about his private life. Tom seemed to fulfill the role of confidant for those guys who, unlike him, did lead an interesting life. When they left, I could not help peeping through my spyhole to take a look at them. Both looked younger or, at least, better preserved than Tom. Several times, when I went to get my post, I had seen his name, Tommaso Zaffarano, on one of the metal postboxes in the hallway. Since our conversation I had occasionally peered inside it to see if he at least got some post.

In the hierarchy of Parisian obsessions, sex occupies an important place. The whole of society seems to be concerned with it. "*Mal baisé*" is one of the worst insults you can say to a French adult, but it is not so much the lack of activity that affects their self-esteem, as the fact that this dearth has become public. The French do not tend to admit to celibacy. They experience it as a humiliation. Very few people confess to not engaging in any intercourse at all, and yet surveys reveal that a significant percentage of the population exists outside of sex. They are anonymous surveys, naturally. I tend to believe that the less contact men have with women, the less attractive they end up being to our gender, but in Tom's case this was not true.

One night I heard something that made me prick up my ears, and which for a moment made me think I had misjudged him. It all began with an unusual squeaking sound from the springs of his bed. I heard the mattress bouncing around a few times, then a silence lasting two minutes and then after this, a moan, but this signaled not pleasure but rather the start of a long and noisy sobbing. The discovery disturbed me, it was so unexpected. I had no idea what its cause might be, but this did not stop me from feeling infinite sorrow for him. I lay motionless for a few minutes, stretched out on my bed, as if instead of offering him my shoulder I were giving him my wall and my ear, until I could not bear it any longer and moved away, convinced I should protect myself: sadness, like almost all moods, is highly contagious. Mine was already extremely fragile; the last thing I needed was to fall into one of those inconsiderate depressions that send foreign students running back to their own countries.

Our second encounter happened midway through December. One afternoon, I had gone out to restock my cupboards at Ed l'Épicier—a pretty crummy supermarket, that much we can agree on, but also the cheapest in the neighborhood—and was heading upstairs with my bags full of the tinned food I planned on consuming that week. When I reached the fourth floor I almost bumped into Tom, who was leaving his apartment and had stopped to rest for a moment at the top of the stairs.

"I'm an old man," he joked. "My mother always said I should do some sport."

"Or find somewhere to live with a lift," I replied. "Even if it's not opposite your dead friends."

He invited me in for another cup of tea. Around that time I was feeling very anxious. My stomach would frequently tense up, giving me a kind of cramp in the guts. Nevertheless, for the first time in two weeks, that afternoon in his apartment I felt strangely at peace, like somebody returning to friendly territory after several days of fierce battle. Unlike the brand I bought in Ed, my next-door neighbor's tea did not come in little paper bags but in a black metal tin containing dried and perfumed leaves. Just as I had imagined from the surname I had seen on his postbox, my neighbor was Italian, but had spent more than fifteen years living in Paris, the city he'd arrived in to study anthropology. He had abandoned his studies two years after joining the department. Since then he had spent his life traveling and working in a range of different jobs, often as a gardener. Now, however, he earned his living as a bookseller in a bookshop close to place de la République, which I often walked past. We talked about Madame Loeffler and how neglected the building we lived in was. It had been a long time since I had talked to anyone and, perhaps for this reason, everything he said seemed interesting. Tom was friendly that afternoon, more than I would have dared to hope after the fracas with the radio.

We drank our tea leaning back on the '70s sofa and stayed there until the early evening, listening to a Ry Cooder record. Among other things, Tom told me that he'd lived in Rome until he was ten before moving to New York with his family. His father, now dead, had been a diplomat.

"And where do you feel like you're from?" I said.

"I don't feel French or totally Italian, let alone American. I'm a creature of borders, really. That's where I feel most comfortable, in those halfway places. Look at the boulevard, for instance. It belongs to the 11th arrondissement but it looks much more like the 20th, over there, on the other side of the cemetery, don't you think?"

"I suppose so," I said, just to say something.

"The countries where I feel most at home are France and Italy. I've being shuttling back and forth between them for many years, and their capital cities are full of immigrants from elsewhere. Lots of them feel at home there, believe it or not."

"I've got a couple of friends," I said, thinking of Haydée and Rajeev, "who, even though they're foreigners here, don't feel like it. Maybe because they've been here much longer than I have."

"It's not a question of time but of being in tune with the city, feeling its magnetism, like the Surrealists used to say. I love Sicily. Have you ever been?"

I shook my head and glanced discreetly up at the clock on the wall. I said to myself that very soon he was going to get up to go and urinate. But Tom noticed.

"Am I boring you?" he said. My hypothesis was proved accurate almost immediately. "I'm just going to the toilet—don't move until I get back."

I did not, in fact, plan on leaving anytime soon. I knew that he would start to get dinner ready in less than an hour and I was hoping he would invite me to join him.

That night he cooked fresh ravioli stuffed with ricotta and a tomato and basil sauce—simple and delicious. He opened a bottle of wine which he drank only one glass of, and set to quizzing me about my life. I don't know if I was just imagining it, but he seemed content to have me in his apartment. He spoke frankly of his childhood in Rome in the '70s and his teenage years in New York. As he told me later, he almost never talked about himself. Even so, with the benefit of hindsight, I can say with all certainty that he did not tell me about what was worrying him most at the time, the reason the shelves in his bathroom cabinet were full of medication. Nor did he mention the dead again. It was as if my presence had transported him to another era in which it was possible to live in the *insouciance* and the happiness of the moment. And nor did it sink in that night that this happiness was unusual for him, even though the expression on his face was very different from the one I had seen him wearing whenever we ran into each other in the hallway, or the night he had showed up at my door to tell me off for my loud radio. When the time came for me to leave, he thanked me for coming and assured me that he had not had such a good time in ages. Only then did he come out with one of his unnerving phrases:

"Having you here in the building is a very special thing for me. Maybe it's a kind of leaving present."

In the same way that an air bubble alters the contents of a sealed flask, the contact with my neighbor broke the climatic conditions of my period of hibernation. I spent the whole of the next day cleaning my apartment. I picked the clothes up off the floor, the used napkins, the tissues containing the remnants of my last cold. I washed the dirty dishes stacked up in the kitchenette and took my clothes to the launderette. I got home and waited all evening, hoping that Tom would ring the doorbell. The sky was already dark by 5:00 p.m., and I had to switch on the electric light and get out a candle or two. Several times I found myself tempted to reach for the radio, but I held back. At around half past six I went out onto the landing to knock at his door. He was not in. What could he be doing? I found it inconceivable that someone would leave their house in weather such as this, unless it were to go to work. The institute was closed, as were the university cafés in the center of town. There was nothing to do on the streets of this inhospitable city. It must have been almost nine when I heard his footsteps on the stairs. I held my breath and watched through the spyhole as he arrived. Before putting his key in the lock he stopped hesitantly in front of my door, but then walked past. Crestfallen, I sat down on the sofa and stayed there, waiting for something to happen. Half an hour later, he returned to announce that dinner was ready.

The previous evening, Tom had finished reading Hoffmann's *The Devil's Elixirs* and had nothing but praise for the writer.

I asked him if living opposite all those graves was not enough for him, and confessed that there were nights when, overwhelmed by loneliness, I was unable to sleep.

"That's why I put the radio on," I said, "so I know that, at least at a radio station somewhere, there are people who are alive, drinking coffee, and just talking peacefully, until three in the morning."

"That's normal," he replied, loftily. "Even though you're in harmony with the place, you're still not used to it."

According to Tom, in order to conquer your fear you had to learn to look directly at it, train yourself to do this.

"So what frightens you, then?" I said, prepared to hear another crazy idea.

"Nothing original. Old age, illness, and death, the same as everyone else."

His reply surprised me. How could he be so sure that other people were afraid of those things? I was weighed down by the present, the lack of meaning in my own life, the enormous space between my breastbone and my back, never my own death, let alone old age, which I thought of as so far away. Tom's fears—even in my worst moments of pessimism, when I shuffled along the streets like a condemned soul—were things I almost never thought about.

"Only someone who really wants to be alive could feel so overwhelmed by the possibility of dying," I said, quite convinced.

A faint smile played across his lips.

"Or maybe only when death checks in with a likely date do we truly become interested in staying in this world."

I began to eat dinner at Tom's every night. Sometimes I would go by the supermarket and then chop up the ingredients in my apartment for him to cook once he got back from work. I learned to buy the fresh pasta on rue de la Roquette, and the dried stuff in the grocer's shop on boulevard Voltaire where they sold De Cecco fusilli. If Tom did not make a sauce, he would use sage leaves soaked in butter and this sufficed for a banquet. We bought own-brand wine from Chez Nicolas; since he barely drank, most of the time I was the one who polished off these bottles.

We had an unspoken agreement that we would not ask each other any questions. All we knew was what the other decided to reveal about him or herself. I had seen framed photographs of his family on his bookshelves, but he never spoke of his parents or anyone else. Nor did I ask him why he took so much medication, or for the reason behind his constant tiredness. I decided to let him broach the subject when he felt ready. Our conversations were nearly always limited to our immediate surroundings: the street, our other neighbors, the shopkeepers in the neighborhood, his work in the bookshop whose name appeared on the price stickers of the books he had in his apartment, novels like Hoffmann's or the complete works of Proust in the Pléiade edition, which I had read in Spanish. Most of them, however, were entirely unknown to me, and I never found out if he had bought them or acquired them by some other means.

"I like your books," I said to him one evening.

"Do you know any of the authors?"

I told him I had read quite a few of them in a library in Oaxaca and that, for years, books had been my only company.

For the second time since we had first met, I felt the force of his gaze upon me.

"You're right," he said. "Books are company. They contain the thoughts and voices of other people who live or have lived in this world. All these authors have in common the fact that they're buried here, opposite us. Even though you can't hear them yet, they speak to us all the time. Not just them, the ones who never wrote a thing, too. You'd hear them if you didn't have the radio on. If you start reading them, they'll seem familiar to you, you'll see." (I thought of all the people I had seen arguing out loud with themselves on the streets.) He paused. I suppose he must have realized that once again I had begun to doubt his sanity. "Let me suggest something: go and stand in front of the bookshelf and choose a book you don't know, any one you like. You can take it, I'll lend it to you."

I stood for several minutes in front of the shelves where Tom kept the authors from the cemetery, arranged alphabetically. I looked over the titles and some of the jackets, but especially the names: Colette, Balzac, Molière, Alfred de Musset, Marcel Proust, and Oscar Wilde, among others. I wondered if they were linked by something other than their final resting place. I decided to take one at random, one that did not seem too long. I knew the author by name, although I had never read him. It was a posthumous publication: *L'infra-ordinaire*. Georges Perec had lived not far from our building. Belleville, his neighborhood, was the one I spent most of my time mooching about in. These streets and buildings were the indisputable protagonists of the book Tom lent me. As the narrator walks along the pavements, he recognizes buildings from his childhood. Some closed as if suspended in time, others utterly transformed. When I realized this, I could not help but leave my apartment and trace the same route he had taken. Perec himself urged his readers to do so: "Describe your street. Describe another street . . . Make an inventory of your pockets . . . What is there under your wallpaper?" It was not a simple distraction or a bit of fun, but a way of seeking the hidden truth in what was most evident, most everyday. Reading the description of rue Vilin, you had the impression that the city hid many things beneath its façades and its "wallpaper," the stories of shopkeepers, of exiles, of people in transit who had lived there for decades; stories of absences, of orphaned children with deported parents, their traces still permeating the façades of the houses. The book said it clearly: we live in the ordinary without ever interrogating ourselves about it and about the information it might give us. "This is no longer even conditioning, it's anesthesia. We sleep through our lives in a dreamless sleep. But where is our life? Where is our body? Where is our space?" he said. I continued to borrow Perec's books from Tom's bookshelves and, although at first I had not set out to discover this author, it was perhaps one more piece of evidence of this objective desire of which he was trying to convince me.

When one of us finished a book, we would discuss it at length over dinner. Tom would cook, I would wash up, and then we would open a new bottle of red. It never occurred to us to invite anyone else we knew. We spent several weeks in total intimacy, including the month of December when people tend to get together, and when classes resumed at the institute, I realized that I no longer cared much about socializing.

CHEMISTRY

I have always been a skeptical man, and so I doubt that a relationship exists in which the magic of the first few encounters does not
end up being pulled apart to reveal its shady side. There will be those
who prefer to live in ignorance in order to remain in the glow of
love for as long as possible. Sooner or later, however, the truth will
come out. You realize that the attractive curls are fabricated every
two weeks at the salon, or that the much-loved breasts owe their
firmness to a talented surgeon and his knife. And, as if by chance, it
is precisely in the detail we most admire where the artifice or trick
is hidden. As far as I am concerned, I would rather know the
mechanisms of seduction as early as possible—even if they then
cease to be effective—than to live with uncertainty, not knowing
when the strings holding up the fragile set will break. If my girlfriend wants to wear a wig to face the world, fine by me; but I need
to be in on the secret to feel at ease. And so, in a way, I am grateful
once again to chance for having allowed me to discover my old
lady's deception. I remember that after having known her for six
months, I found out the cause of her fascinating resignation. We had
screwed more than usual. I was so tired I fell asleep before she
reached orgasm and woke in the middle of the night with the sense
of having some pending chore. Her bedside light was on and, sitting
back against the headboard, Ruth was gulping down water more

thirstily than I had ever seen her do. In one hand she held a little pack of pills, similar to the contraceptives Susana used to take.

"Are you using protection?" I said in a low voice so I didn't wake her children, who that night were sleeping in the room next door. "I thought you'd already gone through menopause."

She looked at me in fright, like someone who is found out seconds after committing some crime.

I took the pills from her hand and read the name of the medicine: Tafil 1.5 mg.

Close up, the pills no longer looked like the ones I had seen years ago, in my first girlfriend's purse. I asked her if there was anyone keeping a close eye on her treatment. And she nodded her head in a childlike way.

"My doctor gave them to me after the divorce. I see him once a week. They've really helped, but I'd like to stop taking them. I feel like they make me numb, as if they cut me off from reality. I didn't want you to know, it's embarrassing."

I told her I preferred to know, and that I did not mind. On the contrary, I agreed with her doctor: if she needed them, it was best for her to keep on taking them.

"And in any case, this way there are no secrets between us," I added, relieved. "Is there anything else you didn't want to tell me?"

She thought for a few minutes.

"I don't think so."

Her voice sounded sincere. With the back of my hand I pushed back the lock of hair hanging over her face and kissed her on the cheek, like a good little girl who has been unjustly told off. I put the pill packet back on the bedside table and turned off the light without saying another word. When I woke up the next morning, the medicine Ruth had been hiding from me was still there. Next to it I saw a glass of water and a packet of even smaller pills I would later learn to identify as "the morning ones."

Ruth took antidepressants three times a day and tranquilizers every night. She did so under the supervision of Dr. Paul Menahovsky, whose clinic on Third Avenue she visited once a week. Prozac and Tafil combined. This was the secret of her unwavering calm, and I could only thank modern pharmacology for having invented a prescription for the woman appropriate for my temperament. Despite what some might think, knowing that this tranquility was not natural but rather induced in her did not disappoint me in the slightest. I would even go so far as to say the opposite. A chemical reaction triggered by medicine is much more trustworthy than behavior based on the circumstances of your life, which are always so unpredictable. What is more, as I mentioned before, I do not believe in love as a kind of spell, but I do believe in a series of pacts and mutual understandings, of shared amusements and of preferences. It is obvious that the little pleasures Ruth and I partook of were not at all compatible with those I procure for myself in moments of solitude and seclusion. It never would have occurred to me, for example, to recite a Vallejo poem to her. Nor could I sit and listen to one of my favorite records with her, or even read a page of Walter Benjamin or Theodor Adorno in her company. No, the interests Ruth and I shared were small, almost trivial, such as good wine, French films, and Polish charcuterie. These interests, as minor as they were, were sufficiently substantial to sustain our shared life, the balance that allowed us to share a space harmoniously once or twice a week. Unfortunately, few things are as ephemeral as pleasure.

As soon as I grew accustomed to it, I ceased to find Ruth's calm and silence arresting. It is sad when you think about it: when two people are not in love, as was our case—at least from my point of view—boredom always seeps in like the mold on food left for too long in the fridge, and this is what happened to us. The day came when tedium crept into our encounters. It was not that I was seeing her too frequently, for we only actually spent two or three days a week together. Nor did she pressure me with too many demands or questions about my life. Her attempts to change the way I dressed—an obsession all women share—manifested themselves in her in the form of sweet, little well-intentioned gifts: a wallet, a cashmere sweater, nothing you could really object to. Nonetheless, the spirit, including my own, grows weak if you stop training it. I had grown far too fond of our Saturday lunches or the afternoons at the movies followed by an intimate dinner, and I was not prepared to give them up. Moved perhaps by this, or by the genuine affection Ruth had for me, I decided to keep the relationship going, even though quite often when I was with her I would busy myself with professional obligations such as editing a set of proofs I had to get through over the weekend, or turning on the television to watch the news.

After a few months, the women at the publishing house began to interest me once again. As I watched them walk past my desk—strategically situated to keep myself isolated from yet simultaneously informed of what was going on in the world—I wondered whether one of them might be the ideal woman whose presence I have sensed so many times whenever I close my eyes to conjure her up. Whenever a new female employee seemed liable to be such a woman, I would concoct some scheme to talk to her or bump into her in the cafeteria. I would wait for her in the buffet line and drag out an introduction or any innocuous question so I could sit at a table with her. A brief chat, accompanied by a slice of quiche Lorraine or cream of mushroom soup, was enough to convince me that those second-rate editors and self-important secretaries could never be the woman I dreamed of. Realizing this, of course, did not prevent me from sleeping with them. But not one of those shared beds seemed worthy of visiting on more than one occasion, still less their owners, whom afterward I avoided whenever fate contrived for us to meet in the corridor or an elevator. I did, however, continue assiduously to visit Ruth's sheets, despite their peach color, despite the nausea which doing so occasionally brought on, and the tedium, too, harder to endure than the nausea itself, for there is no amount of vomit or medicine capable of alleviating a relationship you know in advance has failed. But Ruth did not seem troubled by our foreseeable breakup, or my sickness, or the irritation I wore on my face each weekend like a layer midway between my own skin and the mask of an invited guest. Nonetheless, as unthinkable as it might have seemed to me then, Ruth emerged from her stupor.

One night, about halfway through November—it must have been between three and five o'clock in the morning, I do not recall exactly—the telephone began to ring insistently. As I said before, in my apartment the volume of this device is all but inaudible, but I am a light sleeper and I immediately noticed that the answering machine had come on. The last thing that would have crossed my mind was that *she* might be calling me at such a late hour. I thought perhaps that it was something urgent, maybe some bad news, such as a missile launched at Cuba from Miami, come to destroy the peace of my lair. I chose not to answer, but the telephone rang again and once more the machine clicked on. So it went on intermittently for a couple of hours until my patience ran out and I picked up the receiver, preparing myself to hear about a tragedy from the lips of some recent arrival from Cuba with news of my mother.

"What is it?" I said into the mouthpiece, terrified.

"It's me," Ruth declared on the other end of the line. I recognized her voice, but not the tone she was using. Something must have really been wrong for her to have lost her composure like that.

"What is it, sweetie?" I said, this time with genuine concern. I told myself that perhaps something had happened to one of her children. But soon I realized that there was no objective reason for her call and that once more—with women this happens sooner or later—she had fallen victim to an attack of nerves, the likes of which I never thought I would have to put up with from her.

"It started at noon," she told me. "I called Menahovsky, but he's away on vacation and his assistant didn't dare change my prescription. I don't know what I'm going to do!"

"But what's wrong with you, exactly?" I insisted. Big mistake. I should never have formulated that ridiculous question and I never would have done so had there not been medicine involved. I was afraid this was about an overdose or some kind of poisoning.

"What's wrong with me *exactly* is that I don't have a single reason to live. I feel totally alone at the bottom of a black pit. I can't trust anyone."

My first reaction was astonishment. I never imagined I would hear such words from Ruth's lips. To me, her life—and her way of coping with it—had always looked more like a day out in the countryside than a black pit.

After my initial bewilderment, I was gripped with indignation: once again I was trapped in an emotional spider's web, one of those imaginary dramas that women are so expert at fabricating. For more than three days—the time it took for Menahovsky to return to the city—I had the opportunity to observe Ruth stripped of her eternal calm: a deplorable sight. Not only had she lost her best attribute, but for a few days she turned into a tormented, suffering being, pretty much the complete opposite of her usual self. The worst part of it was that I could only wonder if the real Ruth Perelman was closer to this than to the woman I had known up to then. If that short but intense depression had taken place in total privacy, and I had only heard the faintest echoes of it whenever I called for the latest news, my reaction would likely have been very different. Perhaps I might have felt genuinely sorry—even tenderness and concern—for her, but, as Mario maintains, a woman only suffers in silence if she does not have a telephone close by, and the Tribeca loft was full of the things. That first nocturnal call was followed by six more, all in the early hours of the morning, during which she begged me to come and see her immediately, threatening to show up at the publisher's if I did not. I had to miss work, something that hardly ever happens, unless I have a fever running higher than 104°F. When I got to her apartment building I had to stand on the pavement across the street so I didn't bump into her kids, who at that moment were getting into their father's car. Before it drove off, I managed to see through the back window that the little girl was crying. Although it was cold, the morning light was pristine, as if poured directly from the winter sun. I was about to turn around and make the most of the nice day in Central Park. But I was confronted with an unknown and thus an unpredictable Ruth; who could say for sure that she would not carry out her threat of making a scene at my office? And so as soon as Isaac's car disappeared around the corner, I entered the building and went up to see her. I had seen other women in the throes of a nervous breakdown; Cuban women—a race I try to spend as little time with as possible—are very fond of this kind of spectacle, and so it did not disturb me too much to see Ruth with her bloodshot eyes and her contorted face (and to think that those were the same lips that bewitched me on that first day!). But what surprised me most at that moment was the state of the house. In all the time we had been together, I had never seen her smoke; she had not even mentioned that she had given it up, and yet that morning both the living room and the kitchen, even the bedroom, were littered with cigarette butts. Next to the fireplace, full of fresh ash and coals, I found the shards of a broken glass and, at the other end of the room, a bottle of Hennessy, which led me to think she had spent the night drinking cognac and talking on the telephone. But had she called only me? I could not help asking her, and this too was a mistake.

"Since you weren't answering I called Isaac's house. That bitch who moved in with him last year picked up."

Her vocabulary had suffered a metamorphosis, too. All at once, her mouth had ceased to be silent and was now displaying a totally new and voluble dimension. I would rather not mention her breath. As was to be expected, the idyllic image I once had of Ruth went right down the tubes that morning. Of the woman who had seduced me over dinner at Beatriz's, nothing remained, or perhaps it did: an incorrect prescription of tranquilizers. I could have used this crisis as an excuse to ditch the woman or, should I say, the shell of a human I had before me, but, for some reason I still do not understand, I failed to pronounce the declaration of a breakup. I suggested she telephone the cleaning lady, who luckily was due to come by that afternoon, and after listening to her cry for more than two hours I announced that I was not going to stay for the night. Shattered, I left her house, and walked quickly through the park, my hands in my coat pockets to protect them from the cold. When finally I arrived at my apartment all I could do was seek refuge in music. I went for Stevie Wonder, a songwriter many pretentious types unjustly scorn. *The Secret Life of Plants* was the only secret life I was interested in listening to that afternoon. Before I fell asleep I unplugged the telephone. I was not prepared to let her ruin another night's sleep by ensnaring me with her suffering. Nonetheless, once I was actually in bed, and in spite of how exhausted I was, I found it impossible to fall asleep. All kinds of incriminating ideas had begun running through my mind. How far was this imbalance in her medication going to take her? When I did eventually manage to sleep, the dreams I had were worse than my waking ones. My memory was repeatedly flooded with the morning I left Cuba forever, the troubled face of my mother who, despite the pain she felt, was urging me to leave. Could Mario, impertinent as he was, have had a point when he insisted again and again that I should sign myself up for some kind of therapy? It was one of the longest nights I can recall. The alarm clock went off at six, as usual, and I leaped out of bed in a panic. Before going to the bathroom to carry out my daily purification ritual, I threw a sidelong glance at the front door and saw with a sense of relief that the newspaper had already been slipped under it. Few things comfort me more than receiving the *New York Times* each day. Thinking of the number of people who have had to stay awake or leave home long before my alarm goes off so that I can sit down and read the news over breakfast gives me back some dignity, and makes me feel, in some small way, safe. I left for work without reconnecting the telephone. I would rather run the risk of having Ruth show up at my office than live with the blackmail she was attempting to impose on me. Fortunately, she more or less kept her distance, apart from a few e-mails in which she described her unease in a clumsy and, if I am honest, pretty corny way. This went on for almost a week. On Thursday, in a burst of generosity, I decided to send her a very well-known phrase of Milton's from *Paradise Lost*:

The mind is its own place, and in itself
Can make a heaven of hell, a hell of heaven.

I wanted to let her know I had not forgotten about her but that nor did I entirely believe in her delusional dramas. I assured her that, for the health of our relationship, I preferred to maintain an aseptic distance. We did not see each other on Saturday lunchtime as normal, but on Sunday afternoon I agreed to pay her a visit. I had arranged to meet Mario in a café in Tribeca. Ruth was going to sleep at her brother's house in Long Island that night, and she invited me to have a cup of tea after lunch. I accepted, promising to stay with her until she left the house. Her behavior that afternoon made me believe she was regaining her sanity. There was no weeping or song and dance of any sort, nor did she reproach me for my absence. Nonetheless, the expression on her face told of sleepless nights and a constant state of anxiety. After our tea, she suggested I sit in my favorite armchair. She had bought the *New Yorker* for me and suggested I flip through it while she got ready to leave. I looked at the magazine, but I could not read a single article. They all seemed unbearably pedantic. The late afternoon sun was timidly shining in through the window and, without realizing it, I started to fall asleep. When I woke up, I looked at my watch and saw that more than forty minutes had gone by. I walked over to the bathroom and heard that the faucet was still running. I knocked at the door and asked if I could come in.

"Come in," she said. "I'm just finishing my bath."

Her makeupless face furrowed by the tension of the last few days resembled that of a woman ten years older. Her skinny body moved in and out of the jacuzzi's foam. The languid look she gave me at that moment reminded me of a lobster I had seen a few days earlier in a restaurant in Williamsburg, where Mario and I had dined the last few times we had seen each other. Ruth got out of the water still bathed in bubbles, like an ageing mermaid preparing to die on the seashore. Fortunately she soon covered herself in a white robe. I watched as she dried her hair with the hair dryer and then returned it to the cabinet. Each one of her movements seemed to require a great effort.

"What can I do for you?" I said sincerely, prepared to help her, even to screw her, though I felt not the slightest attraction to her body that night. Ruth stayed silent for a few minutes.

"Come to Paris with me," she said eventually, to my complete surprise. "I have a business meeting, but I can't see myself traveling alone in this state. We could see it as a honeymoon. We haven't had one yet."

The expression grated in my ears like a saccharine, mawkish cry, but I said nothing. Several years had passed since the last time I had set foot in France. The idea of going back to Paris, a city I have so many significant memories of, filled me with glee. I took her by the shoulders and whispered into her ear that I would accompany her to anywhere she asked me.

Ruth left for Long Island and I took a long walk around the neighborhood, waiting for my meeting with Mario. When I got home, I wrote a few e-mails to my Parisian friends. There are certain people I longed to see. If Ruth got better with the change of scene, perhaps I could introduce her to some of them. To Julián Pisani, for instance, to Haydée Cisneros or Michel Miló, whose book I translated into

Spanish more than ten years ago. Although I do not see them regularly, these people have stayed suspended in my affections like abstract and, at the same time, persistent chimeras. Paris bestows a certain depth on its inhabitants and I know that, like me, my friends would also appreciate the silence and peace Ruth is capable of radiating when she is balanced, without questioning the source of that tranquility.

Menahovsky returned on the Monday, and two weeks later my girlfriend went back to being how she was before. When at last I could sit down again, with a glass of wine and a Popular between my fingers, in the high-backed armchair in her apartment, I said to myself that it had been worth having a little patience. Once again, courtesy toward the human race had triumphed.

READING

Even though I lived directly opposite it, I hardly ever went into Père-Lachaise. I loved looking at it from a distance, but I never turned it into a daily walk. Tom had to push hard to get me to come with him. I had not the slightest desire to approach the place with someone who planned on talking to the dead, and before I accepted, I made him promise he was not going to start chatting away to anyone not made of flesh and blood. That Friday he left work at noon. We met at a café in Ménilmontant, where we swiftly had some soup and a piece of quiche so we could get over to Père-Lachaise as soon as possible. Our walk that afternoon was more enjoyable than I could have imagined. Unlike the other visitors, we did not look at the map displayed at the entrance, or ask for a paper one from the guard. We wandered calmly about, with no fixed itinerary, like a couple of carefree tourists venturing out with no expectations, letting their footsteps lead them along instinctively. Tom followed me. He liked the fact that our route was determined by whatever I happened to focus on. If I stopped at a certain tombstone, he would read out the name engraved on it and, if he felt it necessary, make reference to who the deceased was, their profession or the style the monument belonged to. We found more "famous" graves than I would have anticipated. Among them I recall the white marble of Frédéric Chopin's tombstone, almost hidden behind some neatly clipped bushes. His name was inscribed on the white surface with an eloquent simplicity, alongside the beautiful sculpture of a woman. I said to myself that there was something in the fact of dying that could not be expressed in words or in any book in the world. Music was probably the most appropriate medium for doing so.

As the afternoon wore on, the day became steadily colder. It began to get dark and I grew anxious to leave the place. Instinctively, I tried to take a shortcut in the direction of the main gate, but all I did was get us lost. It was then that I realized: a few meters away, a funeral was taking place. It was a secular ceremony, very discreet, not even ten people standing around a coffin made of reddish wood. Next to the granite slab about to slide shut forever stood a white candle, its wick alight, recalling the fragility and beauty of life. When at last we found ourselves approaching the northern exit, I veered off for a moment towards the section containing the ashes of people who have been cremated, the *columbarium*. The term means "dovecote" in Latin, and derives from its similarity to the constructions the Romans built for these birds, full of deep, square cavities for them to roost in.

"As you can see," Tom said, "there aren't any tombs here, just niches. I bought one for myself a few months ago."

Despite his insistence, I refused to let him show it to me. As they fled bewildered from the nameless stones, my eyes alighted on a pale gray gravestone made of cement, onto which someone had taped a red rose. I went over to take a look. It was Perec.

I realized then that, for Tom at least, the walk was not quite as aimless as I had believed. We left and we went to sit in a café with a veranda, situated on the rue des Rondeaux, a simple place, quite deserted. As our waiter served us, Tom took a map of the cemetery from his pocket and traced our route with his fingers, pointing out several graves I had stopped at by chance, and began to draw conclusions as if it were a chart or a genealogy or a tarot reading, in which each name has a hidden meaning or some significance. "First you went over to Colette's grave—that shows your independence and your boldness, but also your literary leanings. Then you stopped at Simone Signoret: a face you never forget." As he talked, I tried to gauge whether he was being serious or if it was a game of some kind, but Tom was not joking, and continued his reading like something out of a Jodorowsky film: "Frédéric Chopin could mean a young death here, but also someone with romantic tendencies. You get emotional very easily. The fact that you stopped at the monument to the members of the Resistance and the Communards' Wall says a lot about your bravery and your rebellious spirit. Kardec's grave I was expecting, and all it does is confirm that you're capable of hearing the voices of all these different people."

Although I knew the most obvious ones, I did not really know who all these celebrated figures that Tom was referring to were, but I did not dare ask any more questions. I was indignant that he could be so impudent as to make assertions about me simply for my having approached such-and-such a grave. I had the feeling I was being put to an absurd test and I reproached him as best I could.

"If you'd told me we were going on this walk so that you could make some kind of in-depth analysis of my soul I never would have come."

"I analyzed you before, that evening we had dinner together for the first time. Today just confirmed my conclusions."

"And what if you're wrong?" I said. "What if in time you find out I'm not the person you think I am, and I don't have the characteristics you've attributed to me?"

"You have the qualities I need," he said, taking my hand.

We ate in silence that night and, almost immediately afterwards, I went back to my house. I curled up in a ball on my bed, telling myself that his bed was on the other side of the wall.

On Saturday, after lunch, he suggested we go and have a coffee at place Gardette, near Saint-Ambroise. We walked a few blocks down the rue du Chemin Vert and turned right when we reached the square. There was a bar on the corner and I thought he was taking me there. Before we reached it, he stopped at the entrance to a building. He tapped in a code and the door swung open. I asked him where we were going and he replied that he wanted to introduce me to someone.

I was worried it was going to be one of the guards from Père-Lachaise whom he waved to every morning and seemed to know personally.

While we went up in the lift, the sounds of some upbeat music reached us, with lyrics in Portuguese.

"It's coming from his house," he announced.

"I thought you didn't know any other living human being apart from me!"

I could smell food. The door opened and a young man with incredibly bright black eyes appeared, dressed in a rough white cotton shirt.

"This is David. A friend who is alive, although not for much longer."

They gave each other a few judo chops (I have never understood why men express affection in this way), and then David showed us where to leave our coats and we settled down in his living room. "You're just in time," he said. "I'm making *roti*." Then two Brazilian girls arrived, and David's girlfriend Marion, a mixed-race French girl. Soon after, we went over to the table surrounded by a relaxed, merry atmosphere, so different from the one Tom and I tended to adopt when we were on our own that I was actually surprised.

Tom really did have friends, people who cared for him and who had no qualms about expressing their admiration for him. I found this out bit by bit, after that first visit, although it was also true that he rarely saw them.

"Thanks for letting him out for the day!" David blurted out at some point over lunch. "We've not seen a whisker of him since you spirited him away."

It also became clear that day that they all knew of my existence and took it for granted that we were a couple. This tacit implication, which Tom did not trouble to deny, made me nervous. I worried they would ask me questions I did not know how to answer and so, instead of taking part in the conversation, I focused on looking around the apartment. David, too, had attractive books on his shelves: all of the Beatniks and the complete collection of Diane di Prima's poetry. At one point I went to the toilet and used my trip to take a peek at the rest of the house, which consisted of a walk-in wardrobe, a bedroom, a kitchen, and the living room we had gone into first. Through a half-open door, I caught a glimpse of a neatly made bed with a brightly colored ethnic throw on it. Each new friendship, especially when there is attraction involved, is a ticket to an unknown dimension, or at least to small portions of reality we are not familiar with. I knew very few things about Tom, had scant understanding of the Anglo-Saxon culture he had in part grown up in, but the experiences of his generation, a decade older than my own, also seemed distant to me and for this same reason were intriguing. It was clear that he felt something similar towards my own personal history and my Mexican origins, but how interested was he in me as a person? This question, and in particular how much he liked me physically, frequently occupied my thoughts and I was afraid to answer them. I chose instead to remain for as long as possible in that place of uncertainty in which all possibilities could coexist, rather than obtain a decisive, negative reply. We ate more than usual and, when we had finished, had the coffee Tom had promised. The Brazilians rolled a generous joint and passed it around the group. Tom and I were the only ones to abstain. When the others started laughing at any old thing, we left and went back down to the street.

As if he had read my mind, while we walked back to our building along the rue du Chemin Vert that evening my neighbor started offering up explanations I had no intention of demanding.

"Did you notice? They all assumed we live together."

I nodded.

"And at the same time they were pretty discreet. Like they were worried about putting their foot in it," I said.

"There was a time when they thought of me as a womanizer," he said, saying the last word in English. "Now they don't quite know how to categorize me."

Although I knew what it meant, "womanizer" struck a discordant note in my ears. It was the polar opposite of how I saw him.

"Why?" I said, disconcerted. I could not imagine him as a playboy, let alone as someone with hypnotic powers over the female sex.

"Before I got ill, I used to be attractive to women."

I smiled fondly at him, like a close relation rather than someone who feels she is being courted, and assured him:

"You still are."

"I'm a shadow," he said, "more than anything. But thank you, you're very generous."

There was a silence of several minutes and then, as if plucking up his courage, Tom announced that he needed to talk to me.

"About how people see us?" I said jokingly, trying to play down the tension that had sprung up between us, but it was useless. Tom did not respond to my attempt and we lapsed back into silence.

"I'm going to Sicily," he said at last, bluntly. "My flight's this weekend."

The possibility of my remaining in our apartment block without him was enough to make my blood run cold. Tom had become my only source of heat, and we were barely into February. I could not imagine getting through winter without him. He explained that in the south of Sicily he had found the ideal place calmly to withdraw from the world and progress in his attempts to have a conversation with his fear. His reasons seemed not only crazy to me but far-fetched. Fear of what? Of continuing to be a womanizer? Of getting involved, of committing? I could not help but feel betrayed. I stared at him in disbelief.

"I was meant to go in December, but I put the trip off by a few weeks, after we first had dinner together. I really wanted to get to know you. I still do."

"How long will you be away for?"

"As short a time as possible. I promise."

That night we had dinner together. His mood remained sombre all evening. I was certain his mind was occupied with matters other than the two of us. When we had finished eating, he got up from the table and wordlessly began washing up. I was tempted to leave. It would have been the logical thing to do. However, something made me stay, clinging to the hope of a happy ending for this meal full of silences. After he'd washed, dried, and slowly put away the plates, my neighbor went into his room and lit a fire. It was like witnessing the images from a film whose soundtrack I had heard from my apartment countless times and which was interrupted whenever I went to visit him. As I watched him, I understood that he carried out this daily ritual of domestic tasks with religious precision, as if each one of the gestures had a meaning and a sequence for him that made him feel secure, or at least soothed him.

When the fire was burning well in the hearth in his bedroom, Tom sat down next to me on the bed. From there we could hear the crackle of the logs and see their orangey light. That night he told me about the state of his health and of the disease he had been living with for several years, working his daily life and activities around it. He spoke of how his body was deteriorating, of his short life expectancy, of the possible treatments. I listened carefully and, when he'd finished I let my eyes and thoughts lose themselves in the fire's shapes, without saying a word. Compared to everything I had just been told, his trip to Sicily for a few days suddenly seemed an incredibly benign irrelevance.

At last my tongue was able to move and said, as if of its own accord, something not at all related:

"Why doesn't my fireplace work?"

"The same reason you don't hear the dead. Because you haven't really tried it yet. Your fireplace is in perfect condition. The chimney has been cleaned once a year ever since I moved to this building. You and I share the same one."

Back in my room, I tried once again to make out his movements, those trips back and forth to the bathroom which before I had not known how to interpret correctly. Next door, the fire was still going and I said to myself that perhaps he too was still awake. My watch told me it was 4:30 in the morning and I decided I could not bear lying awake any longer. I left my apartment and knocked at his door. We stood and embraced each other for a few minutes in the doorway, holding our breath, like two creatures waiting for the imminent end of a secret world. Our mood was sad and stupefied, but also happy at still being together. Then, Tom began to kiss me slowly, as if defying the passage of time. There, beneath the movements of his hands, of his lips and his gestures, it seemed he really did possess what he had boasted of that afternoon, a precise analysis of my sensibility and my needs. All of these sensations mixed with other, very different ones: the feel of his limp, aged skin, the sharp smell of medicine on him, the word "womanizer" going around and around in my head. Tom's voice echoed in my mind with all his scientific terms: hypertension, diuretics, pulmonary and cardiac atrophy, intravenous catheter. We were awake all night, memorizing each other's bodies. Afterwards we had breakfast in the café on the corner while we waited for the gray taxi that would take him to the airport, avoiding any complicated topics. Before getting into the cab he held out the keys to his apartment. "In case there's a problem, or you need something."

He gave me a hug and an absentminded kiss, like someone planning on coming back the same day, in the evening. I could not watch the taxi drive away.

"I met someone," I told Haydée, with no preamble.

She raised her eyes from her wine glass and looked at me with the cautious surprise of someone hearing something highly unlikely.

I told her the details of my friendship with Tom, and for several seconds—an eternity for her—she maintained a respectful silence, and then told me off, offended, for having taken so long to tell her. Then she focused on a single detail: the lack of sex.

"You'll have to find out if that's negotiable."

From the moment I saw him get into the taxi, I heard nothing more from Tom. Not a telephone call, not even an e-mail or a text message. I devoted several weeks to waiting for him, weeks that seemed like years and in which I did nothing else of any importance. I imagined him on the streets of the neighborhood in meticulous detail, like someone calling up a spirit. I looked for any similar features in the pedestrians on the street, whether in their features or their clothes and, after finding an incomplete version of him in every anonymous face, what little I had left of his presence finally ended up vanishing. The pain, meanwhile, was persistent. During those weeks I lost Tom and got him back many times, in an infinite series of speculations I threw myself into without any precaution, still unaware that speculation is a corrosive acid that destroys hope. Instead of accepting defeat, I was damaging myself with a series of imagined promises and deceptions, of telephone calls that were not his, of letters that never appeared in my postbox, of solitary nights I squandered by listening to the sounds of my neighbors, only to verify that his own sounds had gone and that nothing issued from his apartment save a hopeless silence. Things transformed themselves around me as if reality were someone else's patrimony, belonging to those who did not spend their lives waiting. I began to suspect he had gone to Sicily to see another woman. The doubt became a genuine hell. One night, I could not bear it any longer and I went over to his apartment. The fact is, I had wanted to go back there right from the start and had managed to control myself only with great difficulty. Nonetheless, as soon as I had crossed the threshold, I wondered if he had not left me the keys so that I would find it easier to search for a clue that might explain his absence. Emboldened by this possibility, I began to look through the bookshelves and drawers in the house. I opened each drawer in the desk and, whenever I found a letter or a photograph, pored over it. This is how I found the photographs of Michela, a woman not so different from me in terms of physical type: large, dark eyes, very straight black hair, dark-skinned. In several of these images the two of them appeared together, embracing or holding hands. In others, she was half naked. I lingered over these, looking at her body and comparing it with mine. In almost all of the pictures they were smiling or at least seemed happy, in love. They were mostly photographs of trips they had made: the sea, beach umbrellas, wooden picnic tables. None of them had been taken in this apartment where, according to what Tom had said, he had been living for more than three years. Nor in any of them did it look as though they lived together. From the yellowed paper and the clothes they wore, but above all from the expression on Tom's face, I concluded that they were not recent photographs.

I looked at the clock. It was past two in the morning. I felt sleepy. I had left my house in a hurry, intending to stay and sleep at Tom's, to try and recover some of the smell which, when I opened his door, hit me with all its evocative power, as well as our own scent, which must still have lingered between the sheets. But after looking through those photographs I decided to go back home and not stick my nose into his territory again. I managed this for a few days. I went back on the Friday, no longer in detective mood, but simply to feel his presence, make myself a cup of tea, and flick through some of his books.

By the time I had stopped expecting anything, a postcard arrived from Caltanissetta. It was a color photograph in a rather old-fashioned style, as if from the '80s, which showed the gates to a cemetery. On the back, Tom had written a line of Oscar Wilde's, one of his favorite dead people: "The supreme vice is shallowness. Whatever is realized is right," and then added, "Nothing to report." When I first read it, I could not help but relate the words to my meddling in his photographs and belongings. Receiving that postcard, however, was enough to pull me out of the abyss I was in and for a while I was enveloped in this new mood. I discovered lots of things during that time. For example, I realized that spring had begun a couple of weeks ago and the trees were covered in leaves once more. I looked at their branches from the boulevard with genuine rapture, scarcely able to believe such beauty existed, and gave thanks to Tom for having taught me to appreciate it. I dusted off my bike and discovered the joys of riding around on it, feeling the fresh air on my face. I found out how useful it can be going through life with a smile on one's lips; people are less distrustful and behave in a more pleasant manner. I discovered the cocooning sensation of knowing that someone, even if they are on the other side of the world, is thinking of us with love and longing. I discovered the immense power of a few written lines and I also discovered—unfortunately—that this power is short-lived if the lines are not renewed.

And so, no matter how hard I tried to prolong the happiness and security I felt after receiving the postcard, my newly launched smile began to dissolve as I looked in the postbox every morning and verified that there was nothing new inside. No fresh enigmatic little phrase to cling to, never mind a proper letter. Without realizing it, I sank back into the desolation that being abandoned causes in people like me, whose parents did not spend enough time with them or left them at the mercy of life at a very early age. Then, one evening, when I got home, I heard a message from Tom on the answerphone. He said that he missed me and was thinking about me, but left no number where I could reach him. I must have listened to it about three hundred times, at all hours of the day and night.

Since studying was far from being a sufficient distraction, Haydée suggested I find a job to stop me from going mad. She had a point. For years I had been a privileged scholarship girl and I could do with working a bit. I did not have to try that hard to get a job as a language assistant at a secondary school. All I had to do was go to the Paris education board and leave my CV. The work was nothing special, but I found it exhilarating. What is more, although I knew full well that teenagers can be awful, I wanted to teach and to learn from them, from their cheeky, rebellious attitudes. It was an effective measure. The job started early, which forced me to get out of bed at a reasonable hour, and leaving the apartment cleared my mind. The Lycée Condorcet, where I worked, was a few meters from the Saint-Lazare train station, an area I did not know at all and which gave me a new perspective on the city. A month and a half later, the routine had pulled me out of my torpor. I still thought about Tom, but not with the same urgency or obsession as before.

HOTEL LUTETIA

Paris received us coldly, but without the persistent rain that characterizes it. As we drove along the quai de Bercy in the taxi we had
ordered from the airport, I stared spellbound at the cracked
façades, the bridges, and the grand monuments, and understood
that, like Ruth, Paris is a temperamental fifty-something lady with
a great deal of class. I suddenly felt grateful to her for having
brought me back to this city I have always loved and will never
cease to admire. We had booked a room at the Hotel Lutetia, by
Sèvres–Babylone, two blocks from the Fondation Maison des
Sciences de l'Homme, where I did my postgraduate degree. I had
told Ruth that, while she dealt with her business matters, I wanted
to go to my friend Michel Miló's seminar and spend a few hours
in the library there. It was on the basis of this, and not her own
needs, that she chose the area and the hotel where we were to stay.
Ruth had several meetings in the week, but had managed to keep
almost all the evenings free for the two of us. In exchange, she asked
me to go with her on Thursday to La Closerie des Lilas to have dinner with a couple of French designers. On Wednesday, Friday, and
Saturday we would do whatever I wanted. As the taxi negotiated
the traffic that grinds to a halt at dusk across from Notre-Dame, I
wondered if I should introduce her to my friends. It was not Miló
I felt troubled about. Being one of the most cultured, intelligent

men I have ever met, an inveterate optimist and dyed-in-the-wool aesthete, he was used to going out with lovely people of all ages without for one minute taking account of their sex or their intellectual level. I was certain he would not judge Ruth harshly, neither for the impossible gulf separating her mental capacity and mine nor for how much older than me she is. On the contrary, he would appreciate her elegance and good taste, of which I am living proof. I did not, however, expect the same of Julián or Haydée, my Cuban friends, who had been living in Paris since the days of my master's. Although in her presence they would behave with diplomacy and warmth, I was convinced that, as soon as we were alone together, they would let rip with the most corrosive criticisms of the old thing—and thus, indirectly, of me.

The driver turned on the radio, to a program where an expert on Europe's economy was responding to a journalist's questions. His voice was monotonous and failed to hold my attention for long. I thought of Haydée. Now I feel enormous affection for her, but that was not always the case. We met twenty-one years ago, on the trip Susana and I took to Varadero. The girls' fathers were brothers, but Haydée's mother, a Frenchwoman of North African descent, never wanted to live in Cuba. They used to go there for short periods, and only for vacations. Thanks to this, the girls were able to spend their summers together in the best hotels in Cuba, until Haydée began to travel alone and to choose more exotic destinations far away from Latin America. It was my first ever trip to Varadero, unlike Susana, who had been there some five times. Haydée caught up with us a week later. I cannot say I felt an immediate affinity with her, more the opposite. I noticed right away, with some disgust, her exhibitionist, provocative nature, her uncontrollable obsession with arguing about anything at all. In the hours following her arrival, I simply confirmed my first impressions, but refrained from mentioning it to Susana, who was very fond of her cousin—the famous "opposites attract" phenomenon. For the whole trip, Haydée attempted to monopolize my girlfriend with the pretext that she had lots of "intimate" things to tell her and, although I was never able to prove it, I suspect that she tried to convince her to break up with me. Her family saw Susana as a young girl full of possibilities, clinging incomprehensibly to a dead weight. However, Haydée changed her mind pretty quickly. Her attempts at sequestering Susana in her room, where the two of them would chat away until three in the morning, were unexpectedly interrupted when, after a few indiscreet comments from my girlfriend, she learned of my sexual tastes, and from then on her attitude toward me became bewilderingly complicit. I remember one morning, while we were having breakfast out on the patio of that luxurious hotel in which I, as a Cuban, felt like a stowaway, Haydée came out in my defence.

"There's nothing wrong with sodomy!" she shouted, as if no one within earshot could understand Spanish.

I could not help giving Susana a reproachful look for having revealed our private arguments to this crazy woman. I have no idea if Haydée was impervious to our shame or if she enjoyed seeing us embarrassed. Over the next five minutes, she listed all the countries in the world where this sexual practice was not only acceptable, but routine.

"I just can't understand," she concluded, in her accent with its subtle hints of French, "that as a relative of mine you would refuse to engage in it."

With her habitual tact, Susana asked her cousin to mind her own business and then changed the subject. Nevertheless, Haydée's rant brought tangible results and for the remainder of my time with her cousin I could only be grateful to her. After this episode Haydée seemed, if not respectful, at least more forgiving. In her eyes, I was fulfilling a purpose in Susana's life, something to do with ensuring her erotic education and, in that sense, the five-year age difference between us ceased to be an issue. I, too, started to see this wacky, eccentric young woman I had been obligated to share my trip with in another light. Haydée's parents had been too busy when she was young, and this was where her attention-seeking streak came from. The fact is, we grew to like each other, and this remained the case, even after Susana's death. Paris was where we spent the most time together. We used to have lunch at least three times a week in various college cafeterias, until we were so used to their set menus we grew to detest the food they served. Although she was studying at the Sorbonne, I convinced her to come to some of the best classes at the School of Social Sciences, where I was pursuing my master's. She took part in the seminar given by Michel Miló, among others, and it was there that our friendship reached its peak. Along with Julián and Sophie, we formed a group of friends around the philosopher, with whom each of us remains connected in his or her own way.

The taxi taking us to the hotel swung onto boulevard Raspail at last. Ruth took my hand as she stared in fascination at the streets of Paris and its passersby. Although we never lost contact, the correspondence between Haydée and me had grown gradually more patchy ever since I had moved to New York. In the e-mails and postcards we did exchange a couple of times a year, we never spoke about our love lives or other everyday details. She almost always restricted herself to telling me about what she had been reading or the new philosophers she had discovered. I knew from mutual friends that she now lived with a kid from India who, according to Julián—whose judgment I have total confidence in—is a talented photographer. She was still living in the apartment on rue de Lévis she got from some friends of her parents the same year I left Paris, when we held various unforgettable soirées. I could not imagine my Cuban friend living in a couple, this girl who, at least when I knew her, had a new lover every month. Whoever he was, he must be an exceptional man if he'd managed to tame her insatiable appetite. She is one of the few women I have considered an equal over the course of my life. Not even her cousin Susana—for whom I felt a great love, half erotic, half paternal—and I understood each other so well. Haydée can be fiercely brilliant and with her I can be as I am, whole, profoundly close, in the timeless dimension of absolute candor. Few people know me as well as she does, and by few do I feel as loved, in a way that lets me be, that liberates me. Haydée, for me, opens up a space without affectation, without masks, where tenderness and truth are possible, and where silence and loyalty given as a gift—not as a duty—are also possible. And so, after thinking long and hard about it, I came to the conclusion that, were I to decide I wanted to, I could introduce her to the old thing.

Through the windows of the taxi, I saw that night had fallen.

"What are you thinking about, my love?" Ruth said, after respecting my silence for almost an hour.

"The European Union," I said with mild annoyance.

She apologized demurely for having interrupted my musings, and did not open her mouth again until the valet opened the door and took our suitcases from the trunk.

Awaiting us in the room, a gold and pistachio-colored suite with original paintings by Thierry Bisch, was a bottle of Moët & Chandon that Ruth had ordered when she made the reservation.

She drank with the prudence of our first few days together while leaving me to finish off most of it. I do not recall if in my time here as a student I had drunk champagne, but that night I was convinced that it is the beverage that most suits this city, not absinthe, as Mario claims. I felt ebullient, generous, and agreed for the first time to share my memories with Ruth. I talked and talked as never before, telling her details of my youth in Paris, of my beloved friends, ignoring—or pretending for a few hours to ignore—that Ruth had nothing in common with them. I even went so far as to assure her I was excited to be there with her. It was in this generous mood that I screwed her that night. She must have felt some sort of difference because, after we had finished the second time, she wrapped her bare arms around my neck and confessed that for months she had been thinking about the possibility of me moving into her apartment in Tribeca. When I heard this foolish remark, my drunken benevolence suddenly evaporated. I chose not to reply right away. Instead, I laid my cheek on the feather pillow and fell into a deep sleep.

I spent most of that week in Paris holding Ruth's hand, pretending to be in love. This was not premeditated or with any precise aim, but rather in gratitude to her for having invited me on this trip and for her kindness. The fact that she did not mention again the possibility of cohabiting made things easier, although I must admit that the idea pursued me like a shadow. I shuddered to think that she might insist on the matter. Our days in Paris went by overwhelmingly fast. On Wednesday morning I went to Miló's seminar and had lunch with him in a restaurant near Saint-Sulpice. Ruth met us later in the Bon Marché café. Michel's reaction was exactly as I had expected: he thought the old thing enchanting. On Thursday I accompanied her, as planned, to her meeting with the designers.

In the hotel before we left, I let her choose my clothes and paid attention when she made suggestions while I shaved. Over dinner, I spoke only as much as strictly necessary and helped her when her half-forgotten French fell short. Ruth had gone back to the laconic refinement I had so admired that night I met her at Beatriz's house. Dr. Menahovsky's new prescription appeared to be working perfectly, and so on Friday I felt encouraged enough to introduce her to my friends. I arranged to meet them in the hotel bar so we could have dinner in a nearby restaurant afterward. However, only Julián and David could make it, the latter accompanied by a Korean student he was going out with that term.

I was only able to see Haydée on Sunday, the last day of my stay in Paris and the best, by a long shot. I suggested to Ruth that we go our separate ways until the evening, partly because I had spent too many days with her and her infrequent yet ever frivolous chit-chat was beginning to annoy me, and partly because, to be totally frank, I was still reluctant to introduce her to my dear friend. She agreed with no objections and told me she would use the time to visit the stores on boulevard Haussmann, a favorite activity of hers and one I find indescribably dull. I asked Haydée and Julián to meet me near the Père-Lachaise cemetery so that after lunch they could come with me to look for César Vallejo's grave, one of the men with whom I have felt the greatest spiritual affinity throughout my life. They were both delighted at the idea. We arranged to meet at a café in Ménilmontant that the old thing would have considered a real dive but that stirred up all my nostalgia for my austere student days. How right I was to shake her off! More than just a good move on my part, I think I was assisted by divine inspiration. Haydée turned up with her Mexican friend, whom I had not met, a girl with black hair and dark eyes, with whom I felt an uncommon connection, like the meeting of souls Nietzsche spoke of after his first encounter with Lou Andreas-Salomé: "From which stars did we fall to meet each other here?"

Haydée has always had a remarkable influence on my love life. First Susana, and now this young woman who I have not been able to get out of my mind ever since. Another time I would have been offended, or at least irritated, that she showed up, without asking me, with a stranger to the one meeting she had seen fit to grant me. I would have taken it as an act of rudeness worthy of a vigorous telling-off, and yet, from the moment I laid eyes on this interloper, modest and enchanting, unaware, it seemed, of the immense power of her beauty, I felt grateful for her presence. The whole afternoon all I did was observe her, in the café and during the walk we took afterward through Père-Lachaise, with a sort of strange presentiment. Cecilia, that was her name. The condition of being in love is, so they say, the inability to see, and if this woman's name means "blindness," it can only be the blindness that comes from being dazzled.

After our walk through the cemetery, Haydée's friend suggested we go to her apartment, which was a very few blocks away, a space worthy of a philosopher for its austerity and its windows overlooking the cemetery. Being in her studio gave me a chance to verify the similarities there were between us. In Cecilia's little apartment, the walls are devoid of pictures or any decorations or distractions. They are white walls, conducive to concentrating and enjoying the silence. I said to myself that, exactly like I am, Cecilia was a lover of order and cleanliness. Her closet—I came across it on my way to the bathroom—was a narrow space and with only those clothes that were strictly necessary to dress herself. She had never (being in her space was enough to realize this) visited the frivolous stores where my old thing could be found at that very moment, and nor would she invite me, even if she could afford it, to the restaurants we eat in to make up for the deficiencies in our relationship. For the first time in my life, I had met a person of the opposite sex—I find it hard to still call her a "woman"—who was suitable for me. I realized too that not only would my frugal habits and monastic style be comprehensible to her, but that they would adapt perfectly to her way of being. Before having seen Cecilia, I had dreamed of her. I had imagined the exact sensation that being close to her would evoke, the tender atmosphere there would be between us, something that up until that point no creature of flesh and blood had ever made me feel.

I do not know how I managed to leave her house and go back to Sèvres–Babylone. Nor can I explain how I was able to sleep with Ruth that night, even though I resisted touching her, nor how the next day I managed to get into the taxi that would take us to Charles de Gaulle Airport. While Ruth dawdled, choosing magazines to flip through on the flight, I managed to slip away from her for a few minutes and ran to a telephone booth to call Cecilia. Hearing her voice made me feel calm but also utterly impotent. There was so much I wanted to say to her, but I had to hold my tongue so I didn't frighten her. During that brief telephone call, I managed to maintain a casual tone that simply expressed my pleasure at having met her. And it was in this same carefree tone that I slipped in the promise of returning, a promise made mainly to myself, a sort of prediction, an incantation. I barely said a word to the old thing the whole way back. I am not a melodramatic man. In emotional terms I have always opted for an Apollonian sobriety, and for good manners. Nevertheless, it was so hard to maintain my composure and self-control that day! From the airport, I went home to shower and then headed straight for the office. As soon as I had turned on the computer, I wrote the following lines:

Cecilia:

I imagine that one day, one day soon, writing to you and talking to you—or staying silent at your side, with you—will mean not only this limpid joy at opening a window and seeing your eyes behind it. Although brief, our meeting on Sunday taught me how powerful is the desire to sit down to walk around (as dear César Vallejo would have said) in your eyes.

If I were in Paris tonight and could walk by your side, or sit next to you, and gently let Claudio be what Cecilia sees in him, I would be a happy man, happier even than I am right now at the mere fact of being able to write to you.

Thank you for having come along that day with Haydée, for the exact distance your warmth was from me, for existing in me, for being called Cecilia, Cecilia Rangel, and for dazzling me until I went blind.

One either believes in promises or not. Promises are either kept or they are not. But no one can do anything about proof. Proof frees us from the need to ward off uncertainty with promises. Each piece of proof supports itself in the fullness of what it reveals. Promises are human matters, a matter of human will and error, while revelations are a matter of our participation in that which transcends us, which goes beyond us. Ever since the Sunday I met her, I knew that I loved Cecilia in a way that would have no truck with half measures. Perhaps I had seen it with sudden clarity that afternoon in her apartment, or perhaps I had managed to explain it to myself as I walked over to Ruth's apartment thinking about

Cecilia and about the times I had met her before finally finding her in Paris, the times I might have confused her with someone else, the times she might have confused me with someone else, or when I might not have measured up to her. Only a few days ago, I would have thought it ridiculous to say "I love Cecilia," but it is true. I love her in a way that leaves me no alternative: either I accept this love, or I lose her and spend the rest of my days reinventing her with other names, other faces, in other latitudes, exchanging mystery for "wisdom."

RUMORS

Several months after Tom had left, David, the guy from place Gardette, left a message on my answerphone inviting me to a party he was throwing at his house that Saturday.

"Before he left, your boyfriend made me promise to invite you if I had a party. He's worried about you being on your own. He told me you're a bit of a hermit."

I went, after thinking long and hard about it, not because I had any desire to have fun, but so I could carry on finding things out about Tom. Haydée agreed to come with me, but as soon as we walked through the door she left me to fend for myself. I am sure that I would have had more fun if I had not insisted on finding out more about my neighbor's past and future. That night, the apartment opposite the park had turned into a sixty-square-meter bar filled with people from every imaginable country. The music alternated between various styles: soul, while there were still relatively few guests, then Latin, electronic, and retro French. Brigitte Bardot, with "*Tu veux ou tu veux pas,*" Les Rita Mitsouko, and Nino Ferrer were the soundtrack to the high points of the evening. Nearly everyone was drinking wine or beer, although there were a few bottles of vodka or gin doing the rounds, too. Everyone—the Angolans, Swedes, Panamanians, Dutch, South Africans, Brazilians, and Koreans who were there that night—knew and were fond of

Tom. Almost all of them, too, considered him a lost cause. It was not hard to get them to talk about their history with him and the influence he had had on their lives. They did so with the fond nostalgia one's dead or seriously ill friends tend to inspire, making one forget about the traces of any quarrel or disagreement one might have had with them. I was not able to interrogate David as I had meant to. His role as host—which he carried out to perfection—prevented him from stopping to talk for any length of time to his guests. I did, however, manage to speak to Nick, a writer from New York who had been a friend of Tom's since childhood, and an Italian called Ricardo, who worked with him at the bookshop. They were the only two who did not sum up their friend's disease as a "tragic, inevitable condition," but instead speculated, showing tact towards me and affection for him, on the possibilities medicine offered him. Both made jokes about Tom's eccentric character. They told me, for instance, that in the last few years, since he had been diagnosed with the disease, he had invested a considerable sum of money acquiring niches in different cemeteries across Europe. They also spoke of his recent penchant for horror fiction. They were hopeful that our relationship might cheer him up, give him more of a desire to live. They told me his trip to Sicily could turn out to be beneficial, since Tom loved the place.

"Be patient with him, please," Ricardo said, in his Neapolitan accent. "It's like he forgets himself when he's there, as if time didn't exist. He'll come back really keen to see you, I'm sure of it."

Neither of them, however, had the slightest idea how long this would take. He had traveled to the island before for several months, with no set date for coming back. I tried to find out where he was staying, but no one I spoke to really had any idea. Someone mentioned an aged aunt, others a friend of his mother's. In short, it was impossible to locate him.

"What about Michela?" I said. "Is there a chance he's with her?"

Bewildered, Ricardo and Nick looked at each other; they both thought this a ridiculous notion.

"They stopped seeing each other years ago," Ricardo said.

I tried to find out more, to discover exactly what had happened between them, the nature of their relationship, how long it had lasted, how it had ended and, above all, which of the two had been the abandoned party. But neither of them wanted to go into details.

"It lasted quite a few years," Nick said, "and I'm sure it was important, but lots of things have happened since they broke up, too."

"You're a lot like her!" the Italian said, quite drunk by that point. "Not just physically, but your accent, your personality. Maybe that scared him. It must do . . . No man, especially a sick one, could survive two women like you."

"Two women like what? You don't even know me!" I said, indignantly.

"Ignore him! He's talking nonsense," Nick protested, forcing his friend to change the subject.

I looked over to the corridor to see where Haydée was—I had last seen her circulating between the living room and the kitchen, drinking first gin and then wine from various bottles that David was offering his guests. Eventually I found her in the queue for the bathroom, struggling to stand up. I suggested we leave immediately, without saying goodbye to anyone but our host, and that is what we did. As we were going down the stairs, my friend tripped and fell in a painful way that seemed to go on forever. When at last I reached her, spread-eagled on the hall carpet, she would not get up. She had twisted her ankle, and we had to call David to get someone to come and help move her. We had planned to both stay at my place that night as she had arranged to meet a friend at a café in Ménilmontant on the Sunday. Walking home in this state, however, was unthinkable, let alone climbing four flights of stairs. David offered to put us up, but Haydée refused vehemently, and so we had to take a taxi back to her building, which luckily had a lift.

And so I was back to staying in one of the first rooms I had lived in in Paris. Apart from me, almost nothing in it had changed. The same books on the bookshelves, the same Cuban masks on the walls. Being back there was like having gone off on a trip around the world and then come back to where the journey had begun. Maybe for that reason, or thanks to the whiskey still flowing through my veins, I had a strange dream in which I saw myself walking down the boulevard de Sébastopol under a glowering, rain-filled sky. I did not have a very precise idea about where I was heading, although I did have the sensation I was hurrying, perhaps due to the cold. Wanting to find out the time, I went into a telephone box and there, sitting on the floor inside, I saw Ricardo—Tom's Italian friend—flicking through the Yellow Pages, stiff with cold. I asked him what he was doing and he said, quite naturally, that he was looking for the number of the Greek god Helios.

"It's not under 'H,'" he said. "It might be under one of his other names, or in the Sicilian section." I noticed that his tongue was stained black, like the monks in *The Name of the Rose*. Ricardo looked curiously at me and asked:

"What about you, are you still waiting?"

I nodded.

Then he handed me a piece of paper with a telephone number on it, the same number as the telephone booth, and said very seriously:

"When you get tired, call me. I'll have something to tell you."

"What is it? Tell me now," I insisted. "I can't bear the uncertainty."

"I can't. You're not tired yet."

I woke up with an incomprehensible feeling of hope and gratitude, as if the dream had been a premonition. I never, in fact, received another postcard from Sicily, not then or in the months to come.

I spent the whole morning in the apartment on rue de Lévis with Haydée and Rajeev, just like old times. For breakfast we drank the delicious vanilla tea they made there every morning, but this time Rajeev went to find some croissants as a treat. Haydée's ankle was still hurting, although her hangover was far more conspicuous and pungent. We sat for several hours in the kitchen, chatting and looking at photographs of Rajeev taken in India and Cuba.

Over the morning, Haydée's ankle got better, and although walking was still difficult, by around one o'clock she felt like going out again. She told us she could not rearrange her plans: her cousin Susana's old boyfriend was visiting Paris and she had promised to go to Père-Lachaise with him.

"Either of you fancy coming?"

"I thought you were scared of my neighbors," I said, remembering her shock the first time she saw my apartment. Rajeev and I exchanged a knowing look. Only someone in love would think that Haydée could change, I remember thinking. I told her that I would just make the journey on the métro with her, no further, but on the way Haydée told me so many stories about her beloved cousin Susana, who had been dead for many years, and about her ex, that I was curious and ended up going with her to the café where they had arranged to meet.

When we got there, the New York Cuban was waiting for us. At his table I saw Julián, another friend of Haydée's I knew only superficially. From the familiar way they were talking, slapping each other on the back occasionally, I could tell that theirs was a very close bond. When they saw us come in, Claudio stood up to give Haydée a hug. Seeing them together, I understood how important this man was to her and how enormously fond she was of him. Our friends' true friendships are always somewhat intriguing. Meeting these people is equivalent to discovering an essential component of their lives. And so, despite the misgivings they can sometimes inspire, we adopt them, with resigned acceptance, like distant relatives it is impossible to be rid of. When I saw how moved Haydée was, I realized what a privilege it was to accompany her and be a silent witness to this reunion. I did not mind that I felt excluded or at least set apart from this friendship. It was enough for me simply to observe my friend's happiness. And this is what I did. At least for the first half an hour, I simply watched them, curious, listening to them speak in the island slang that Haydée, out of consideration, toned down so much when she was talking to me. Little by little, without any of the four of us making an effort, I joined in with the group and, thanks to the wine and the warm, relaxed atmosphere around the table, I began to feel part of the gathering. Like Julián and Haydée, I began to tease the recent arrival, who seemed to be enjoying my presence. When we had finished lunch I forgot, for the second time, my promise to slip away and instead went with them to the cemetery, defying Tom's memory, which prowled the place like a tangible shadow, much more dangerous than any specter. What was it with men? Where did this new interest in graveyards come from? I asked myself if it might not be me and my own interest in graves that attracted this kind of person. Nonetheless, unlike Tom, Claudio did not seem to have any esoteric inclinations. His aim, as a simple or obsessive reader, was to look for the grave of one of his favorite authors. Someone in New York had told him that Vallejo could be found in Père-Lachaise, and this was why he had arranged to meet Haydée in this part of town, wanting to use the afternoon to do a bit of necrological tourism.

When we got to the main entrance, Julián asked the guard for a map, something I had never done, and stopped in front of the list of "illustrious dead" by the gate, with more than three hundred names on it—a ridiculous number if you take into account the fact that there are an estimated two and a half million bodies buried in the place. The list, in alphabetical order, helped us to orientate ourselves and to establish that César Vallejo was not on it. Claudio, however, did not give up. Convinced that the French did not know the Peruvian poet well enough to give him a mention, he marched off, taking for granted that we would all follow him. So we went in search of the grave, knowing full well that it was a capricious enterprise, perhaps destined to fall short, and yet also trusting in objective chance, which Haydée summed up in Santero code:

"If Vallejo's out there, he'll lead us to him. In all his existence as a poet he hasn't had a more dogged fan than Claudio. He's got to repay him for that kind of loyalty."

When I heard this, I thought of Tom and of how pleased he would have been with this Caribbean creed. I felt a pain in my chest I chose to ignore.

We did not manage to get very far along the winding paths of Père-Lachaise. Despite her stubbornness and her attempts to hide it, Haydée was still injured and we were all concerned she would get worse if she forced herself to walk too far. When we got to the third avenue in the cemetery, Julián suggested we sit down on some large steps and asked Haydée to show him her sprain. The ankle had gone blue, nearly black. Claudio, accustomed to New York hours, offered to go and buy a bandage. We had to tell him that at 6:00 p.m. on a Sunday evening it was rather unlikely he would find a pharmacy that was open. I looked down at him from up on my stone step. The light was shining on his face and made him seem several years younger. Under that almost supernatural sunbeam, he looked familiar to me. I would not be able to say where or when, perhaps in the photographs Haydée had at her house, but I was sure that I had seen him before. He had stood up impulsively, and now did not know what to do. So he amused himself by reading the inscription on the grave to our right.

"It's Kreutzer's grave!" he shouted, as if we were a long way away and could not hear him.

But he was all on his own. No one else knew who this was.

He had to explain that he had been one of the best violinists in Chopin's time.

"Beethoven's Violin Sonata No. 9 is dedicated to him. The famous Kreutzer Sonata, which inspired the title of a Tolstoy novel."

Haydée gave an ironic smile.

"Yeah, right. That novel everyone knows."

I wondered what Tom would have thought of Claudio and the tombs he liked so much.

It had begun to rain. Fine drops of water were falling on our heads. The guard walked past, very close to us, ringing his little bell.

"*Ça va fermer, messieurs, dames!*"

"What shall we do about your leg?" Julián said.

I suggested we go over to my apartment to have a cup of tea. I would have something in a drawer somewhere we could bandage her ankle up with.

Haydée mentioned the stairs.

"We didn't sleep there last night because of them, remember?"

"If you like I'll go up on my own and bring you down a bandage," I said. "But we've got two strong men with us today who can carry you upstairs."

Claudio took charge of carrying her up to my apartment. I was glad I had not slept at home the previous night. As a result it was tidy, with no dirty glasses on the little table or Haydée's fag ends stubbed out on dirty plates.

I saw Claudio give me an approving look.

"Would you like a glass of water?" I said. "You must be exhausted."

After making several flattering remarks about the simplicity and austerity of my home—completely unintentional—he downed three glasses of water, slurping like a horse. Then he sat down heavily on the sofa next to poor Haydée, who was staring silently at her foot. I offered everyone a mint tea and, while the water was boiling, went into my room to look for a bandage in the chest of drawers. In the living room, none of my guests spoke. The silence went on for several minutes, until the soft notes of a piano could be heard: Claudio had put a disc into my CD player, an Albéniz concert played by Alicia de Larrocha, which he had bought in FNAC before meeting us.

Miraculously I found the bandage, among a tangle of T-shirts and underwear. I put it on the coffee table and went back to the kitchen to turn the gas off and pour the hot water over the mint leaves.

Not much else happened that afternoon. After drinking our tea with pine nuts, Moroccan- and Belleville-style, my guests left, each to go back to their homes, except for Claudio, who was flying back to New York first thing the next day and had a dinner to attend close to his hotel. We said goodbye very naturally, certain that there was already a growing complicity between us. I told him not to forget his CD, but he refused to take it with him. As soon as I had closed the door, I sat down on the sofa to carry on listening to it and, not long after, fell asleep. In the morning, Haydée's friend rang me from the airport to say goodbye. It was a brief but warm call, and confirmed the good impression I had already formed of him. He thanked me for inviting him to my house and said he was very glad to have added me to his list of Parisian friends. Then he hung up, but just before doing so, as he replaced the telephone on its cradle in the booth, I caught the sound of another animal sigh.

Several hours later, a new message popped up on my computer screen.

Claudio had sent me a declaration of love, quoting César Vallejo.

At the moment the message from New York arrived, the first in a long series, my world, as paradoxical as it might sound, was made up of an absence. It was a world in negative, where everything was a reminder of someone not there. The places and objects of my daily life, the boulevard outside, the main door to my building, the windows in my apartment, and the view from them of the sprawl of Père-Lachaise and the treetops, the walls in my room, the sheets on my bed, the radio playing; everything betrayed Tom's absence and, as such, all these objects were frustrating to see and to touch. Claudio's message, those terse, unexpected lines that expressed in all candor his happiness at having met me, had a similar effect. They underlined the lack of communication between Tom and me, our lengthy silence. Waiting for someone, at least in this way, is equivalent to canceling out one's own existence, loaning it out for an unknown period of time, exchanging it for a meaningless, absurd doubt. To be obsessed with someone who has decided to absent themselves is to gift minutes, hours, and whole days of our life to someone who has not asked for and does not want them; it is to condemn those minutes, hours, and days to the dimension of lost time, of the futile; to waste the infinite number of possibilities that this time offers us and trade it in for the worst of all options: frustration, suffering. I read the e-mail three times, quite taken aback. How easy it seemed, all of a sudden, to sit down and write a few friendly words to thank someone for an encounter. How sad that Tom—whatever his circumstances might have been— was unable to make such an effort. Before I replied, I decided to go for a walk to shake off my mood. It was a brilliant morning with a clear sky, an unusual day for this time of year. But that sun, that beauty, were also painful for me. Absence prevailed like a toxic rush of water spilling over uncontrollably, soaking everything. I felt angry with myself for not being able to enjoy the lovely weather and the new friendship hovering into view in my life. Who was Tom compared with the force and splendor of nature? An insignificant individual among several millions; more than that, an intangible memory. How much did it matter that he was not here in a city so overflowing with beauty? *Avec des si on mettrait Paris en bouteille,* they say round here, and this is exactly what I was doing: bottling the city, turning it into a compressed, gray miniature, impossible to enjoy. When I got home, I switched on the CD player with the album Claudio had left behind and remembered his face in the cemetery, illuminated by that strange late afternoon light. After trying out two or three possible replies, I decided to write this:

> *I'm still trying to decipher the familiar sensation I felt when I met you, almost as if I recognized you.*
> *In any case—know that it was a pleasure.*

As I listened to the record, I made another mint tea and stood for a long time in front of the window. I thought of the lives of those million or so people now buried over there: I thought of the intensity with which many of them would have passed through the world, struggling to leave something valuable behind so that they would be remembered forever; and I thought of all the other people whose names did not feature on the list of celebrities and whose biographies had passed into oblivion. Did they feel anything? Did they think, as Tom claimed they did? What if our existence were a kind of mold, a mold like the one a sculptor or a metal worker uses? I wondered. If each experience we have while we are alive, each emotion, each thought, were equivalent to a record made just once and then listened to passively, again and again, with no possibility of modifying anything—would we waste time in the way we do, tormenting ourselves with painful thoughts and ideas to be repeated for all eternity? I stood and thought about this for a good while before concluding that we would. The most likely scenario was that, even if we knew this were the case, we would not stop doing it. I am afraid it is a kind of inertia, I told myself, an uncontrollable behavior like that of insects, which we like to think of as so stupid—and which, at the same time, seems strangely familiar—when we see them carry out their repetitive routines, not to mention flying close to a flame or smashing into windows (an image, incidentally, which appears with suspicious frequency in literature). But supposing that, on the contrary, informed of the definitive nature of our time on earth, we could choose how we wanted eternity to play out, what would we choose to do, to think or to say? What would our final judgment look like? I could not find an answer. That night I received another message:

It seems that exactly the same thing happened to us both. I know what that recognition is, Cecilia. You'll know it too, when you see me again.

The sun stayed out all the following week, and little by little, I began to notice the beneficial effects of the Indian summer on my state of mind. Tom never wrote back to me after that first postcard, and nor did he call after that first message and, although I had not forgotten his scent, his closeness, his tenderness (which, despite the silence, I did not totally mistrust), I began to think more and more of Claudio and to enjoy his frequent letters, as if life had somehow determined to compensate for such scarcity with the sublime silver tongue of this Cuban. When a relationship, no matter how intense, opens up so much space for uncertainty and frustration, it makes room for other interests, other hopes.

On Wednesday I decided to go back to the swimming pool I occasionally went to and which I had not visited since Tom left, partly because of the cold and a little bit due to the paralyzing apathy I was dragging around with me. As I was leaving my building, I found a package in the postbox. It came from New York and was in the shape of a CD. I had time to go up and open it in my apartment, but I was afraid to hang around. I decided to leave it for when I got back. Before setting out, I had a look in Tom's postbox, stuffed with bills and junk mail. The pool helped me to relax and meant I came back hungry. I made some pasta and poured in sauce from a jar. I opened the package in front of the steaming plate of food. It was *Dark Intervals* by Keith Jarrett, whom I had never listened to. Before I put it on, I washed up the plates and tidied the kitchen. When I had finished, I realized I had another e-mail. It was a set of instructions for listening to the CD:

Cecilia—I suppose by now you'll have received the package. I decided to send it because I need to explain a few things to you, and because I know that I wouldn't be able to say anything either as exactly or as frankly precise as what this piece of music says and what I hope it tells you about me. Close your eyes and listen to "Americana." When you get to 2:19, or 2:56, or 4:16, or 5:25, or 6:11, imagine me by your side. Or put on "Hymn," and listen to as much of it as you can from 1:11 onward. This is what I am trying to tell you, imperfectly, like taking you by the hand, like being on the road right this minute, heading somewhere, watching you look at what is near, at what is far away.

I must admit that I did not pay any attention to these instructions, but they did give me a clue as to the personality of this new friend Haydée had described as "odd." It was not the only time. More than inspiring repulsion or curiosity, such a level of precision bored me. And so I listened to the CD the same way I almost always listen to music I put on at home, carefully and quietly, in front of the window. Then I wrote to Claudio to thank him. From then on, I began receiving CDs with instructions for listening to them as he would suggest. There were messages, too, in which he asked me to go to a certain park or museum and observe a sculpture from particular angles, how far I should walk from the front of the piece to one of the cardinal points, and how best to tilt my body so as to bring such and such a detail into focus. How on earth did he have such a good memory? Did he get this information from a notebook somewhere, with things he has scribbled down during his years in Paris, or was it simply a kind of madness? Looking back at it now, I am inclined to think it was the latter.

Claudio:

Today was an incredible day, just as how I imagine days in New York to be. It was cold, but the sky was intensely blue and the sun was shining. I went out for a swim this morning for the first time in ages. Afterwards, I went home and sat down to listen to Dark Intervals, *which arrived in the post today. Thanks for sending it. It's great that your rhapsodies in the key of Jarrett reach as far as Paris, but can I ask you a favor: please don't idealize me. I can't bear to disappoint people.*

UNCERTAINTY

Ever since returning to Manhattan, I have been trying to avoid Ruth as much as possible. Being with her fills me with despair now. Her snobbish frivolity, the attitude she has of a spoiled little girl who has obtained everything she has without lifting a finger and yet still indulges in the luxury of getting depressed; it insults me. The last thing I want is to hurt her and this is the main reason I continue to spend time with her, at the price of a guilty conscience. As I feast on delicacies in her Tribeca loft, I think of Cecilia. I imagine her sleeping, or eating breakfast alone, across from the cemetery, deprived of my embrace, face to face with that implacable lucidity that characterizes her, with no one to protect her, to guide her along that painful path I know so well, the path of beings such as she and I, incapable of deceiving ourselves. While Ruth chatters away, plays with her nails, chooses a tablecloth to go with the vase of roses she has put on the table this evening, and takes out bottle after bottle of the most expensive wine to indulge me, the remaining embers of the desire she once made me feel are slowly dying out. In their place has arisen a nostalgia for this other life being lived far away from me, with nothing I can do to stop it, or almost nothing, apart from writing to Cecilia with everything I cannot say to her in person.

I cannot deny that I have gone back to those peach-colored sheets and yielded to sessions of violent sex. Sometimes there is a force in my body I can only release through acts such as these. But in the morning, whether I awake on the satin sheets or in the sobriety of my own room, the first thought that comes to my mind is Cecilia, the existence of Cecilia, and her absence, painful like a snakebite. It is then that looking at Ruth sleeping by my side becomes unbearable. If before I was not satisfied with my deficient existence with her, the sensation it gives me now is of lying in a bottomless vacuum, certain of not finding myself where I should be, of failing in everything I do. Cecilia, meanwhile, gives me inner peace. All I have to do is think of her to feel it.

November was a strange month and very different from the rest of my life in New York. I was euphoric at having finally found the ideal woman, at her constant presence in my fantasies, and at her positive reaction to my messages. Even so, I was still visiting Ruth. One part of me, the most honorable and moralistic, demanded I put an end to this habit. If now I had the intention of being as far as possible a better man, of reaching my full potential, it was due to Cecilia, not to Ruth, and especially not *for* Ruth. Why, convinced as I was that this certainty in my life I mentioned before was finally before me, did I not act in this spirit and send the old thing packing once and for all? It was getting harder and harder to hold a conversation with her, and I felt less and less like sleeping curled up next to her. Not even sex interested me now. Meanwhile, the correspondence with Cecilia, no matter how scant it was, kept me in a mood that favored sublime feelings over physical sensations. Instead of such elation strengthening my spirit, however, I saw myself acting with hideous faint-heartedness with regard to Ruth. Now, perhaps to excuse my behavior, I tell myself that the experience of love, when it is as indisputable as this, brings with it the threat of revolution, of radical change, of *renversement*. And no matter how much we avoid—or put off, as was my case—making abrupt, untimely decisions, everything seems to be on the point of collapse, of an earth-shattering tremor. When a love of this magnitude appears, when it foists itself upon you, the fragility you feel is enormous. And it is natural and inevitable that you look for something to cling to, no matter how absurd or mistaken this might be, so you don't feel you are being swallowed up by the abyss: work, everyday habits, but also relationships with the people who make up your universe prior to the shattering encounter. This, at least, is how I explain to myself my cowardly attitude toward the old thing. Ruth gave me all the security that Cecilia took from me merely by existing, by having appeared in my life. Unlike Cecilia, whose feelings I knew very little of, she was happy with me, was happy spoiling and indulging me, welcoming me into her aura of luxury and comfort. I harbored no doubts about this and could only acknowledge her constant benevolence. I felt grateful, concerned about her, and doubtless a certain amount of affection. No small thing, although not enough, either. Nevertheless, as soon as my moralistic side began pressuring me to let her go and honor my undeniable love for Cecilia as I should, I was flooded by a feeling not dissimilar to grief. On a couple of occasions, as I relaxed in the armchair in the loft after a sumptuous dinner, watching as Ruth dutifully cleared the table or arranged some magazines on the bookshelves, I tried to organize in my mind the reasons for a breakup, the way to express it. Then I recalled the vulnerability she had displayed in the days prior to our trip, the naïve enthusiasm with which she had voiced her wish to live with me. The childlike expression on her face would seem suddenly defenseless—far more than usual—and the explanations about our inevitable breakup would vanish before I could even formulate them in silence. It is not that it was impossible for me to do without Ruth—far from it; but thinking about breaking up with her made me start to miss her. The need to end the relationship sharpened my affection and made me suffer prematurely. Moreover, to be totally honest, my practical spirit would frequently oppose the breakup, and not without reason: Ruth lived in New York, Cecilia did not. My work was in this city, and everyone knows how hard it is to find a job as flexible and well paid as mine was. It is true that my love for Cecilia justified anything, including leaving everything behind to set myself up in Paris to try to make a life by her side. However, reason and prudence, two deities I have paid tribute to my whole life, advised me to wait before making a decision like this, before giving up something that meant a daily escape from the tensions of working life, before hurting someone who had only ever been infinitely patient, caring, and good to me. If things went well with Cecilia, if I managed to make her feel something similar or in proportion to what she inspired in me, then I could try to get her to live in New York to finish her studies, without having to give up my job. To do this, however, it would be necessary to act with tact and caution. Give her time to take things in, not force anything. My strategy with Ruth would have to be equally judicious so I didn't cause hurt. Sooner or later—of this I was convinced—I would have to shake her off, move our courtship toward the terrain of friendship, but the transition would need to be stealthy, almost imperceptible. And this is what I attempted after our return from Paris. The problem, as ever, lay in that feminine ability to detect danger, to correctly read any sign of inattention or lack of interest. From the moment we got back, Ruth started asking me all the time what I was thinking about. She would wake several times in the night, dreaming that I was leaving her. She even began to jealously interrogate me about the day I had gone to see Haydée, as if her subconscious understood that this meeting signified the turning point in our story, the moment the scales had tipped down toward a definitive "no."

November was, as I said, a very strange month. Receiving each reply from Cecilia, no matter how brief, filled me with joy, with affection, with hope, and, at the same time, made me wish desperately that time would pass so that I could see her again. I started looking up tickets to Paris as a habit, seeking out and comparing the costs. Every day, during my lunch break, I would sit in front of my computer with a steaming coffee on my desk and search the various flight comparison websites I knew, mainly American, but some French ones too. To tell the truth, I would have been able to wait, to prolong this stage of chaste love, of the communion of two souls, to the furthest possible limits; I would have been able to delay for as long as possible a physical encounter with her and eventually seduce her with my words, take all the time I needed to invalidate with good reasoning each and every one of her impediments and fears. However, the knowledge and experience I have acquired over the course of my life about the female sex told me that in order to consolidate the attachment, a physical encounter was necessary. Women need this, even if it is just the once. No words, no matter how passionate or profound they are, are able to make a mark on their hearts if not preceded by at least one or two caresses. It was important to me, too. Before I began distancing myself from Ruth in any way, I wanted to corroborate what I already knew, and to ensure that Cecilia felt exactly as I did.

*

Six weeks went by in this unusual rhythm, swiftly when it came to my emotions and epistolary advances toward Cecilia, slowly when it came to my ailing relationship with the old thing, to which I did not dare give the necessary lethal injection. Cecilia and I wrote to each other daily, sometimes several times a day. At first her messages were reserved, circumspect, even; but little by little, probably influenced by the zeal of mine, we gradually established a confidence between us. And although her letters were not long and amorous like the ones I sent her, it was possible to read in them a certain disposition for romance. One afternoon, in a short message, she expressed a clear wish to see me. It was then that I made the decision to visit her. The December holidays were upon us. Just as I did when I was a student, I bought a ticket for the 24th, the best way I know of to ensure a quiet, empty flight.

CECILIA'S VERSION

I spent that Christmas Eve at Haydée's house. Neither she nor Rajeev had grown up in a Catholic household and so dinner was a very secular, informal affair. Accustomed as I was to my own family's blowouts, impossible to wriggle out of, that Christmas dinner felt like the best of my life. We were joined by a couple of Indian guys and a Venezuelan friend of Haydée's, whom I had seen at other parties. The meal—curry with dried fruit and coconut milk, accompanied by basmati rice and *saag paneer*—was delicious. We opened several bottles of champagne, although I drank no more than two or three glasses. The next morning Claudio was arriving from New York and I wanted to avoid a hangover at all costs. According to Haydée, traveling on this date when everyone else comes together to celebrate was one of the man's eccentric habits. I, however, saw it as an excellent way of ducking out of this annoying evening, and evidence of the affinity we shared. I returned to Ménilmontant shortly after midnight. The previous afternoon I had bought croissants and orange juice to give Claudio for breakfast. After making sure my apartment was clean and tidy, I set my alarm and went to bed. My plan was to get up a few minutes before he arrived so I could get dressed and lay the table calmly, but in the end this was not possible. Instead of letting me know the time his plane landed at Charles de Gaulle, as I had supposed he would, he had given me the rough time he would show up at my house. It was a miracle I was awoken by the sound of him coming up the stairs, energetic strides that gave away his height and his robust constitution, so unlike those of Tom. I did not even have time to wash my face. I opened the door and, to make up for my disheveled appearance, made an effort to give him a huge welcoming smile. Claudio left his suitcase by the door and waited for me to get his breakfast. In our own continent we are used to eating far more than what I was offering him. I told myself that he must have a raging hunger after his transatlantic trip and felt embarrassed at having nothing but pastries, juice, and coffee in the cupboards. He said nothing, however, and just ate without taking his eyes off me. I was silent too. His arrival had caught me off-guard, although the aftereffects of the champagne were also making themselves felt. It was an exceedingly awkward moment, and I even started wishing that he would leave. I thought about putting on a CD, but said to myself that choosing one was too tricky a matter, one I was not capable of resolving. Resorting to Jarrett or Albéniz would have been an exaggeratedly romantic gesture. I suppose that Claudio must have noticed my discomfort and that it was to dispel it that he took me in his enormous arms and carried me to my bedroom. Fortunately, he did not attempt to make any kind of sexual move. I found his tall, strong body, his curly hair and gray beard, his large nose and his hands attractive, but they also seemed unknown and intimidating to me. Everything, from our meeting in the restaurant to his return to Paris, had happened too fast for me to take it all in. I am sure he realized this. After a few minutes, which to me felt eternal, due to my increasing timidity, Claudio asked if he could have a shower, and I seized my chance to get dressed. His plan was to go for a walk in the Montmartre cemetery, on Christmas Day itself, to continue looking for Vallejo's grave. I liked the idea. Indeed, as incredible as it might sound, I had never taken the time to go and visit any other cemeteries in the city. What is more, something told me that the obvious alternatives, such as hunting for a street market or walking around the Christmas village that springs up at that time of year in the Champs-Élysées, would seem rather dull to this man who knew every inch of Rodin's statue of Balzac.

We sat on the métro to Blanche, and there, convinced that the poor man was going to pass out from hunger at any moment, I suggested we take a seat in the first *brasserie* we saw. The price of the set menu was entirely beyond my budget, but I said nothing. Luckily, he insisted on paying. As we ate, Claudio asked me the obligatory questions, the ones that two people who are attracted to each other but still do not know each other ask. He wanted to know, for example, where I had grown up, what my family was like, and where I had studied. He told me a bit about his childhood in socialist Cuba, too; he spoke of his mother as an exemplary woman to whom he owed everything, including his having gone to a good school and having been able to leave the island; he told me about Susana, Haydée's cousin, whom he had loved a great deal. The most painful thing that had happened in his life had been this young woman's unexpected death, from which—this at least was the impression I got—he had never quite recovered. This conversation was important to us both. I, who had gone through my mother abandoning me at a very early age, was able to comprehend the sorrow in his eyes, and, as he told me all of this, I felt certain I would end up loving him.

The cemetery in Montmartre was very different from Père-Lachaise. First of all, it lies several meters below street level, in the hollow of a disused mine. It is a fanciful place, messy and bohemian like the legendary neighborhood of Montmartre once was, when it was inhabited by artists. An information booth was still open at the entrance, quite incredible on Christmas Day. The woman behind the desk asked us in a friendly voice if we were looking for a relative, so we asked her about the poet.

"Valley-*oh*?" she inquired, after making us write the name on a bit of paper and looking down her printed list. "He's not here. You'd be better off looking in Montparnasse. I'm almost certain he's buried there."

We went in to look at the graves of a few other writers, among them Koltès, with whom Claudio felt great kinship, but also Zola and Théophile Gautier, one of my favorites as a teenager. Getting to know other cemeteries was like visiting different countries without having to leave the city. Compared to Père-Lachaise, for example, Montparnasse is much more modern and orderly. While in the first there are graves that seem to be made of crumbling bones or old rags, almost organic, consumed by the worms of time, or in the shape of a monument, terrifying to go near because they seem to be aware of everything that happens around them, in the second, the tombs are newer, cleaner. The inscriptions on the stones are easy to read. By this I do not mean that the place lacks character—it has that in spades—but it is a more twentieth-century character—closer to that of Sartre or Serge Gainsbourg. There is not that mishmash of periods I see from my apartment. The Peruvian poet was, in fact, buried there in Montparnasse, but so too were Julio Cortázar, Emil Cioran, and Eugène Ionesco. I cannot express how surprised I was to discover that Porfirio Díaz, ex-president of Mexico and a native of Oaxaca who had settled in Paris, just as I had, was resting there, next to so many other illustrious characters to whom he would surely have nothing to say.

The cemeteries of Paris are located in the four extremes of the city: Montmartre to the north, Père-Lachaise to the east, Passy to the west, and Montparnasse to the south. As we walked back to Bastille, Claudio told me that, before they were built, the city's main burial ground was in the center, by Les Halles market, exactly where place Joachim-du-Bellay can be found today. It was closed towards the end of the eighteenth century after a terrible epidemic, caused by mishandling of the bodies. Since then it has been forbidden to bury the dead within the city limits. "There are so many bodies under the ground that we walk on every day!" I recall thinking. As if that were not enough, there is also the network of Roman catacombs that stretches out beneath the city and holds a huge number of bones, too. I concluded that living in Paris, no matter where one is, means living on top of someone's burial place. The entire city is an enormous graveyard. If spiritualist theories are correct—and I am more convinced by them every day—then we all must have been possessed, at least once, by a soul in torment.

The more I think of it, the stranger it seems to me to have explored all these cemeteries with Claudio and not with Tom. Unlike my neighbor, Claudio was interested not in the dead, but in the cult of writers. To him the graves were devoid of any kind of mysticism or occult significance. What he sought was a purely aesthetic pleasure, something that gave me a certain sense of security.

That night we slept together without any reserve on my part coming between us. If I was rather awkward when it came to social matters, in terms of sexual experience I was a genuine novice. What I had prided myself on for years in Mexico had, since I arrived in Paris, and especially since my friendship with Haydée, been the source of disgraceful embarrassment. Claudio was infinitely patient with me. I do not know if he realized the extent of my ignorance, but he never once hinted that he did. What he certainly did understand (and I do not doubt that he enjoyed this) was that I was a blank page upon which each and every one of his instructions—he gave them with music and on trips to museums, but also in bed—would remain inscribed for all eternity. I do not mean to brag, but I think I learned fast. Claudio returned to New York and I caught up with him there a few weeks later, in my February holidays.

CLAUDIO'S VERSION

Just as the Muslims depict paradise as a garden filled with virgins, in Cuba I always used to imagine it as the North Pole, a white and spacious place where, instead of palm trees, there was ice, and instead of clamorous noise, a perfect silence. This is why, ever since I first arrived in New York, my favorite season has been winter. Unlike my compatriots, I consider this period quite edifying, a time of purification. The cold, especially when the temperature drops well below freezing, not only cleans out our respiratory channels but also strips us utterly of the unbearable laziness caused by good weather, in particular in tropical climates. When it is 5°F outside, no one thinks of squandering their life away in a hammock, or shuffling around in a pair of flip-flops. On the contrary, winter impels us to cut down on our movements, to walk quickly, avoiding any unnecessary diversion, any passing temptation. Every one of our cells is active, producing the necessary fuel to keep us functioning properly. You only have to look at the global economy to realize that the cold countries function better than the hot ones, and the northern, mountainous regions are more lucrative than those populations on the coast, where the only thing people produce is the kind of music that encourages dancing and debauchery, beats that incite animal sex, the excessive consumption of cannabis . . . in other words, stupefaction, and via the fastest route I know of. This is the reason, contrary to what Mario and my other detractors claim about my being a miser, I aim to turn on the heat as little as possible and make do with the warmth given off by the other apartments in the building, inhabited by spineless Latinos or Asians, who waste their electricity. As at any other time of year, I shower every morning in cold water and thus appreciate far more my cup of hot coffee at breakfast.

When I leave the house, I endeavor to walk with dignity through the streets of my neighborhood to the bus stop, not with rapid, embarrassing movements, or any of those unnecessary grimaces that feed like parasites on the faces of the other pedestrians. I imagine that I am an officer of the Austro-Hungarian Empire, treading the paths that lead to his regiment's barracks. Sometimes I even imagine I am winter itself, and that it is beneath my frozen whip that these commoners quiver. With majestic dignity, I walk slowly up the steps of the bus on my way to the publishing house. People look at me enthralled by a sensation of envy which also contains a certain amount of admiration. No matter how hard they try, they cannot control their moans and bleats at the chill I leave in my wake. Burying their noses in their coats, they swap information on the day's weather forecast. Listening to them, I think of their miserable lives and of how different the world would be if these people knew how best to make use of the seasons in order to strengthen their character. But it is useless. Over the years I have learned that the masses are a lost cause, and taking pity on them is as fruitless as trying to educate them.

On Thursday, December 25, at 9:30 in the morning, a taxi from the airport dropped me at the door of no. 43, boulevard de Ménilmontant. I punched in the entry code I had been sent and climbed the four floors to wake up Cecilia. This, at least, was my intention. She was waiting for me with the door open. She was wearing, I remember it well, dark-gray flannel pajamas, her hair hanging loose but not messily over her shoulders. She looked lovely just out of bed. It was the second time in my life I had been with her. Someone more skeptical or conventional would say, and not without a certain degree of accuracy, that we were two strangers. But it was not wholly true, either. Cecilia felt familiar to me in every way. I recognized—who can say how?—her scent, her features, her way of speaking and moving, her softness, and the exact space between us. In any case, she seemed much more known to me than Ruth's presence, to which, by now, I should be accustomed. As soon as she saw me, she took my suitcase and put it on the floor, behind the door. Then she took my hand and led me to the couch in the living room, the same place where only a few weeks earlier we had sat listening to Albéniz with Haydée and Julián. It was cold. Outside, a steady drizzle fell and through the windows of her apartment, instead of the trees and the sad monuments of the Père-Lachaise, we could see the mist and the reflection of a glowing streetlight. I had no appetite. I had eaten practically the same thing on the flight, but I forced myself to eat again so I didn't offend her. In the meantime I imagined her breasts, just like the ones painted by Diego Rivera, whose murals I had seen in Chicago. As soon as I had finished, I carried her to her room and lay down beside her on the bed, where the humors left by her body in the night still remained. This fragrance, which I remember now with astonishing clarity, intoxicated me like a cloud of opiates. Even though I had an erection of equine proportions between my legs, Cecilia seemed wrapped up in other thoughts and I chose not to force anything that morning. At around eleven, I took a shower, changed into clean clothes from my suitcase, and waited for her to get dressed. If there is anything that makes me feel uncomfortable it is not having showered. In Cuba, when the lights went and the pump could not get the water up to the tanks on the roof, I used to carry buckets of water for the whole family. Surprisingly, it did not bother me in the slightest that she refrained from showering. I told myself that perhaps she had acquired local customs, somewhat laxer than those in America. In any case, her scent was clean and fresh at all times and, unlike my own, had no need to be tempered. The rain had almost stopped, and a ray of sunlight was showing through the winter storm clouds. I suggested we eat something in the 18th arrondissement, and then, if the good weather continued, visit the Montmartre cemetery to see if that was where Vallejo was buried, since we had not found him on our previous visit to Père-Lachaise.

We ordered the *menu de midi* at a modest *brasserie* by the exit to the Blanche métro stop. I admit that I enjoyed the moment she took off her jacket and her breasts were outlined once again beneath her sweater. This time, perhaps due to the cold, or because my proximity was starting to have some sort of effect, her nipples stiffened in my direction. As I said before, I do not tend to ask women I associate with anything about their past life. Nonetheless, with Cecilia I broke not only this rule but others to do with basic survival, incapable of doing otherwise. That afternoon, as we ate our salad and *steak-frites*, I asked her a long string of questions as they occurred to me. I wanted to know what she had been like as a child and a teenager, who she had grown up with, how long she had lived in Paris. She told me about her childhood with her grandmother in Oaxaca, a city I have never been to, but which I imagine surrounded by volcanoes and full of old buildings and exotic birds. She told me about her father, who traveled back and forth between Oaxaca and Mexico City, of the great affection that bound them together. She told me of her mother, whom she remembered very little of, and of how, in love with another man, she had fled the family home to be with him; of the arts degree she had completed at a provincial college and the library given by the painter Francisco Toledo to the city he grew up in, which gave her years of reading. Oaxaca was not Havana, of course. The complete opposite, in fact. However, there were similarities between our formative years, or at least I thought I could identify a few: the difficulties in buying books in our cities, our love of libraries. Cecilia had not grown up in an overcrowded home, but she had been semi-neglected. She used to spend a lot of time alone in a big old house, inhabited solely by her infirm grandmother. Neglect and overcrowding are, as I see it, two sides of the same coin. In both situations you are isolated, and each causes desperation and anxiety. Although Santería is scarcely practiced in Oaxaca, her neighbors, like mine, did have very ingrained beliefs and practices. I imagine that the rejection of these delusional customs had an influence on her character, which above all is rational. Something similar happened to me thanks to Facundo Martínez and the many rituals his family used to perform out in the yard. Everything Cecilia told me about herself that afternoon only increased my desire to remain by her side, to guide her, to protect her with my own body from any inclement elements. After we had eaten, we walked up to avenue Rachel to enter the main gate to the cemetery. We could not find Vallejo in Montmartre, so instead we visited the graves of Stendhal, Zola, Théophile Gautier, and Koltès, for whom I feel a great affection. Bernard-Marie Koltès. One great source of pride for me is having lived in Paris when he was still alive and when very few of us knew him. Of course, it would never have occurred to me to importune him unnecessarily with my presence. It was enough to know we shared the same city. We took the bus home at around six that evening. Cecilia suggested we buy a bottle of wine from Chez Nicholas. It was a very affordable red that tasted as good as one of the old thing's finest vintages due to the simple fact that I was sharing it with Cecilia. We slept together that night and before dawn broke we made love three times. If I use that expression it is not because I have suddenly become corny. I am very aware of how banal it frequently sounds. Nevertheless, there is no better way to describe what occurred between our bodies early that morning. Cecilia and I did not screw, we fucked—an extremely vulgar word that I only employ when absolutely necessary. We simply extended to the physical domain the way we had felt for each other since the moment we first met.

My stay in Paris lasted exactly three nights and four days, the time my employer allows before they start deducting it from holidays. We saw no one. Not Haydée, not Julián, not even Michel Miló was informed of my passing through Paris on those dates. We concentrated on enjoying each other's company, pretending we lived together, even—life as a couple, like the one I had dreamed of by her side: silent, unhurried, frugal, brimming with mutual affection, but without exaggeration. I will not deny I thought of Ruth quite a few times, nearly always to scold myself for having been unable to send her packing before I left. I felt guilty for jeopardizing my relationship with Cecilia because of this commitment I had failed to confess to. Sometimes I worried about Ruth, too. I had not told her anything about my trip. I had simply said that I planned on working this weekend and that it would not be possible to see her. After getting on the plane I had turned off my cell phone and had not turned it on again, not even once, to see if there were any calls from her. I was also worried about how to find a way to clear things up when I got back to New York. It was ridiculous to wait any longer. These thoughts, however, were brief, and occupied very little space in my mind. Cecilia's presence would immediately take hold of me and the strength of my feelings toward her would redeem me from any past offenses.

On Sunday, in the Montparnasse cemetery, we finally found Vallejo's grave. We had eaten at a sushi place on rue de la Gaîté that Cecilia, who loved Japanese food, went to quite frequently. After lunch, we walked together to avenue du Maine to enter by one of the side gates, where there is a list of the famous people buried there, and where, at last, we found his name. It was not easy to find him—I believe the map was badly drawn—but we got there in the end. In my pocket I was carrying a compact edition of his collected poems, which I planned to take out once we had found the place. However, we were not the first visitors to the poet's grave that afternoon. Two of his readers had beaten us to it. One was a professor of Quechua at the University of Paris, the head, as he told us, of the department of oppressed, minoritized languages. As I did, the man knew several of Vallejo's poems by heart, but, unlike me, he was not shy about reciting them in public. Moreover, he assured us that on many of his visits to the tomb, when he always brought *pisco* brandy and boxes of cigarettes as a gift for the dead man, he had been lucky enough to converse with the writer's spirit. When we told him how we had searched through the different neighborhoods of the city, he explained that Vallejo had first been buried in Montrouge, in the 14th arrondissement, but that in 1970 his widow had managed to get him moved to Montparnasse, as he had dreamed of. When we got back to her apartment, I took out my book and read Cecilia fragments from *Trilce* that seemed as if they had been written for her. She listened attentively with her eyes closed until she fell asleep.

Now that it rainshines so pretty
in this peace of a single line,
here you have me,
here you have me, from whom I might hang,
so that you may satiate my corners.
And if, these brimming,
you overflow with greater kindness,
I'll draw from where there may not be,
I'll forge from madness another sumpage
insatiable urges
to level and love.

I left Paris in the early hours. My flight was on Monday, December 29 at eight in the morning, French time, which meant I was just able to get home, take a shower, and leave my suitcase before heading to the office in the early afternoon, ready to surprise all the staff at the publishing house with my newfound, inexplicable happiness. Nonetheless, the joy I prophesied for myself lasted a very short time. As on the previous occasion, my good mood hit rock bottom as soon as my feet touched American soil. My days with Cecilia had been too good, too promising to allow me to take up my daily life casually once more; bringing an end to them seemed not only intolerable but also genuinely stupid. I was not scared of denying myself pleasure, but at the idea of losing her. We had arranged that she would come to visit me in New York during her February break, but how could I ensure that nothing would prevent us from seeing each other or separate us once and for all? Like my mood, the temperature also took a dive that Monday. There was no snow, but the piercing chill sliced through my skin.

Cecilia,

I can hardly concentrate on my work. I miss you. What's the weather like over there? Who are you with right now? Doesn't it seem absurd to you that we're not together today, that we're not going to the theater and to eat sushi on rue de la Gaîté, then back to your apartment, knowing that we can stay in bed until late, pressing our bodies together and keeping each other warm with our own heat and with a desire that is now fearless, without masks? I feel as if I'm missing a part of my newest nature, my newest me, of which you are flesh and reflection: I miss—and "miss" here is a viscerally physiological act—your eyes, your mouth, your tongue, your fingers intertwined with mine, the sound of you breathing, the smell of your breath, your taste, your neck, your shoulders, your back, your voice. I really miss your eyes. Your voice and your eyes. What we feel and sometimes do not dare to say to each other, what you make me feel that I do not dare to say, what your smile and your breath say to me, even though you yourself don't dare to repeat it.

I spent the first week transformed into a physical wreck, a slave to nostalgia and impossibility, fighting against unease and physical absence. Several times in the morning, as I corrected galleys at my desk, I was gripped by the urge to call her on the telephone. Most of the time I found it impossible to resist. Luckily—this is what I think now—after ringing a few times the France Télécom answering service would click on. I hung up, ashamed, not daring to leave any trace of my distress in a message. I chose instead to send her anxious e-mails, where I could confirm over and over again that my feelings were real.

On Friday, after almost eight days of silence, Ruth called me at the office. Contrary to what I had predicted, she had not called my cell phone once during my absence and I found no messages from her on my answering machine at home.

"Hello, darling," she said that Friday morning, with the same fond, friendly tone as ever. "Did you manage to work in peace over the holidays?"

Her voice, which I had neither expected nor wanted to hear at any point in that agonizing period, had the effect of a healing balm. I accepted her invitation to dinner, unable to resist. And, once we had finished feasting and I had enjoyed my glass of cognac in front of the fireplace in her apartment, I could not resist screwing her, either. In the morning, as we breakfasted on buttered bagels, coffee, and orange juice, Ruth announced some good news: in my absence, she had spoken with a friend of hers, an official at the UN, about the possibility of my being recruited as a permanent translator for the organization. According to what she had been told, it was very likely, given my experience and my record at the publishing house, that I would be given the post.

I left the house feeling enthused about work but a real asshole in terms of personal matters. I needed to speak to her, not to tell her that there was someone else, but to inform her once and for all that I could not go on seeing her. Despite what you might think, it was not the possibility of the job that had prevented me from making things clear. I am still convinced of the generosity of her spirit and that, even if we had broken up, she would have continued trying to find me a post at the UN. No, my trouble was cowardice, plain and simple. Never in my life had I acted in such a shameless fashion.

On Monday I went back to the publishing house and back, too, to exchanging e-mails with my Parisian girlfriend. Cecilia's messages were less frequent than mine. Whereas I sent her around two or three per day, she would reply only two or three times a week. The only effect of her sloth was to increase my desire, and when the wait between one message and another grew too long I felt an unease bordering on anxiety. It was during this period we spent apart, from my visit in December until her trip to New York, that I had a chance to discover one of her less dazzling sides. Our sudden separation after three such intense days together had probably not done her any good either, and it took no time at all for the effects of this drastic change between passion and absence to make themselves felt in our correspondence. Three weeks after I had returned home, Cecilia's messages stopped being so amorous and, gradually, an increasing ambiguity began to manifest itself. The frequency with which she sent them diminished, too, and they became sporadic. Below are two of her "letters":

> *My darling:*
> *Since you left, Paris has become an igloo where it's always raining. Being with you was like falling into a long, warm embrace. I miss your skin and your solid, bear-like body. I can't wait to see you again in New York soon.*

And, a week later:

> *Claudio:*
> *There are times when I just want to forget about the world, and to obsess over something meaningless. This is what happened recently, on the days I didn't write to you. I'm fighting a battle*

with myself. I have a few undesirable habits that cause me a lot
of anguish and which I find hard to break out of. Ever since I met
you I've been trying to open myself up to the possibility of love so
I can fight back against all the frustration, all the helplessness I
feel. But sometimes it all takes over my life. Why would you
want me to write to you from a place like that? If I had to choose
which sea to drown myself in, I'd go to Sicily.

    Please don't stop writing. It does me good to read your words.

After I read this message, I closed down my computer and went out
for a walk, thinking all the while of Cecilia and her low moods, so
different from Ruth's pharmacological crises. I am certain that in
her case, pills would have had very little effect. What is it that we
love in another? I believe it is style—the thing that lies beneath
what they call "chemistry": a more or less permanent way of being
in the world, an indefinable way of helping others to know themselves, to accept themselves. I said to myself that, in the end, our
minds are a constant battlefield. Cecilia Rangel, like anyone—and
more so at the age of twenty-seven—is an unstable element, an infinite series of attempts, of errors and successes. I already felt so
much affection for all her shifts and fluctuations. When I got back I
wrote to her:

Cecilia:
Nothing you can reveal to me about your "invisible" sides can
surprise or scare me. There will be things that seem more useful
or productive or benign than others. But it's not possible to love or
respect someone in parts, selectively. Here is a poem by Salvatore
Quasimodo, which I discovered years ago, one day when I felt
just the way you do:

Ognuno sta solo sul cuor della terra
trafitto da un raggio di sole:
ed è subito sera.

I hope that, one day soon, wherever we might be, you and I will feel
that the same ray of sunlight is piercing us.

On February 7, after bargaining for several days with her reticent side, Cecilia touched down at John F. Kennedy Airport, where I went to pick her up and take her home.

BARS ON A WINDOW

Looking back, that trip to New York seems far more extreme than it did while I was in the middle of it. To begin with, the weather was colder than I had ever experienced; not even in that first winter in Paris had I suffered so much. The sky, unlike the one Claudio had described in his messages, was more overcast than in the French capital. The snow had begun to melt a couple of days earlier, filling the streets with a filthy, frozen slush. It was impossible to go anywhere without special boots, which I did not own, and I did not much feel like it in any case. Each morning, Claudio leapt out of bed at six on the dot like an automaton mechanically repeating the same movements: the way he put his feet on the floor, the amount of time he spent in the bathroom. It was not deliberate, but, from under the covers, I could hardly fail to notice the sounds of the shower and the coffee machine, just as I used to listen to my neighbor's. I did not enjoy this one bit. To a certain extent it alarmed me for what it said about Claudio and his temperament. It revealed very different facets from those he exhibited with me. While his behavior towards me was caring, pleasant, protective, the sounds he made in the morning betrayed a rigid attitude and an intolerance of chaos. He particularly hated it when the telephone rang, its almost inaudible tone making him flinch. When he had finished showering, he went into the kitchen already dressed and perfectly spruced up, a serene expression on his face. Every morning he extracted items from the drawers and kitchen cupboards in the same order. First the bottom one, to take out the coffee scoop, then the one next to it with the napkins and, lastly, the cupboard where the cups were kept. Then he took out the coffee and the milk from the fridge and turned on the Krups machine to make his espresso, which was all he had for breakfast. He drank it standing up, by the kitchen window, through which nothing was visible apart from a minuscule balcony on the building opposite and an equally tiny patch of sky. When he had finished, he quickly washed up the cup and the spoon, and then put them back in their respective places, as with the milk and the ground coffee. Every single one of Claudio's glasses and all his cutlery and crockery were identical and had to be put away in a particular order which he explained to me on the first day, proud of his ingenuity, and requested that I not alter it. The name of this domestic policy was "stock rotation" and its aim was to give the same use to each object, without privileging or neglecting any of them. To achieve this it was essential always to put things away at the back of the drawer, or underneath the things that had not been used yet. Something similar occurred with his clothes. The shirts circulated on their hangers in the wardrobe, the trousers on their shelf, as did the underpants, in their identical white design. The only thing that escaped this rotation were his shoes, which he had far fewer of: a pair of black boots (the same ones he had worn in Paris on both trips), white tennis shoes that he also wore in the week, and a pair of Birkenstock sandals. One might expect that someone who arranges his house like this and behaves in such a way on a daily basis would possess a very rigid kind of character, but in his case this was not true. Claudio was still the loving Cuban Haydée had introduced me to several months back, the same one who with his letters had helped me to get over—to a large extent, at least—my obsession with Tom. Nonetheless, New York consumed him totally. The day I arrived, we had dinner at a sushi restaurant in his neighborhood. After that, we did not go out again. Claudio worked until 7:00 p.m. and then went to the gym, which he could not do without. While I waited for him, I sat dying of boredom. He would generally come back from work with some Chinese food and, once our plates were clean and back in their place, he would ask me to sit next to him on the sofa to listen to music in silence, or else we would watch a documentary about robots. He loved military androids and other machines that simulated animals, like a robotic pack mule or BigDog, which he found impressive and I, although I never dared tell him so, thought were pretty ridiculous. Given my confined state, such diversions were insufficient. One of us would almost always fall asleep before the video ended and the other would have to sort out moving us both towards the bedroom. In New York, our bedroom encounters were much less regular than on his last trip to Paris. We slept in each other's arms, but our love seemed to have migrated towards chaste, sibling-like territory.

Claudio's place was not exactly comfortable. Scarcely bigger than my own apartment, it was full of boxes of files and correspondence. Stacks of newspapers were piled up in the corners and by the bookshelves. The stone walls were stylish but not very cozy in a cold climate like New York's. Most of his books were philosophical treatises, utterly impenetrable to me. I could not even entertain myself by looking out at the street because, as strange as it might sound, there was nothing outside the window. I know that it was bad form to snoop around in his private papers as I had done once before in Tom's apartment, but at the same time, I did not have very many options and I should say in my defense that, before doing so, I held back for several days. On the Friday, however, I could not bear it any longer and, after a long, drawn-out lunch sitting on the sofa in the living room, I decided to attack the first box. They were nearly all letters from his mother. She described her pain at having let go of "the person I loved most in the world." These, if I remember correctly, were her exact words. After reading for hours, by now fully committed to my espionage, I began making an inventory of what Claudio kept there. I found a small envelope containing postcards Haydée had sent him from Paris and, with it, more postcards from different friends. I discovered manuscripts of poems that seemed to be by Claudio himself, and also a book of aphorisms, underlined and with comments by someone called Michel Miló. Eventually, in a box hidden behind many others, I hit upon what I had been looking for: letters from Susana—a dozen similar-looking envelopes, tied with a white ribbon, along with a silk handkerchief, a couple of official photographs showing her face in black-and-white, and a few other small personal belongings. I knew that I was on the threshold of a very intimate space and so I chose to think long and hard before defiling it. What is more, we were talking about a dead woman, and Tom had clearly warned me that the objects of the deceased must be respected if one does not want to suffer the consequences. Taking advantage of the rain having stopped, I put on my coat and, well aware that my shoes might get ruined, went out into the street. I wanted to surprise Claudio with a tasty home-cooked meal, so I went out to look for a supermarket where I could buy all the ingredients, from onions and garlic to the most basic condiments, since there was nothing in his kitchen cabinets but sealed packets of coffee, crackers, and cereal. In a shop on 86th and Broadway, I bought a bottle of wine and everything I needed to make moussaka and a salad.

I returned to the apartment and called Claudio's mobile to let him know my plans, but he never picked up. I tried to get hold of him at the office, but no luck there either. The receptionist told me he had left an hour earlier than usual. I told myself he had probably gone to the gym early so as to get home sooner. I went over to the shelves, put on a Ry Cooder record, and began to cook. As soon as I heard that liquor-soaked voice, I could not help thinking of Tom and asking myself where he might be hidden away this winter, a year after our symbiotic phase, during which I had learned to cook this dish I was now making for Claudio. As I chopped up the peppers, I opened the wine and drank a couple of glasses until I reached a subtle, functional level of drunkenness. The record came to an end and I decided to put on an album by David Byrne to go with my happy mood. The moussaka bubbled calmly away in the oven, giving me time to lay the table and create a romantic atmosphere with the light of a candle I found in a cupboard in the kitchen. Dinner was ready, but Claudio still had not shown up, and had not even been in touch. I rang his mobile phone again with no reply. No one answered at his office at all. Outside it had begun to snow. As the minutes passed, my hunger and misgivings spiraled out of control. I finished the bottle of wine and angrily devoured the salad, followed by the main dish. Before I went to sleep I decided to defy the laws of respect for the dead and go back into Susana's letters. With the exception of a few postcards, they were almost all from the same year, dated between March and December. The handwriting was tiny and shaky, the lines abnormally squashed together. Rather than correspondence designed to be read, it looked like evidence of an exhausting, highly confused inner monologue. Nonetheless, it was enough to read a couple of them to the end to understand that they were full of reproaches and accusations. She felt alone and, in a sort of tedious refrain, kept asking Claudio to tell her "the reasons he had abandoned her." I could not read all of them. There were too many pages and too much pain for what I was able to cope with right then. I put everything back in its place and returned to the sofa to resume my vigil, and eventually fell asleep.

I woke up shortly before dawn with a headache and the impression that I had carried on reading Susana's letters late into the night. I felt sorry for her, as well as an impossible urge to help the woman. I went into Claudio's bedroom, hoping he had come back home, but the bed was untouched. This time, however, the red light on the answerphone announced that a new message had arrived. It was from him. Despite my attempts, I could not work out what time he had left it. In the recording he informed me, in a strange voice, a kind of cautious whisper, that he was fine and that I should not worry. He would come back in the morning to explain things. Instead of pressing STOP I must have pressed the button that played all the old messages by mistake. The tape began to play and I heard a whole string of messages in English, full of threats and expletives that I did not fully understand but which left me quite astonished. It was a female voice, a smoker, and sounded like a woman a lot older than Claudio himself and who, every two or three insults, also called him "love" or "sweetheart."

One likes to think that the ties that bind us to others are fixed and eternal, especially affection. However, people change a great deal according to where they are and the circumstances they find themselves in. Since I met Claudio, I had been receiving on average two messages a day, sweet, supportive e-mails, occasionally tinged with some didactic or corrective urge I had not paid attention to. We had also spent four very intense days together in Paris, during which I felt I had got to know him intimately. Up until this moment all our encounters had taken place in the city where I lived. As a sports commentator would say, I always played at home and he away. This is why, with a little perspective, it is not that surprising that in New York I came up against someone so different from the Claudio I knew. I did not exactly notice the change right away, although, now that I think about it, if I had opened my eyes I would have been able to spot a few signs. As it was, I chose to trust him, to believe blindly in his love, in his honesty. Of the first I had no doubt, just as I had had none about Tom's feelings for me, but honesty is a virtue that grows scarcer by the minute.

After listening to these messages, it was impossible to get back to sleep. I went back to Susana's letters and found a few notes Claudio had written to her. The similarity to the e-mails he sent to me was embarrassing. I cleared the table, tidied up the kitchen according to his crackpot "stock rotation" system, and sat down on the sofa to wait for him to come back. All kinds of explanations ran through my mind. When I grew tired of speculating, I decided to phone Haydée. It was ten in the morning in Paris and I was not worried about waking her up. She did not have an answer either, but hearing her voice made me feel at home. When I told her what had happened and how my last week had been, her verdict was categorical:

"I do love Claudio, but he's a real bastard. Don't stay there. Come home right away."

And this, in short, was what I did.

INSOMNIA

The radar some women have for threats—imminent or not—from their fellow females aligns them with snakes and other venomous animals. I still have no idea how Ruth found out about Cecilia's arrival in New York, because I had told no one, not even Mario, my only friend in this city. Perhaps she consulted an uncommonly skilled fortune-teller or perhaps—and this would be consistent with the practical side she sometimes displays—she hired a private detective to spy on me. The thing is, ever since Cecilia touched down in the city, I began receiving one telephone call after another from Ruth. At first they were seemingly innocent, and then, later, aggressive. I refrained from replying. Then the text messages began. Every fifteen minutes she would write, asking if I was still at the office, if I was at the gym or "dealing with someone important." The obvious sarcasm told me she knew what was going on. Even so, I managed to stay calm enough to collect Cecilia without giving anything away. We got into a taxi that took us home from the airport and, to compliment her, I asked the driver to put on the Alicia de Larrocha CD I had given her the first time I had gone to her house. That evening, after we had taken her suitcase back to my apartment, I invited her to dinner at one of my favorite Japanese restaurants, on Columbus Avenue and 77th Street. Far greater than my astonishment at having Cecilia in my city, like I had dreamed of for so many months, was the spiraling terror that something, or rather *someone*, would manage to separate us. I have told myself over and over again that the fault lay entirely with me. If instead of endlessly avoiding breaking up with Ruth I had spoken to her honestly and put the distance we needed between us, nothing would have been able to get in the way of the pure, intimate space both Cecilia and I deserved. In spite of her tiredness from the journey, and the time difference—in Paris it must have been three o'clock in the morning—Cecilia noticed that my face looked tense. She took my hand and, looking into my eyes, asked me if I was happy she had come. Her question moved me deeply.

With great difficulty, we managed to survive Ruth's venom. In spite of the cold and the melting snow, we returned home with no mishaps other than stumbling a few times on the wet streets. That night, Cecilia fell asleep in my arms before I could take off her clothes. Instead of being disappointed, I enjoyed just being there with her in silence, listening to her breathing. Her loose, dark hair was spread out over my chest. I took off her pants, pulled the covers over her, and got in next to her. However, as soon as I had switched off the light, I heard the answering machine come on. I got out of bed and went over to the telephone to see who it was. My suspicions were confirmed: it was Ruth, in a nervous state similar to the pharmacological imbalance she had slipped into before our trip to Paris. In between sobs, she hurled ridiculous accusations at me, threats that went from showing up at my office and making a scene to killing herself that very night. I looked at the screen. Twenty-nine messages had been left, starting at 6:45 that evening, and they were almost certainly all from her. Ever since I had met her, being with Cecilia had let me attain an unprecedented state of happiness, but that night my elation was overshadowed by dread at the old thing's threats.

I could not go back to bed without deciding on my defensive strategy, and so I sat down on the couch and started going over it in my mind. Meanwhile, the telephone rang twice more. It took all the self-restraint I had not to answer. In the end, I opted to disconnect the machine.

I awoke unexpectedly the next morning in the same position on the sofa. When I went back to the bedroom Cecilia was awake, reading a novel whose title I do not recall. I apologized for not having slept with her.

"Don't worry," she said. "We've got lots of time. There's fresh coffee in the kitchen. Shall I get you a cup?"

I imagined her a few minutes earlier, walking hungrily around the apartment in search of something to eat but not daring to wake me. There was very little in the cupboards. Even so, she had managed to get breakfast ready. It was the first time that someone had been in my territory. No one, other than me, had ever eaten in my house. It was quite likely that she had dropped crumbs all over the floor and left the sink full of dirty dishes, but none of that mattered. If anyone deserved to be inside the fortress, it was her.

Instead of discouraging Ruth, all my silence did was heighten her anxiety. At around midday, as I was preparing to leave my desk and go down to the cafeteria for lunch, my cell phone rang again, insistently. I decided to confront her once and for all.

"Now you listen to me," I said, in the coldest tone of voice I could muster. "I don't know what pill you've taken, but you're out of your mind. How dare you leave those insulting messages on my answering machine? What right do you think you have? I don't recognize you any more."

"Who are you with?" she replied, shamelessly. "Where did that girl living in your house come from?"

It was obvious someone was giving her information.

Ruth knew full well that I never invited anyone into my lair, and so it was not too hard to convince her that it was a relative of mine, a cousin who had come from Miami to tour colleges.

"She's trying to get into CUNY and she came over for an interview," I lied. "Please don't call my house in the middle of the night again."

"If you've got nothing to hide," she said, "then why don't you answer the telephone?"

"I won't tolerate you spying on me or insulting me like this. Just tell me what I can do for you."

She was, she said, in a café at Penn Station, a few blocks from my work. She begged me to have lunch with her. She wanted to see me "to apologize." It was the last thing I felt like at that moment, but I agreed just to calm her down. At first I acted haughty and resentful, but in truth I was troubled by remorse and outright terror at driving her mad again. Gradually, as I saw that she was coming to her senses, I too relaxed. When we parted she made me promise I would introduce her to my cousin on Friday night. It was a mistake, no doubt about it, but at least she stopped bothering me for the rest of the week. The next few evenings, after I left the gym I would make a quick stop at a Korean restaurant near my work and come home with hot food. After we had eaten, Cecilia and I would sit on the couch to listen to my favorite CDs. Cecilia does not listen to music; she surrenders herself to it. She melts into the notes in such a moving way. For the first time in my forty-two years of life, I was in the company of a being endowed with sufficient sensitivity to enjoy music as much as I do.

The week went by without any other complications. On Friday I decided to come home early, straight after work and without going to the gym, to disconnect my cell phone and the landline and shut myself up all weekend with the woman of my dreams. While Cecilia and I were together everything else could come to a standstill. However, Ruth's cunning surpassed all my expectations. Just as I was about to leave the office, she appeared in the lobby and took me by the arm.

"I hope you don't mind me coming to find you?" she asked, in such a cheerful, enthusiastic voice that resisting was futile. "I thought we could go to that French restaurant you really like, get something to take home, and tell your cousin to meet us back at my place."

All I could do was follow her. As we made our way to the restaurant, I pretended to call my cousin to tell her of the plan and told her that I could not get through. As I did so, I saw several calls from Cecilia appear on the screen, which showed how desperate she must have been. I had my cell phone on silent so that Ruth could not hear it. She did not leave me alone for long enough in her Tribeca loft, either, to let Cecilia know why I was taking so long. I scarcely ate a thing at dinner. Not even the *confit de canard* could awaken my appetite that night. My stomach felt as if it were obstructed by a recent scar. Ruth, meanwhile, smiled and blathered away like never before. I waited until she had finished dessert and, as soon as she had, got up from the table to get my coat.

"You're leaving so soon?" she asked.

"I'm worried about my cousin. Maybe she lost her key and can't get into the building."

"But she has your number, doesn't she? She'd call you if there was any problem." Her voice had grown shrill again.

"She's not answering. I dialed her number several times and it just goes straight to voicemail. She might have left it in the apartment."

"Well, let's call the police, then." Her tone was more desperate than sarcastic.

"I'd rather go back, if you don't mind. I'll call whoever's necessary if I don't find her at home."

"Of course I mind!" Ruth screamed at me, holding the Opinel knife she had been cutting slices of cheese with and putting it to her throat. "I'll kill myself if you go back to that slut!"

We struggled for a few seconds, during which time I tried to take the knife away from her. I realized that her arm was shaking. I pulled it roughly away from her neck and as I did so, the steel blade sliced into her collarbone. Her neck began to run with blood. It was a superficial wound, as I realized when I dabbed it with cotton pads soaked in alcohol, but at first neither of us could tell how deep it was. As I cleaned the blood off her, the old thing began to cry. That night, more than ever before, her sobs were like those of a little girl who has been unfairly treated. I tried to calm her down by sitting her on my knees and this was how I ended up screwing her. It was, without a doubt, one of the best fucks of our time together and was repeated several times until late into the night when, as ever, I was overcome with nausea. In the bathroom, between retches, I managed at last to ring Cecilia and leave a guilt-ridden message on the answering machine at home.

I got back to my apartment at around nine. As soon as I walked through the door, I realized Cecilia had gone for good: her suitcase was not there, and the CDs and books I had given her each evening when I got back from work were stacked in a little pile on the couch, where only two nights ago we had listened to Philip Glass's soundtrack to *The Hours*.

II

REUNION

The abrupt end to my romance with Claudio upset me far less than Tom leaving had done. I returned to Paris happy to be there, ready to celebrate Haydée's birthday with her and her friends. Over the following weeks, Claudio sent dozens of messages I never read, not even out of curiosity. I was convinced I had escaped just in time from a disastrous relationship and felt satisfied at that. As soon as term began again, I went back to the seminars at the institute and my job as a language assistant at the Lycée Condorcet. My life went by in a routine fashion, with no big surprises. This sensation of calm and relief, however, rather unusual since my first arrival in France, did not last long. One morning, as I was getting ready to leave the house to do my weekly shop for tinned food, I heard the unmistakable sound of Tom's footsteps on the stairs. I peeped through the spyhole and saw him looking more tired than ever, dragging the same suitcase I had seen him leave with.

Before long we had re-established a daily routine similar to the one we had had before he left. We ate dinner together every night, and on the weekends we sat in front of his fire, talking until dawn. My first impression had been right: his health had suffered a setback during his time away and this, more than my happiness at his presence, helped me to lay aside any resentment. We started again our walks around the neighborhood and the cemetery, this time without any objections from me. He told me that in Sicily he would take his daily walk in the Cimitero degli Angeli di Caltanissetta, of which he had sent me a picture; a more modern cemetery than ours, with grandiose, ochre-colored monuments. He liked it so much that he had acquired a niche, despite already having one in Père-Lachaise. As he put it, he had been unable to resist when he had found out the price.

"When I die, you'll have to take some of my remains there," he quipped, although my blood ran cold when I heard this.

Every evening after I left the school, I would meet Tom at République and we would walk back to our building together. Sometimes, while he cashed up, I went to look at the table of new titles he was so scornful of. In his opinion, books had to pass a strict test of maturation, which meant they could not be read until at least ten years after their author had moved to the neighborhood opposite us. Only then was it possible to know if they had survived the test of time or not.

He liked walking, whatever the weather, but it was obvious that it wore him out. This is why I was so insistent on our taking the métro or the bus that went up Parmentier and dropped us at the roundabout. Then there were the stairs in our building. Walking up the four flights of stairs was enough to leave him breathless. It was not always easy for me to keep my distance, or to avoid asking questions about his health. Although he was obsessed with the idea of his own death, he spoke very little of his illness. It was as if he was ashamed of all the things he could not do, as if he found it hard to find the balance between excessive effort and prudence. If Tom hated anything in this world it was for people to consider him disabled in some way. One evening when I got to the bookshop,

I found him sitting on the floor in the stockroom. His face was a greenish-gray color. I was very worried, and suggested he ask for some sick leave so he could recover.

"You have no idea what you're talking about," he said. "If I step out of the line I won't be able to get back in again."

I went back to the shop and waited, looking at the shelves until he came out again pretending that nothing had happened. I am sure that someone outside our relationship, someone like Haydée or Rajeev, would find it hard to understand why I did not try to convince him to step out of "the line," to use his expression; why I did not go with him to the Institut Pasteur, where he had his weekly checkup; why I did not care for him in some other way; but I knew that if he appreciated anything I did, it was the way I did not treat him as an invalid.

The end of winter came sooner than we had expected. By April I had already read a third of the books on Tom's shelves. I began to write up my thesis on Latin American authors buried in Paris, spending hours in the library reading biographies and books on Cortázar, Ribeyro, Vallejo, and Asturias. I stopped going to the university café and instead, after teaching, went to the canteen at the high school where I taught. Tom and I ate together once a week, the day he saw his doctor. If it was a sunny day, we would go for a walk afterwards along boulevard Raspail or in the Jardin du Luxembourg. When he came out after the consultation he looked different, kind of shocked. He said that the doctors drained his energy. It did him good to walk among the trees in the park, watching the people strolling about with no worries. How different these walks were from the ones in Père-Lachaise! In the Jardin du Luxembourg our mood was far lighter. We enjoyed spotting certain familiar characters: tramps, old ladies with their lap dogs.

"Unbelievable," he would say, mockingly. "You take me out for a walk among the bushes and flowers in this bourgeois park as if I were a poodle, even though you know I'm a graveyard jackal." But this only happened on Thursdays. The rest of the week Tom stayed in our neighborhood. I remember that June as a period of feeling particularly happy, not unlike how I had felt a year earlier, when I had received his only postcard. I had the sense of having drawn back a dark veil that, unbeknownst to me, had for years obscured my view of the world. I was moved by the resplendent trees, as well as the sky, kinder and more luminous than ever. It was not simply the euphoria of being in love. Rather, it was a sort of reunion with myself and with what surrounded me. The mellow feeling of being at home and—behind this modest happiness—a constant sense of gratitude.

Then summer came, and the holidays, which on this occasion we did spend together in a village in Brittany, three hours from Paris, in a cozy little hotel rather like a five-star B&B. The doctors had advised him not to travel too much, but the clean sea air did him good. Despite his body's endless fatigue, Tom's mind was alert and he was in a jokey mood. We spoke a great deal about the past and how it had influenced our characters. I felt trusting enough to confess I had gone into his papers in his apartment. Tom was not surprised at my meddling, but when I mentioned Michela his expression grew serious.

"Did you go to Sicily to look for her?" I said, forcing myself to use a conspiratorial tone, prepared to settle all my doubts.

"In a way," he said. "It was there that I met her."

I understood then why he had bought a niche in the cemetery there. I told myself, not without bitterness, that Michela had enjoyed the best years of this wonderful man. He would have been able to travel with her and very likely to enjoy being a fully erotic person. I felt so jealous I was dizzy.

I said to myself that pain sends people mad and that perhaps it had been due to his breakup with her that he had become ill like this. I decided not to ask any more questions. What little I knew was enough to obsess me. Few things are as difficult as shaking off jealousy. Although I was not able to accept the presence of the dead, I can say that Michela's memory, if not her ghost, accompanied us for the whole trip.

When we got back to Paris, we paid dearly with Tom's health for our jaunt, plus interest. In September, he could no longer walk to the bookshop from home, and climbing the stairs took him twice as long. I decided not to renew my post at the Lycée Condorcet. Whenever Tom could manage without my help, I spent my time doing research for the thesis. One Thursday at around 2:00 p.m., as I was coming out of the François-Mitterrand Library laden with books, Tom called to tell me that he was in hospital. That morning he had gone to his appointment at the Institut Pasteur and the doctor had forbidden him to go back home. He had not taken a change of clothes and asked me to pack a suitcase for him. When I asked if he needed anything else, he said, I could go and buy him a new pair of pajamas.

ROBOTS

When Cecilia left, I fell into a state of emotional suspension. I was dazed, and it took me more than three days to work out how to react to what had happened. I am certain that this period of stupefaction worked against me. If I had tried to locate her immediately, the very same Saturday she left my apartment; if I had called Haydée and begged her to help me find her; if I had gone to the airport to prevent her from boarding the plane that would take her back to France, as doubtful as that plan was to succeed, things might have played out differently. She would surely have forgiven me. Instead, I concentrated on my work at the publishing house and on perfecting my routines of order and cleanliness in the apartment. I spoke to my trainer at the gym and asked him to up my training so that, when I got home in the evening, I could flop down on my bed without succumbing to the temptation for nostalgia or any other kind of sentimental nonsense. I read Seneca and Michel de Montaigne, and listened over and over to *The Goldberg Variations* played by Glenn Gould, whose curative powers have never ceased to amaze me. When the weather permitted, I went out to walk for hours around Central Park. As generally occurred now after each of our encounters, Ruth did not appear again for a couple of weeks. She thus avoided my fury raining down on her. I did not call her either, of course.

I did, however, write Cecilia countless messages. I sent her CDs and ordered flowers to be sent to her little apartment in Ménilmontant via the internet. I never got any reply. I bore her silence not as a humiliation, but as a well-deserved punishment. Eventually, in a fit of angst and humility, I called Haydée, prepared to be scolded. True to her character, but above all to our pact of sincerity, Haydée was sharp with me.

"You behaved really badly and you know it," she said. "It's best you don't try and find her. She's in love with someone else."

I absorbed her reply in silence and, as I helplessly assisted in my own collapse, allowed her to tell me in great detail about the vacation Cecilia and her boyfriend had taken recently to Brittany.

In March, I had a call from Ruth to tell me that the job at the UN had gone to another of the candidates. I carried on working hard at the publishing house and increased the number of pages I edited daily. I also stopped going down to the cafeteria at lunchtime. I was not hungry and saying hello to people in the buffet line or anyone who decided to sit down at my table felt like torture. I got into the habit of skipping this meal and, unsurprisingly, was too tired to go to the gym in the evenings. Lacking a reason to live does not justify a man letting himself go. I needed to carry on working, carry on with my life plan, carry on making and saving money for my retirement; needed to support my mother until she did not need me anymore. And, once she had died, I had to become a neat, respectable old man and pay for my retirement home with my savings. In those months I fell prey to an excessive number of flus and other such viruses. The doctor prescribed me antibiotics on three separate occasions. The last time I had no choice but to ask for a short period of leave from work, since I could not even sit up at my desk anymore. As I was not managing to get there, I canceled my membership to the gym, although the worst thing was not this but the great disdain I started to feel toward myself. What was I becoming? I, who had always had my life and my emotions under control, had now turned into a poor specimen of a human like those wretches the street teems with, sniveling on the escalators in the subway.

No matter how many eminent minds have ruminated on the topic, I have never been able to consider depression a genuine illness. It seems, if anything, to be a symptom or rather a self-indulgent attitude that a ridiculous number of people seek help for and, naturally, a very profitable business for the pharmaceutical industry. This is why, ever since I can remember, I have dismissed anyone who claims to be depressed as if it were a philosophical posture. Taking advantage of my fragility, the most horrendous memories I have began to pop up with alarming frequency. I relived my grandfather's arrest, and the day a teacher at my school smacked me on the head in front of my classmates. I relived the morning I found my mother sobbing, out on the patio, unable to explain to me the reason for her distress. I relived Susana's funeral, the expression on her mother's face, racked with pain. Susana. As if my malaise had invoked her spirit, I would often feel her presence in the apartment, her eyes on the verge of crying, looking at me reproachfully. To avoid thinking of her—or of anything—I would spend hours in front of my laptop, searching for soothing images. I cannot explain why, but spaceships landing and planes piloted remotely bring me an indescribable sense of peace. Nevertheless, as soon as I closed the laptop, the memories began pursuing me once more.

Convinced I had lost my mind, I called Mario and asked him to have dinner with me that same evening.

"My God!" he cried as soon as he saw me. "You're as thin as a rail! Please don't tell me you're ill."

We sat down and I let him order for both of us. Many months had gone by since we had last seen each other and I had to go back to when I first met Cecilia to give him the whole story. Mario listened to me without saying a word. In his eyes, I recognized genuine concern and an urgent need to rescue me from that state.

"I don't know, brother. I think this time I really have flipped out," I said, once I had finished my tale.

"Relax, you're not crazy," Mario said, with the kindest tone of voice I have ever heard him use. "No more than usual, in any case. You're just a man like any other, and men go through these sorts of phases. You know, a midlife crisis, all that shit. What you've got is a damn big dose of depression."

I felt my eyes popping out of my head.

"But I don't want to be a man, don't you see? I want to be a robot!" I shouted, turning all the other diners' heads.

Mario sat back in his chair. The terrified look on his face pushed me totally over the edge. I almost grabbed him by his shirt collar.

"I want to be a machine! I want to be a robot! I want to be an infallible machine!"

Right away, the manager of the restaurant came over to our table and asked us to leave. We did so, convinced it was the most prudent response. We walked in silence to the entrance to the subway. As we said goodbye, Mario suggested, almost fearfully, that I make an appointment to see a psychiatrist.

"If you decide to go, let me know. I know one of the very best."

Mario's advice did make a certain degree of sense. If I did not have the necessary presence of mind to return to my habitual state (and

God knows how I hated myself for this), the best thing to do was to see a specialist. However, I preferred that no one find out about my weakness. Calling Mario or anyone to ask for the number of a shrink was beneath my dignity. I had to find another way. When I got home, I decided to send a text message to Ruth's cell phone and ask for her doctor's number. "Get back to me soon," I wrote, "a colleague at work needs it urgently." The reply appeared right away, along with an invitation to have dinner, which I ignored. Dr. Menahovsky's appointment book was full. After persisting for a long time with his secretary, I managed to get an appointment in two weeks' time.

AUTUMN

It was early October. The leaves on the trees had already acquired a blazing red hue. To get to the hospital, I had to cross Paris on practically all the modes of public transport that exist in the city. I took the métro from Père-Lachaise to Châtelet, and then got the RER commuter train that took me to the suburb of Antony. When I got there, I got on a bus, which went over the motorway to the commune of Petit Clamart, where the clinic was located. It was a small village, and each place the bus stopped at corresponded to a stage in the life of its inhabitants. The first one, for instance, was the primary school. A few streets further on were the college and the gym, then the town hall and, next door to this, the church. A few streets beyond this, the bus went past the cemetery, stopping eventually by the hospital where Tom had been admitted. Unlike the center of Paris, these suburban streets were lined with trees and low bushes. The journey would have been quite pleasant if it had not been for the last two stops. By that point I was very used to Père-Lachaise, whose graves had lost any disturbing association for me. The cemetery in Clamart, on the other hand, was unknown and, precisely for this reason, ominous. It was characterized by an aseptic uniformity—the gravestones as well as the flowerbeds with their bright little flowers—and a total absence of drama. It was, in short, a petit bourgeois Catholic cemetery in a village where the last thing people wanted to do was to draw attention to themselves. Several times as I went past, I wondered what the difference was between being buried in a common grave and in a place like this. It is likely (I never had the time or the inclination to verify it) that among its dead there were no celebrated or distinguished people, no one except for the deceased of Petit Clamart, as invisible and anonymous as its living. People with a low profile, who had settled there a few generations ago, businessmen and -women who kept the local economy going, schoolteachers, and local officials. Once the bus had crossed the road that formed the edge of the village, it stopped outside the clinic and then continued its route to the terminal.

After having gone for years without talking—or hardly—about his health, in those weeks Tom's clinical history became the main subject of our conversations and my thoughts. In order to calm me down, he told me that it was a passing phase, a kind of limbo in our daily lives, and that soon we would be sitting in front of the fire again, joking about his time at the clinic. I talked a lot to him about his apartment, our building, and the neighborhood. I passed on greetings from the newspaper seller and the baker, even if I had not seen them for days. I brought him flowers and chocolate, books and magazines he was in no condition to read, because the substance they were injecting him with meant he could not concentrate.

Antoine-Béclère Hospital, where he'd been admitted practically against his will, specialized in respiratory diseases. The doctor who saw him every week at the Institut Pasteur was also the head of the cardiology department and sent his patients there. Tom's illness was abbreviated to PAH (pulmonary arterial hypertension). It consisted of an abnormal inflammation of the right valve of the heart, which had stopped pumping the necessary quantity of blood to the lungs. Nobody had managed to discover the real causes behind it and, in his case, after making sure that no other members of his family had suffered from it, they opted to accord it an idiopathic origin. As he told me, it was not the first time he had ended up in this place. He had been admitted to the same sanatorium once before, while they examined his reaction to different substances. This time they were testing his response to a relatively new medicine, whose English name, Flolan, brought to mind (at least for us) an altered state of consciousness ("'Relax and float downstream,' as in the Beatles song," Tom had said, trying to lighten the mood). It was a very strong vasodilator that not only irritated his veins but also made him feel tired, sick, and permanently dizzy. According to Dr. Tazartès, Tom's quality of life would improve a great deal if he managed to adapt to his new medicine. Thanks to Flolan, he would feel less tired, would be able to walk up and down stairs and to get about much more easily, to cope with changes in altitude and, equally as important, to get his sex life back. In exchange, he would have to wear at all times a square cartridge the size of a double-C battery on his left arm and extremely carefully recharge it twice a day. A specialist nurse was going to come and demonstrate the procedure. The fact that this apparatus would be installed in his body felt to both of us like a disaster disguised as good news. Neither of us had imagined having to live with this kind of intruder. Nor did they ask us if we agreed to it. It was the only possibility they offered, since, for them, the previous medicine had stopped having an effect. At some point it was decided that I would also attend the nurse's training session so I could help him if he ever lost consciousness. They outlined several other equally terrifying scenarios, which we did not enjoy thinking about but were perfectly possible, and which it was better to start getting used to. Sometimes, the only way to bear the present is to invent promising futures, to dream of all one might do when the unacceptable is over. Tom and I decided to take a trip to Mexico as soon as he got out of that place. Oaxaca would be our reward for this difficult phase of adaptation to the new treatment. We imagined ourselves walking down the streets and little plazas of my native city, with its timber roofs, high walls, and wrought-iron balconies. We looked up photographs of hotels on the internet, deciding where we would stay. The truth is that, for the moment, the trip to Mexico did not feel all that close at all. Tom continued to be in pain most of the time, whether due to the effects of the medicine, the catheter needle that burned his skin when it dripped, or the frustration at being shut up indoors. It was obvious that he was suffering from being held captive and that he missed his independence. He could not get out of bed except to go to the toilet. His left arm was punctured by a tube that dripped an amber fluid, and the stand for the ferocious liquid did not have any wheels to move it about.

I spent my mornings and afternoons in Tom's room. At around one, I ate lunch with him from the tray the nurse placed on his bed. We looked like a Japanese couple with our legs crossed, sharing the same *tatami* mat. I nearly always bought my food in the visitors' café on the ground floor, next to the gift shop and the florist and where, on more than one occasion, I bought him a sunflower or a bird of paradise flower to cheer up his room. There was no single time when he did not moan about the taste of his food or the smell of mine. Although he was much thinner than usual, he was still attractive. You could see it in the way the nurses looked at him and treated him. Instead of hospital clothing, he wore the red-and-blue-striped pajamas I had bought him, and they allowed him this freedom. After lunch, Tom would lower the head of his bed and ask to be left to sleep. Then I would take my computer out of my bag and write up my thesis on the bedside table by the window until he woke up again. If he felt like talking, I closed the laptop. He would ask me to tell him about my childhood in Oaxaca or show him photographs of the few trips I had gone on. As well as records, films were our main source of entertainment. We preferred lighthearted feature films with heartening story lines, comedies that occasionally bordered on the daft, such as *When Harry Met Sally*, or *Four Weddings and a Funeral*. Visiting hours finished at 7:00 p.m., but they never said anything to me about staying until late, although I did so every day. At around nine, when the sky and the grounds around the hospital grew pitch black as only the countryside knows, Tom would suggest I go back home. I always found the moment of leaving stressful. At first, the very idea of being separated from him, of leaving him alone in that room with its stink of detergent, was enough to lower my spirits. By that time, there were hardly any other outsiders in the building. It was an odd moment, when you could sense a different atmosphere, similar to what happens in theaters behind the scenes. The night nurses looked more relaxed, but above all it was in the patients that the changes could be seen. In the corridors, or hidden behind the emergency room doors, a drip connected to one hand, they would gather together in small groups to share a cigarette, something totally prohibited within the hospital. Rather than a transgressive or shameful experience, what was reflected in their faces was a feeling of relief. Smoking, for them, was comparable to a visit from an old friend, an inseparable companion who in the majority of cases had brought them here and from whom they could not be parted. As they filled their lungs with smoke, they chatted and laughed in low voices. Sometimes they would also succumb to violent, collective coughing attacks. In one of his best essays, entitled "For Smokers Only," the writer Julio Ramón Ribeyro, afflicted with lung cancer and to whom I had devoted a chapter of my thesis, tells how, even in the final moments of his disease, he fails to stop seeking refuge in cigarettes. Smoking is a consolation, despite the devastating consequences of tobacco use.

The worst thing was going back home again. As soon as it got dark, Petit Clamart ceased to be a merely unpleasant place and became terrifying. The bus stop was on the other side of the *périphérique* and the only way to get to it was via an underpass covered in graffiti and stinking of urine, which would have served perfectly as a location for any police drama. The echo of my footsteps bounced around the tiled walls, highlighting the place's isolation, but that was far preferable to sensing a presence at my back. Once I got there, I had to wait for several minutes before I saw a bus coming and when one did finally appear, it was not always the right one. Sometimes, instead of the direct bus, the first to come would be one that took me to an even more remote suburb of Paris, from where it was possible to get on the RER. I then had to decide between the uncertainty of waiting and the highly impractical yet comforting detour, and I almost always opted for this alternative. Throughout my life, I have always tried to carry a book in my bag, preferably a novel, to kill the time I spend on public transport, but in that period I found it impossible to read. My eyes needed to drift to the window, filling themselves with moving images, lights, cars, the faces of people, tired but healthy, who were sitting in the seats next to me. In those months, I still had enough enthusiasm to respond to the occasional smile of a Muslim mother on her way home, her veil slightly lopsided after a long day at work.

*

One morning at around half past ten, shortly after I had arrived at the hospital, the wretched specialist nurse appeared in Tom's room to show us how to handle the cartridge they were going to attach to his left arm. When I recall this woman I feel almost as confused as I did that day. She was wearing the white uniform of the hospital and yet had somehow managed to make even that outfit look alluring. The trousers, unusually close fitting, perfectly outlined the shape of her thighs and hips. Instead of the regulation thick-soled shoes, she had on a pair of pointy high heels. Her red hair was gathered into a high bun, almost exactly on the top of her head, and she wore glasses in the shape of a cat-like eye mask. The way she had of sitting on the edge of the chair, her legs apart, and, above all, her way of holding the syringe in her right hand, in the casual yet greedy manner of a junkie, reminded me of drawings by Milo Manara, the Italian erotic cartoonist whose books Haydée had stockpiled in her apartment. The way Tom watched her was worthy of a comic book too. He seemed to have quite forgotten the little matter of the cartridge and the discomfort that the surgery to fit it would entail. His fascination with the nurse made me feel a mixture of jealousy and joy at realizing that, in some secret place, he still had such urges. When the woman had finished her task I was incapable of repeating the procedure she had shown us, and in fact Tom was, too, because the following day he asked if they could schedule another lesson so we could take in the information. Two days later, the nurse returned, and we both attempted to concentrate more on the technical part and not so much on the choreography. We learned how to load the blasted thing, but above all we learned about the risks of any mistake in preparing the substance just when it came to filling the receptacle itself: the smallest bubble of air could cause thrombosis or an embolism. Imagining myself filling this instrument, overcome with nerves after one of Tom's fainting attacks, the urgency to inject him, the fear of not doing it properly, was enough to make me feel dizzy. I felt like refusing to learn, or to take on such a responsibility. But what, realistically, was the alternative? If I did not do it, who else would? Even so, I felt optimistic enough to ask the nurse, outside the room, how we could refill the cartridge on a plane, and if the product's effect or the dosage might change because of the altitude or a different atmospheric pressure. I told her we had a lot of trips planned, and that we were even thinking about spending some time in Mexico. The nurse's reply was unambiguous and not without wisdom:

"It's best you concentrate on the present for now. It's important to familiarize yourselves with the substance before you start thinking about traveling anywhere, whether it's on a plane, in a taxi, or on the métro."

MEMORY

A downpour was falling over New York once again. I was ill and I suppose it was my fever that brought me to a state of consciousness similar to hypnosis. I believed I was back in Havana and was still a teenager. The humidity was unbearable. I had positioned myself at the entrance to the yard more than an hour ago, waiting for Regla, my neighbor Facundo's cousin, to arrive. When she appeared, she had on a pair of tiny shorts that revealed a large portion of that taut, bountiful ass of hers, as well as her thighs in their entirety. Her sleeveless top showed part of her waist, too. There were still several hours to go until the bathtime ritual, but the one-peso coin was already in my pocket, permanently in contact with my erection. Facundo came over and put his hand on my shoulder. Half conspiratorial, half mocking, he invited me to come over to his house "to watch the show from the front row." I looked down at his arm resting on mine and, strange as it seems, realized that the texture and color of his skin were identical to those of the young girl. I readily accepted his invitation. From the kitchen we could hear the music on the radio and the smell of freshly cooked black beans. We sat in the living room of his house eating junk for a long time, as his cousin went back and forth with her mop and rag, performing the most disturbing dance. The protuberance in my pants was more than obvious and Facundo was staring fixedly at it. After a while, he suggested we go into the bedroom where he slept with his brothers, totally deserted at this time of the morning. Regla had gone out into the yard, and so I quickly stood up without her seeing me and followed my neighbor to his room. As soon as we were inside he threw himself down onto one of the bunk beds, took off his shirt, and stretched his arms out behind his head, like a bear.

"Make yourself comfortable," he said. "You can take off your clothes if you like."

Overwhelmed by the heat, and above all by my member on the verge of exploding, I followed his advice. I stared in astonishment at my penis, which looked as if it was trying to escape out of the side of my underwear. I noticed it was dripping a clear liquid. Facundo had come over to take a look, too.

"I can help you, if you let me," he said, looking me in the eyes. Right away, he took my cock between his two enormous hands, as black as his cousin's cunt must have been. He kneaded it for a couple of seconds and I did not put up a fight, but then, almost immediately and without asking my permission, wrapped his mouth around it and left me to ejaculate between his huge lips, even pinker than his fingertips were. In my Manhattan apartment, I could sense once again, as if I had gone back to that very same day, the heat and the humidity of that room in El Cerro, Facundo's hoarse voice asking me to turn around so that he could relieve himself next. And I remembered the sheets brushing against me and the docile way I allowed him to penetrate me with his member while mine grew stiff once more, ready to start all over again and to put it in his ass, similar in shape and proportions to Regla's coveted backside. We spent I do not know how long like this, until the excitement waned and I began to feel the pangs of remorse. That afternoon, when the girl went into the bathroom to bathe as she always did, neither I nor Facundo hid to spy on her. He went out through the yard, happy as Larry, to play football in the park, and I shut myself up at home, bewildered and scared to death by my transgression. I imagined myself before a judge, as the local president of the Committee for the Defense of the Revolution shouted accusingly at me: "Faggot! You fucking faggot!" For years I managed to keep this memory hidden, but from time to time it would resurface to torture me, almost always with disastrous consequences. For instance, I foolishly revealed it ten years later to Susana who, after our trip to Varadero, had grown fond of this position which I, too, enjoyed like no other. I told her because I was very drunk that night and had no control over the words coming out of my mouth; I told her because, even though I had never again had an experience like that in my life, the guilt had not stopped plaguing me for years and I needed to get free myself of it, I told her because I needed someone to share this weight with me and play down its importance, I told her because I trusted her blindly and was sure that her acceptance of me was unconditional. But I was wrong. From that point on, Susana began to question my sexual preferences, to insinuate that I secretly desired one or another of my male friends and I do not know how many other ridiculous things until, tormented by her suspicions, I decided to distance myself from her. It was after the episode with Facundo that I stopped seeing the Martínez family so often, and instead spent my time despising them in secret. A few months later I made friends with Mario and sought refuge in as many of the white, submissive daddy's girls as he could introduce me to at his parties. I tried to forget about my first experience, learning by heart the mechanisms of female pleasure, but I did not achieve this in any lasting way until I met Susana. Never again did I focus my attention or desire on a black girl. After Facundo's, the darkest I caressed was Cecilia's Mexican skin.

"PINK MOON"

There are few places where you get to know people as well as in hospitals. Visiting Tom every day allowed me to become very familiar with his less entrancing aspects. It is true that his medication had a high dose of adrenaline and this increased his irritability and bad moods, but knowing the reasons did not stop it from bothering me. When you exist in a confined space, the smallest things can take on exaggerated significance. The way food tastes, the way objects are arranged on the bedside table, the position of the blinds, any change in routine—it was all disproportionately apparent. Even I had become a factor that influenced his state of mind. Whenever I spoke, I felt as if I was walking across a minefield, and the last thing I wanted was to awaken the irritability that was waiting for the slightest reason or pretext to emerge.

A few weeks after he had gone into hospital, Tom's family sent reinforcements. I will never know if he had asked for help or if he had just accepted their offer. One Monday morning, I met his cousin Valeria, a slim, tough-looking woman in her forties who had grown up in Switzerland. She was staying somewhere very close to the sanatorium, in the house of some other relatives. This is why she always arrived an hour and a half before I did, in time to hear the doctor's report.

Tom's best moments, the periods when he was at his most lucid and energetic, were the mornings. All his sense of humor, his jolly character, and his flashes of genius were active before midday. In the afternoon, however, he worsened considerably and spent many hours sleeping. This was my chance to get some work done on my thesis, and there was not a single day when I did not attempt this. But, to tell you the truth, I found it very hard to concentrate. I needed a great deal of coffee to do it, and at the time it was my main source of fuel. While Tom napped, Valeria and I would go down to the hospital restaurant to have one or more cappuccinos and to talk, to clear our heads. Little by little I began to piece together the story of this woman who was so strange in my eyes. For instance, I found out that she had worked for years as a bilingual secretary and had left her boyfriend to go on a long spiritual retreat, from which she had returned even more withdrawn. She was a pleasant enough person but excessively tense, and her stiffness hid any trace of Italian warmth or tenderness.

It was starting to feel cold, although there was no way to predict the remorseless weather that was to set in that winter. The wind blew hard, but the light was still bright and rousing, and the trees went on with their struggle to hold on to the splendor of their foliage. An autumn jacket or a medium thick coat was enough to keep one warm. At the time I was wearing a wine-colored corduroy overcoat with a belt I tied in a knot at my waist, a skirt in the same material, and ankle boots in a petrol blue. I carried my things in my laptop bag. Sometimes I also carried a small gift for Tom: a book, or a liter tub of Berthillon ice cream (my favorite brand in the whole city), despite the considerable detour I had to make to buy it on my long trek out to Clamart. I much preferred the mornings to the evenings. That year, the building in Ménilmontant assumed a more desolate air than ever, and sleeping there was cold comfort. When I got home I had a hot bath and switched on the radio. I had gone back to it like an addict to an old vice. When I was in the mood, I listened to my answerphone messages. Sometimes it was my father, or my director of studies insisting I hand in the progress report on my thesis so my grant could be renewed, but the person who called the most was Haydée. I had not spoken to her since Tom had gone into hospital. The messages she left on both my mobile and my landline sounded urgent, but even so, I found it impossible to reply to them.

Aside from our time in Brittany, being with Tom in the hospital was the closest we ever came to living as a couple and yet we very rarely chatted, laughed, or enjoyed our time together as we had done before. The distress at being stuck inside and the uncertainty surrounding the advances in his treatment came pitilessly between us. It was as if the Tom I had met two years earlier had split in half, and one of the halves—the one I needed more—had once again set off on a long journey with no return date, not to Sicily, but to an ambiguous land where I ran the risk of losing him forever. Alone in my apartment, which I scarcely managed to heat with the electric radiator, I thought often about the possibility of him dying. I also thought of my own life, and my prospects. For me, everything led to Tom. The route from my birth and my childhood in Oaxaca, my love of cemeteries, the books I had read and the ones I had studied followed a path, at times straight, at others winding, which led to our meeting. My role as his companion in the hospital not only connected us incredibly closely, but was also the most important experience of my life. I, who had always considered myself useless, had at last the impression that I was good for something.

*

One afternoon, as Tom and I sat in bed together watching *Dick Tracy*, a simple move to shift our position turned into more intentional, risqué entwinement. Then came the kisses, the lips and the tongues; a perilous coming together we knew was made all the more urgent for how rash and yet unavoidable it was. Several times, a silhouette appeared at the frosted glass in the door, like a warning that someone could come in at any moment and yet, even so, we allowed ourselves to get carried away, throwing caution to the wind, until Tom's energy ran out and he fell asleep. I left the room in such a state of excitement I felt it was obvious to everyone I ran into in the corridor.

I cannot say if it was related or not to this encounter—it still torments me to think of it—but the next day, Tom's health had deteriorated. The doctors decided to up the dose of Flolan to revive him. I watched him sleep for several hours while struggling away at my thesis, hoping with all my might that I had nothing to do with this turn of affairs. As it began to grow dark, Tom woke up, calmly raised the head of his bed as if nothing had happened, and asked if he could have dinner. Then he asked me to put some music on, whatever I had on my computer.

"You suggest something," I said. "What would you like to listen to? I might have it if you're lucky."

We both knew this was very unlikely: our musical tastes were pretty different. He was a connoisseur of a branch of Anglo-Saxon music, in particular jazz and anything from the '70s, while I had quite an eclectic collection of CDs that I had copied from my various friends over the years. He felt like listening to something by Nick Drake, preferably a record called *Pink Moon*. I typed the name into the search field and saw that I would be able to give him what he wanted. Almost immediately, the guitar and Drake's introspective voice filled the room. Then something happened that I had not expected: just as he had a year and a half ago, on the other side of the wall separating our apartments, Tom began to cry. He cried for several minutes. When he had stopped, he said: "It's so sad for a man to die so young when he still has so much to give to the world." He was talking about the singer, of course, but also about what might happen to him. I told him that in Drake's case, it was not so obvious, but that lots of equally young and talented musicians had given up on life. We spoke about Elliott Smith, whose death had shaken us both, and also Jim Morrison, the most visited of our neighbors in the cemetery. When he heard me defend suicide, Tom looked at me, resentful and incredulous. I thought I could understand him. He was facing physical and psychological suffering for exactly the opposite reason, while I, with no idea what it was like to be in his shoes, was praising those who had given up on life prematurely. A few days later, Tom entered the operating theater on a trolley so that they could implant the cartridge, which from then on he would have connected to his aorta. His mood was confident, enthusiastic. It took a day and a half for him to recover from the operation but, once he'd done so, it was clear how much he had improved.

RUNNING

I was anxiously awaiting the day of my appointment with Dr. Menahovsky, who would—or so I hoped—give me the prescription I needed to be able to sleep again and to resume the austere, disciplined life I had been leading until not so long ago. That Saturday, for the first time in almost three months, I got out of bed as soon as the alarm clock instructed me to and went to take a shower. I looked at my naked body in the mirror. It seemed to me that, as well as the weight I had put on, there were more gray hairs at my temple and on my chest. Muscle spasms rippled all across my back, but even so I diligently carried out my scrupulous hygiene routine. As on every Saturday, I put on my sneakers and chose my clothes according to the stock rotation rule. Up until that point, everything was under control. But when I went to prepare my essential morning espresso, the coffee machine refused to react. All I got out of it was a few short, explosive exhalations, like a cat farting. It is unconscionable the degree of security household appliances can give to us. They simply have to break for the very structure of our existence to be disrupted and our world to crumble. Standing before the inert machine, I felt a mixture of rage and self-pity, difficult to describe. I almost punched a hole in the table. I looked at the clock. I still had enough time to go out for breakfast. What I really wanted was to eat a plate of fried eggs and bacon, but yet again, I drew on my reserves of restraint and asked for a dish of kiwi fruit and strawberries, as well as the espresso I had been denied at home. Dr. Menahovsky's clinic was on 57th Street, between Lexington and Third Avenue. It was a glorious morning and I decided to walk through the park. People were cycling or rollerblading, exercising their bodies as they should. I, meanwhile, walked along, bloated from my malaise and the extra pounds this had made me gain in the waist and thigh areas. When I reached the building, the doorman informed me that the elevator was not working and I had to walk up seven flights of stairs. When she saw how much I was sweating, the secretary offered me a glass of water. She then made me fill out a form, where every imaginable disease was listed, as well as some I had not heard of. I had to put a cross by whichever ones I was suffering from. Menahovsky, the demiurge who had created the mellow Ruth, was a short, wiry old man. His appearance would have been rather sinister if it were not for the good-natured expression on his face, with its white, padlock-shaped beard. His head was bald and his spectacles round and metallic. Over his rather sporty-looking outfit he wore the compulsory white coat. Despite the beautiful furnishings in his office, I did not feel comfortable in that place. Nor did I manage to relax when he started asking me questions about my past and present life. Nevertheless, I tried to answer him as sincerely as I could. I told him about my breakup with Cecilia and the memories preying on me recently, in particular the death of my first girlfriend. I assured him that, before, I had been a methodical man who stuck to his habits, capable of imposing many restrictions on himself. The doctor asked me for the details of Susana's death and my voice broke when I tried to relate them, so I chose to give him a much shorter version of events. He also asked me about my sexual activity, and whether or not I regularly had wet dreams. As his line of questioning grew more and more intimate, the doctor came closer and closer to where I sat on the couch on his chair on wheels. Then, eventually, he spoke to give me his diagnosis. As he saw it, my problem lay in a post-traumatic disorder I had been carrying for several decades, an obsessive-compulsive neurosis, and a recent but far from negligible bout of depression. He asked me if I was prepared to take medication.

"Frankly," he told me, "you don't have much of a choice."

After writing out the prescription, he suggested I come back in eight days to check what effect the first dose of psychiatric drugs had had on my state of mind.

I left with the formula for my new personality tucked away in the inner pocket of my coat. As I walked down the stairs, I thought about the absurd diagnosis I had just been given. The word "disorder" seemed excessive to me. It was without a doubt not a term that could be applied to me. "Disordered" referred to a life like Mario's, for example, whose sporadic work with no fixed hours allowed him to wake up at odd times and stay up late drinking several nights a week, or to the life of the kids I so often saw smoking marijuana around the edge of the park. Who diagnosed all those people? Who decided whether or not they should take psychiatric drugs? Where did the cycle of medicines such as these end? It seemed to me that to start playing "trial and error" with different substances to alter my brain chemistry was a move just as dangerous—just as indulgent— as drugging oneself with LSD or marijuana. I was thinking about this as I got to Central Park and, as I walked along its paths where occasionally a runner would emerge, absorbed in their workout, I contemplated these individuals for a few minutes. Despite their attire, almost always tight and ridiculous with fluorescent colors, these runners looked to me like the standard bearers of good habits.

Of all the users of the park, they were the ones who seemed to me the most healthy. I told myself that no one could accuse them of leading an insalubrious life. I looked down at my feet in their white sneakers and thought to myself that it was to this social group and no other that I should belong to. In the name of all the values I had defended throughout my life, I began jogging through the park, slowly, not overdoing it, trying to measure the rhythm of my steps and my breathing.

That same week, I signed up to join a small group of beginning runners, led by a trainer. Every day, at around half past six in the morning, the trainer and the members of the group jogged up to my house and waited for me at the entrance, never once stopping moving. After we had collected everyone, we went to Central Park, where the training lasted until nine. I stopped being the first one to arrive at the office, but the noble cause meant I did not care in the slightest. The trainer imposed a strict diet and routine on me, including warm-ups, sit-ups, sprinting, and long-distance running. Slowly but surely, I incorporated all this into my life with the same seriousness I had previously devoted to the gym. The set hours and the new diet had a most beneficial effect on me. The fat turned into muscle, and my apathy into energy. I began to feel happier, more secure and, above all, to regain my self-respect. Running brought me so much pleasure that I wondered why I had not started doing it before. I did not see Dr. Menahovsky again. Six weeks later, my brain chemistry had changed enough that I was able to stop thinking about taking the medication. My treatment consisted of a mixture of pheromones in high quantities and dopamine, substances I obtained from the exercise. In three months, I was already running six miles in the morning before work, and on weekends, the trainer made us do ten. We were training with a goal of entering our first marathon. The idea thrilled me. I saw myself as an athlete from Ancient Greece, pursuing the physical triumph that would bring him closer to Olympus. What is more, according to what I had heard from some of the other runners, the enduring sensation after one of these races is similar to being reborn, and this was exactly what my body was asking for: to be reborn as someone different, someone better. Symbolically, I chose the marathon in Mexico City to start with. It was my way of getting closure from Cecilia. I wanted to leave behind, in her own country, the convalescence I had gone through after our breakup. I cannot say that my time on the run was particularly memorable. I was poleaxed by the altitude as well as by nerves and my lack of experience. Nonetheless, I reached the finish line and, as I did so, I felt a happiness I had never felt before.

Visiting Cecilia's country knowing that I had lost her forever and managing not to slip back into a state of lethargy was the irrefutable proof I needed that the marathon had worked. I went back to being not just the methodical, steady person of before, but an entirely new being, even more strict and resistant to sentimentality.

NEW PLACES

Tom felt fine with the cartridge in and was convinced that from now on his health would only improve. When he discovered that a friend of his was coming from London to visit him, he suggested I use the weekend to take a break. I had traveled very little since I had arrived in Europe, and liked the idea of visiting Barcelona, so I bought a ticket from a budget airline and booked two nights in a hotel in the Gothic Quarter. The sea air helped to dispel the stress I had been building up over the last few months. The weather there was much milder than in Paris, and I was able to be outside almost all the time. I rang Tom several times on the Friday. I also called the hospital, and wrote a couple of messages to Valeria. On the Saturday I withdrew a bit more, and on the Sunday I disappeared altogether, assuming that if there were any bad news, they would get in touch immediately. I visited a few bookshops, and went to a piano concert at the Palau de la Música. I recall a long walk along the seafront, from the Mapfre Tower to the neighborhood of El Born, during which I resolved to shake off all my worries and, as if my life depended on it, not think of anything except for where my feet were going. Then I devoured a plate of *arroz negro* with a couple of beers and, after going back to the hotel, slept for more than twelve hours. I woke up late in the morning, grateful to Tom for having ordered me to get away. For the first time in months I felt the urge to have a casual, easy-going chat with someone and so I rang Haydée, but the conversation did not go exactly as I had thought it would. After spending half an hour telling me off, she blurted out what she had been wanting to tell me for weeks: she was going to have a baby. She told me that when she had got the news she had been shocked and quite worried, but after talking it over with Rajeev, who even now in the twenty-first century, was categorically against abortion, she had decided to keep it.

"He believes that reincarnation isn't just a possibility offered by his culture but an actual fact. Can you believe it?"

"I can," I said. "Tom thinks that people who die stay in this world, with us. There's not much difference between the two theories."

We laughed, but there was no lightness to it. I spent the day drifting about with the sense that I had been far too relaxed, telling myself that nothing in life mattered except taking care of my boyfriend.

I went back to Paris that evening and, after dialing the hospital's number several times without success, unpacked my suitcase and fell asleep. The telephone woke me at half past six, when the sky was still pitch black. I struggled to get out from under the duvet.

"Cecilia?" Tom's cousin said. In her head was the possibility that someone else might answer in my apartment. "Where have you got to? I left you an urgent message."

"Sorry, I was so tired I didn't see it. Is something wrong?"

"Quite a lot's happened since you went away. Tom's just been moved into intensive care. It's not good news."

I felt as if the temperature of the floor was rising up through the soles of my feet until it reached the center of my chest. I insisted she tell me, and at least dispel the uncertainty, but Valeria refused to say anything on the telephone.

"Tom wants to tell you in person. It's best you come here right away."

Despite its impenetrability, this phrase calmed me down. I told myself that at least he was not unconscious. I put on the first items of clothing I came across: a pair of enormous baggy trousers and an ancient jumper. As in the days Tom and I had first met, I left my hair just as the pillow had styled it and left the house with my coat buttoned up unevenly. I walked to the taxi stand, prepared to spend my last hundred-euro note. I did not take my computer, or even a book.

The intensive care unit was right at the furthest end of the hospital to cardio. It was a darker place, its windows pointing north. You had to go through several doors to reach the new room. The first thing I noticed was the presence of a monitor measuring his cardiac arrhythmia. He was lying down but awake, with an artificial respirator in his mouth. His skin, bluer than ever, stood out in the failing, wintry light from the window. His face looked sad. He asked me to come closer, and when I did he took the respirator out so he could speak. He explained that his illness had gone from stage three to stage four, where Flolan was no longer an option and the only possibility left was a heart and lung transplant. He looked into my eyes, waiting for my reaction. I sensed that during my absence he had been wondering how I was going to take such a piece of news. I was surprised at this. How could what I thought or felt matter to him? I wished I knew what he could see in my eyes. I was not indifferent to the news, but a heart and lung transplant was something so big that my brain was unable to take it in, just as I have never been able to get my head around distances in space, light-years, or numbers with more than nine zeros. I squeezed his hand and spoke to him as one speaks to someone at the dentist, about to have a tooth out.

"Let them operate, if they have to. Don't worry. You'll get through this, too, I'm sure."

Some hours passed before I was able to assimilate the scope of the new status quo, the risk and the uncertainty it implied: nobody could know when a donor might appear. The only option was to wait in the hospital until the time came for surgery, and then the convalescence period. If everything went well, he would have to stay in bed for another six months until they gave him the all-clear in the summer.

"Why would you want to get out before then anyway, when the weather outside's so awful?" said Fred, the nurse, trying to cheer Tom up. Tom smiled out of politeness. As soon as we were alone again, he said jokingly to me:

"You see? This is what I wanted, a change of rooms. It's warmer here, and more comfy. Look, we've even got a TV."

In fact, we never switched the device on. We did occasionally watch a film on my laptop, as we used to, but it was always my choice. In the room next door, on the other hand, the television was always switched on, and at a considerably high volume.

"It's my destiny. I'm either going to be bothered by my neighbor's radio or that Congolese gentleman's TV."

"So long as you don't fall in love with him too, we're making progress . . . How do you know he's from the Congo?"

"That nurse is a gossip. He tells me what goes on in the other rooms. Monsieur Kilanga's got a huge family; his kids take it in turns to watch series with him."

The nurse Tom was referring to was Fred. He was one of those provincial Frenchmen, short and corpulent, easily distinguishable from the Parisians by his jolly character and friendliness. He would joke with the patients and cheer them up, telling them stories about the daily life of the hospital in a cheeky tone of voice. A man with a vocation for service.

That same afternoon, I began paying close attention to Monsieur Kilanga's room—I had already come across his relatives a couple of times, mainly a girl in her twenties who came to visit him often. Sometimes, when he went to check on him, Fred would leave the door ajar and you could hear them talking. Monsieur Kilanga was a very tall, sturdy-looking man, who to me—for some unknown reason—looked as if he had served in the military. I supposed perhaps he had held an important post in his country. This was why he was able to be treated in France and bring his whole family over. The most likely reason, however, was that they were immigrants.

Fred the nurse called him *chef*, which seemed to please the man.

"I need light," Monsieur Kilanga would say, in his booming voice. "Please open the blinds."

And Fred would oblige, putting his hand up to his temple, in a sign of obedience, even though you could raise the blinds from a distance using the remote control.

Around this time, it was four or five degrees below zero outside. There was no snow yet, but occasionally a frozen rain would fall, like tiny knives that stuck to the skin. I swapped my corduroy trench coat for a brown one with a big furry collar, which made it look more elegant than it really was. All the tension and the staircases in the métro had made me lose several pounds. I enjoyed looking at my reflection in the windows of buses, in lifts and sliding doors. The expression on my face was fragile and interesting. I still had not finished the thesis, and so I lugged my computer all along the passages of the métro and the corridors in the hospital, from Tom's room to the visitors' restaurant, on the bus and on the RER. I would sit down with it at any table, my headphones on, and listen to the serious, melancholy voice of Meshell Ndegeocello who, with her peculiar, moving appearance, made me think of Monsieur Kilanga's daughter.

Unlike the ones I had got to know in the cardiorespiratory unit, the nurses in intensive therapy used to leave the doors to all the rooms open. Since Tom's room was at the very end, I found it impossible not to peep into the neighboring rooms. This is how I came to see an old woman feeding her sick daughter, a young blond man connected to a respirator, and a teenage Indian girl, with a heartbreaking expression on her face, lying in bed and staring at the line where the wall and the ceiling meet. To avoid being suffocated, I would go down to the visitors' restaurant, but when I got there the people coming and going, the clatter of the plates and cutlery, and the ringing of telephones seemed surreal and ungraspable to me.

OBSESSIONS

I found out from Mario that Susana had only stayed in Cuba to win me back. Mario was good friends with her sister and had spoken at length to her before she had gone on vacation to Spain with her whole family. At first her parents objected to Susana staying behind, but she had made such a huge fuss that they gave in. They could never regret this enough. It is difficult to explain clearly the reasons for our breakup—if I know anything it is that we loved each other intensely, with all the power first loves tend to have. What drove me, then, to split up with her? When you are young—this is what I think now—you grow bored very quickly with routine. I had been going out with Susana for several years by that point, during which time I became perfectly integrated into her family, and to her it was obvious that we would at some point get married. But I was not at all keen on this idea. Her doubts surrounding my sexuality also played a significant role, doubts that had been generated the day I told her about my absurd, inno-cent episode with Facundo. Living with her constant suspicion was impossible to tolerate. If the fear that I was attracted to men profoundly affected Susana, our separation unhinged her com-pletely. I knew she was suffering, that if she had chosen to stay home alone instead of going away with her whole family it was in order to see whether, once the stress of exams had passed, I would change my mind about breaking up with her. My decision, however, was set in stone, or at least that is what I felt at the time. To avoid giving her false hopes I stayed far away from her, in spite of her letters, her visits to my house at all hours, and her persistent telephone calls. The times when we did meet by accident at a party, or in a mutual friend's house, I opted to slip away immediately. It was a mistake to treat her like this. I should have foreseen that her temperament would never allow her to bear such rejection. I repeated this to myself a hundred times on the afternoon when her mother, fresh off the plane from her vacation, turned up at my house to see if her daughter was with me. Then came three days of total stupefaction in which we searched the city and its surroundings; we went to the police and the coast guard; we even went to the morgue and looked at dozens of bodies that were not hers; we asked all our friends in Havana and the ones who lived in other cities and, more than anything, we tried to keep ourselves busy day and night, in any way possible, so guilt would not consume us. Whereas before I had not even deigned to see her, when her parents came back I installed myself in their house, like another member of the family, occasionally allowing her mother, as crazy as it might sound, to comfort me when the anxiety and remorse overwhelmed me. Not then nor afterward did it occur to her to think me responsible, as many people do, for her daughter's disappearance. Nonetheless, I knew full well what role I had played. Finally, at the end of that interminable period—much longer, it seemed, than it really was—moved by a sort of intuition or presentiment, I asked for the utility room to be opened up, where she and I used to sleep with each other as her family wandered unawares around the house. It was there that I found her, her body already half decayed, hanging from a rope with her eyes and mouth open. It was those bulging blue eyes that pursued me on my sleepless nights on the Upper West Side, forcing me to go out running in the park every morning to try to forget them, at least for part of the day.

VITAL ORGANS

The rain falling over Clamart was dark and heavy. Without realizing it, we had stopped talking about the future. We tried to be nice, even lighthearted with each other and the staff. It was our way of being optimistic and the optimism was a superstitious measure we had tacitly adopted. Tom fell asleep and, as usual, I tried to work for a couple of hours, but was not able to concentrate. He did not wake up that night, or the following morning. He had fallen into an unconscious state that, according to the doctor, was due to a drop in his potassium levels. He told me it was nothing to worry about: all that had to be done was to add more salts to his intravenous fluids and increase the adrenaline to raise the heart rate of that exhausted organ they were about to extract from his body. I sat down to wait for him to open his eyes. Ever since Tom had arrived in this hospital, the only available place to sit with him was a hard aluminum chair with a plastic seat. Valeria and I took it in turns there throughout the day.

"They really don't care about us visitors here," I said to Fred, who was emptying the bedpan in the bathroom. "Just look where they make us sit."

"Most people can't stand being in here for more than ten minutes," he said, "even less in intensive therapy. They turn up all stressed, with their boxes of chocolates and their bunches of flowers, which only get taken off them in reception anyway, they say hello, and then they leave straight away. People can't bear to think about hospitals, never mind actually be in one. You deserve to have a sofa brought in to your husband's room."

As I chatted to Fred, I heard voices in Monsieur Kilanga's room. A woman was shouting: "*Get out! We don't want you here!*" At first I thought it was a family argument, the girl in the corridor and her brother fighting in front of their sick father; one of those tactless moments towards the dying that at times are unavoidable. Little by little, other voices joined in with what sounded like a brawl. I began listening more closely. I managed to make out words, then whole sentences. The exhortation for someone to leave was repeated several times. It was not just the girl shouting—there were one or two others, as well. Who were they trying to get out? And why was this person so desperate to stay put? Could he or she not come back once everyone had calmed down a bit? Tom still had not woken up, and so, curiosity getting the better of me, I left the room to go and snoop through the frosted glass next door. I could not really see anything, just the silhouettes of a group of individuals who exceeded the regulation number of visitors standing around poor Monsieur Kilanga's bed. I realized it was a ceremony. Nevertheless, despite my efforts to decipher the aim of the ritual, I could not determine whether his children were trying to encourage their dying father to pass over to the other side once and for all, or if, on the contrary, the one they were trying to drive out was death. I was engrossed in this when Fred appeared at my elbow and, very gently but forcefully, asked me to move away from the corridor. A few minutes later, Monsieur Kilanga's relatives came out of the room. I heard their voices as they made their way noisily to the exit. Only the girl who was always there remained. She stood sobbing outside her father's room, waiting for the nurses to carry out the routine procedure.

It was Fred himself who came out of the room to tell her that her father had just died.

When I went back to Tom's room, which had somehow become my own space, I saw that his eyes were open. I felt a profound sense of relief, which I chose not to show. I simply smiled, and asked him how he was. He took my hand with a huge effort and, beneath the respirator, smiled back. I could not bear it any longer, and so I summed up what had happened.

"Monsieur Kilanga died," I told him, with a lump in my throat. Tom squeezed my hand gently.

"I don't want to know."

As I said before, I never received a religious education. Although he was conservative, my father was an atheist and, after my mother ran off, he had prohibited my grandmother from indoctrinating me with Catholicism. Even so, for the first time in my life I began to pray, in my own way, to whoever was out there and might be able to help us. At the entrance to the hospital, on the bus on the way back home, in the street, any time I heard a siren or saw an ambulance speeding along, I begged that the organs for Tom would "appear." Wishing for a death, even that of someone we do not know, so as to remove, vulture-like, the most essential parts of a body is something horrendous and I was very aware of this, but nothing in the world could have made me stop. I wondered too if wishing for someone's death really was equivalent to wishing them harm. Did the dead suffer just as we did? Perhaps it was worse to be alive and to be profoundly wretched . . . When I prayed for my boyfriend to keep on living, I did it far more for me than for him. Considering the gravity of his condition, Tom was at the top of the list. He was not going to have to wait years, as happens to many patients. But what would happen if no one who was generous enough to donate their organs left this world in the next few weeks? Tom would be gone forever. In that case, I said to myself, all I would have to do was jump from the fourth floor to be reunited with him. I was consoled by this option. I remembered our conversation about Nick Drake and other musicians. I told myself that if people with that much talent had opted for suicide, then it could not possibly be such an abhorrent choice.

When they found out that he was waiting for a transplant, Tom's friends began showing up at the hospital. As well as the ones who lived locally, such as David and Ricardo, others came from abroad. No one would admit that they had come exclusively to see him, but it was obvious they were here to say goodbye, and I suspected that Valeria had contacted them to suggest it. I understood her: she was the most rational and practical of the three of us. Nonetheless, I could not help but interpret her decision as a betrayal. This was how I met Cyd and his wife, who lived in a big hippy mansion on the outskirts of London with their four children; Ghislaine and María, two plump lesbians, ruddy cheeked and very affectionate, who brought us tea and ginger biscuits from Holland; and Max, a friend from Ireland who had been in the IRA and who gave Tom an iPod loaded up with music from the '70s. Ingeborg, an ex-girlfriend from Germany, arrived from Boulder, Colorado, to spend a Sunday morning with him and insisted that Valeria introduce us. She took my hands in hers and told me she had come to leave behind any sense of acrimony or bitterness from the past.

When at last she left, I went over to the room, anxious to see how the visit had affected Tom, and to my annoyance found that a nurse was changing his incontinence pad with the door open. This was how I discovered that he had lost all control over his sphincter. His body was shutting down at an alarming rate. His scrawny back showed each and every one of his vertebrae. His arms and legs, which had once been muscular, were barely more than bone, which was why his hospital dressing gown was always hanging off him. His eyes, bigger every day, gave his face the appearance of an extraterrestrial. And yet even so, I heard him complain very few times. He went through all these tests with a composure I found incomprehensible.

I never found out if it had been his idea or his cousin's, but around this time a few religious objects started to appear on the shelves in his room. Valeria put an old statue of Saint Anthony of Padua, something his family had left him, by the window, and an iron cross in the shape of a four-leafed clover. Since it was forbidden to have an open flame in the hospital, Valeria brought in a little lamp that looked like a candle. On the other side of the glass, it was snowing and the reflection from this little altar gave the room a cozy, new atmosphere. I congratulated him on the idea, and in an anxious voice he said:

"I spat blood twice today. The doctor says my lungs are suppurating and they'll have to cauterize them. They're going to put a catheter in at my groin and thread it up through my back until they reach the wounds."

It was obvious he was really frightened.

"They'll put you to sleep and you won't feel anything," I said, with feigned calm.

Then Valeria explained that his heart was too weak to cope with the anaesthetic.

*

A few hours later, Tom left his room on a trolley headed for the pre-op room. I accompanied him as far as the white automatic door where there was a sign prohibiting unauthorized personnel from entering. The nurse advised me to go home. There was no way of knowing what time they would be finished. I obeyed without a sound, but the whole way back to Paris I felt guilty. Valeria was not at the clinic either, and the most likely outcome was that Tom would return to his room without a single friendly face he knew to welcome him. It was snowing when I emerged from the métro. Unlike Petit Clamart, the streets in the 20th arrondissement had stayed clear of snow until then thanks to the heat generated by all the inner-city bustle. Now, however, Ménilmontant was covered in white, too. Without taking off my coat, I went to make an herbal tea in the kitchen: a blend of calming flowers to banish the stress. Before I finished it, I decided to look for the key Tom had given me to his apartment. In his place—I was certain—I would find the strength I needed to keep on believing in a future together. Except for the cold, everything was unchanged. The table with the teapot on it, the books, the fireplace. It was as if Tom were still living there and might come back at any minute. I switched on the stereo and began listening to a CD from the last morning we had spent in his house: *Get Rhythm* by Ry Cooder. A carefree, optimistic album. I told myself that, if he'd come back that night, Tom would have run a bath and stayed lying in it until he felt relaxed. I decided to do the same. The hot water eased my anxiety. Afterwards, I wrapped myself in Tom's bathrobe and then put on the faded pair of pajamas I found under his pillow and which, out of vanity, he had not wanted me to bring him. The smell of his house, so different from the one his body had acquired in the hospital, was like a warm, familiar blanket that encouraged me not to give up. I was not sleepy and, to distract myself, I tried to take advantage of the fireplace in his room. I was not able to light a fire that time either.

At half past ten I called the hospital to ask if the operation was finished. After going through a maze-like series of recorded messages, a real live person informed me that the operation had indeed finished fifteen minutes ago.

"He's recovering. He'll be taken back to his room in a couple of hours."

The snow was still falling. I hung up, put my clothes back on, and called a taxi.

I arrived a little before twelve. His bed was empty and I was afraid, but was calmed down almost immediately by a nurse on the night shift I had not seen before.

"They're about to get him set back up in his room. You can wait here for him. Do you need a blanket?" she said, taking it for granted that I would spend the night in the hospital.

A few minutes later, they brought Tom in. I was surprised to see him sitting up on the trolley, as the nurse adjusted the height of the bed so he could move Tom onto it. He looked like someone who had just come back not from the operating theater, but from a war. His pupils were dilated and his jaw clamped tightly shut. His expression betrayed the enormous amount of adrenaline flowing through his blood at that moment. "Poor Tom. What are they turning him into?" I remember thinking. If before I felt slight distrust towards the doctors who used guesswork to increase and decrease his levels of potassium and painkillers, of Flolan, and of who knows what else, from that moment on I began to harbor frank resentment towards them. I knew that they were doing whatever they could to save him, I knew that if they had cauterized his lungs without anaesthetic it was to stop him from drowning in his own blood, and yet, nonetheless, I hated them for torturing him with all of this.

Tom moved his head slightly so that I would understand he was grateful for my presence. Then he brought a tissue up to his mouth, spat into it, and screwed it up again, throwing it into the wastepaper basket in the corner of the room with a precision that confounded me. His appearance was deranged and at the same time extremely alert. I just smiled lovingly at him. Then he motioned for me to come closer.

"Who's that man standing in the doorway?"

I shivered. There was no one in the room but us. I did not want to tell him he was hallucinating.

"It must be some other patient's relative," I said.

After two or three days, on an afternoon when I was hanging around near the staff office, I happened to overhear a conversation among the doctors on duty. They seemed to be urgently trying to locate Dr. Tazartès. When they finally managed to get hold of him, they told him that an organ had turned up. As soon as I could, I went over to ask if it was for us. They told me that for the moment they were not authorized to say anything, and that I should wait to hear more. Luckily, Fred was there, and when he got a chance to talk to me without his colleagues seeing, he explained that they would have to carry out some tests to check the compatibility of the heart and a few other things.

"Cross your fingers," he said. "You might just be in luck."

I felt as if my own heart was about to burst from anxiety. I went to look for Tom's cousin to give her the news, but she had gone down to the cafeteria to have something to eat. The doctor rushed in and began checking Tom's vital signs. Then he left, and things took the same course as usual. When Valeria came back to the room, I told her what had happened and she went to ask the nurses herself if it was true. She came back out into the corridor with a calm expression, a little disappointed, and confirmed what I already knew deep down.

"There is an organ, but they're not going to give it to him because he's too weak. We'll have to wait until he gets better and then put in another request."

It was another patient in intensive care who was taken to pre-operative care on a trolley that night. Since whoever it was was lying down, I could not see which of them was the chosen one. I hoped that it was the teenage Indian girl who would receive those extra ten years of life.

That night, I went back to Tom's apartment. I lay down to sleep in his freezing cold bed. Something of his old smell still clung to the sheets and the pillowcase, and so I slept with my arms wrapped around it. The Tom in the hospital bore little resemblance to the one who had lived in his house and whose presence remained there like a scarce and precious substance. Which of the two did I know better? The question bubbled up in my mind and I could not find an answer. Of the past Tom, I knew very little. It was all I could do to cobble together a hazy history of his family and his most important love affairs. As I had done nearly two years ago, when he was on his trip to Sicily, I began sniffing around in his cupboards, in the boxes he kept on the top shelf of his wardrobe, in the photograph albums on one of the bookshelves. It was not voyeurism, but an attempt to grasp him somehow, even if to do so I had to steal his secrets, the fragments of his life before he met me. I stayed up all night, going through the pictures of his childhood, of adolescence, of his trips and his numerous girlfriends. What did Tom think about in the solitude of his hospital room? Quite probably about the very thing I was looking for in his apartment. About his past, about all the combined pieces like a mural telling an epic story through images. What place did he reserve for me within this story, the woman who was accompanying him on his final days? Did the months that had gone by in my company—three of which had been hellish—have any weight compared to so many other years of happy courtship with other women? It was impossible to know. As I went through the photographs, I finished off the tea with the Mariage Frères label that we had opened on my first visit to his place. Like the tea, his possibilities of life had run out dizzyingly fast. I thought once more of the organ they had denied him and of how absurd it would be to cut short our lives together at this point. I could not resign myself to the idea. I was prepared to do anything, even to kill myself, so that we could stay together. And the truth is that I had very little keeping me in the world. My family felt a long way away from my reality. The pain my father would feel after my death would be, I was convinced, less than what I felt at that moment.

If it was inevitable that Tom leave this world, I wanted to go with him. To go together. To go together. To go together like someone immigrating to another country with their partner. I could not sleep, and so I started repeating this phrase like a mantra for a long time. Later, insomnia's unpredictable logic led me to count up all of the famous people who had gone mad or died of sadness in Paris, almost all of them through depression or heart conditions: Éluard, Balzac, Doré, Montand . . . The city, and I knew this more than anyone, was conducive to this. I remembered Beethoven and his hallucinations. The send-off organized by Gustave Doré, who, the night before he died, invited all his friends to a *brasserie* and jubilantly raised a glass with them all to toast his imminent end. I saw this scene in the form of a dream. Doré's round face with a handkerchief at his neck. And then it was not Doré anymore presiding over the farewell get-together, but Tom and I, sitting at the head of the table. And the dinner guests? Haydée, Rajeev, David, Valeria, and my whole group of goth friends from Oaxaca.

On December 3, the doctor informed us (with Tom present) that there was no longer anything they could do. With the possibility of a transplant ruled out, it was a question of waiting until his body failed completely and no one could say how long that would take. From now on, all his efforts would be focused on soothing the unbearable pain in Tom's chest, as well as the feeling that he was suffocating. They moved us into a standard room, away from intensive care, and also away from the waiting area, to give our room to a new patient. The walls of this new room were light green, or what some people call "aquamarine." None of the three of us could believe what was happening. Once the nurses had left the room, Tom asked Valeria to leave us alone for a minute.

"I want you to promise me something," he said, taking out the respirator so I could understand him, which, even without it in his mouth, was very hard. "No matter how unhappy or alone you feel, never take your own life."

"If I died too," I argued in my defense, "we could stay together."

"We'll be closer than you imagine and, if you listen hard, you'll be able to hear me."

"That's not enough for me," I said. "I'm coming with you even if you don't want me to."

I admit that I responded harshly and with no consideration for the state he was in, but there was no room for kindness anymore.

We were a couple negotiating our future. I was not going to compromise on something so important.

"Suicide," Tom said, in the most serious tone of voice I had ever heard him use, "is a crime in spiritualist law and you pay dearly for it. We all have a mission in life and it is up to each of us to find it. Passing through this world without discovering what it is is equivalent to wasting your existence. If you want me to die in peace you have to promise me that."

I was silent. By deciding to go with him I was trusting in those spiritualist laws on life after death and the possibility of being reunited with one's loved ones in some intermediate world. If these laws were against me, my only possibility—an uncertain, desperate possibility, on that we can agree, but valuable precisely because it was the only one—was being closed off to me at that moment. There was nothing for it but to promise what Tom asked. And so this was how, against my will, I signed my life sentence.

The day went by slowly until it was time to eat.

"Talk to me!" he begged. "Say something, please!" But I could not find the words.

At around five, Tom asked Valeria to call his Sicilian relatives in Paris—cousins, uncles and aunts, and family friends—to see who was able to come and see him. We all gathered one night in his hospital room as if it were a party and not the premature wake full of drama I was afraid of. They were singing in dialect until dawn broke. Even though we did not all speak Sicilian, everyone joined in with this trance-like joy. The night nurses cooperated, not only turning a blind eye, but also by bringing seats and putting the staff coffee machine in the room for us to use. At some point, I looked at the monitor that measured my boyfriend's heart rate: for the first time since I had known him, the rhythm of his heartbeats was constant once more. After dawn, things changed. The nurses were no longer as understanding, and ordered us to clear the room before the doctor arrived. The members of the family, of which I too now formed a part, said goodbye and left for work with tears in their eyes.

On Monday, December 4, at nine in the morning, Tom left this world and passed into what he liked to call "the neighborhood over the way." Valeria and I asked the doctors to leave his body untouched on the bed for as long as possible, according to his beliefs, to help him to adapt to his new state. His remains were divided up between the Cimitero degli Angeli di Caltanissetta and Père-Lachaise. Although it was true that he had had other niches in various parts of the world, not a gram of his ashes was sent to another country.

MARATHONS

I spent an entire year traveling the world in search of new challenges. After Mexico, I ran marathons in Chicago, Berlin, and New York, and the Saint Silvester Road Race, which is held in São Paulo. There are people who claim to have mystical feelings during the race, like some kind of brotherhood established among the runners. All these assertions sounded to me like the product of an exaggerated, sentimental imagination, if not odious lies. Although running brought me a sense of pleasure and well-being, it took me a long time to get over the distasteful sensation I got from people. In a marathon, other people have to be invisible and considered only and exclusively as potential opponents. This is not easy to achieve. The sweat and even the breathing of others can, if we allow them to, lead to an uncontrollable sense of disgust. Runners perspire, spit, and endlessly exude every substance from their bodies. I admit that on more than one occasion the breath of some individual running very close to me made me start retching. Once, I had to interrupt my run and vomit behind a tree. And yet the worst thing is not the runners but the public: overexcited people, most of them drunk or intoxicated, who show up to have fun, to sing stupid songs, wave banners, eat hamburgers and hot dogs behind the barriers, an attitude that goes diametrically against the spirit of athletics. One of the greatest satisfactions a marathon can bring, however, is that it pushes us to surpass our limits, not only physical but also mental. Little by little, by sheer force and willpower, I overcame, if not my repugnance of these hordes, then at least my vulnerability to their noxious stench. And I was proud of this. The more I managed to ignore the existence of others, the better my concentration was on myself and on my performance. I know of no pleasure that comes close to that of beating my own records. More than endorphins, so often talked about in magazines at doctors' offices, it was the certainty I was turning into someone strong and resilient, a sort of modern Titan, which made me feel euphoric, a true addict of the sport. Nonetheless, my view of things changed radically while I was running one of the marathons I had been most excited about and for which I had trained tirelessly. I was a mere few miles away from the finish line, and I should say I was one of the first to achieve this, when a tall red-headed girl fell over at my feet, overcome by what was clearly an epileptic fit. Seeing her rigid body in the throes of convulsions, salivating like a rabid dog, I felt a mixture of disgust and fear. For a moment as brief as a lightning bolt, I thought about stopping to help her. At school I had been taught how to give first aid to someone undergoing this kind of attack: you had to remove any objects or pieces of clothing the person could injure or strangle themselves with, and move them onto their sides until the attack was over. However, that morning I resisted the temptation for heroism and chose instead the stoic discretion of the athlete concentrating on his performance. No one would stop me from reaching the finish line as soon as possible. And so I swerved to avoid the woman, like you avoid an orange or any piece of rotten fruit in your path, and proceeded with the race. A few yards further on, I found myself flying through the air, the victim of an explosion that shook not only those of us who were there on that day, but runners and the press the world over. I woke up in the ambulance, listening on the radio to the voices of the nurses who could not keep pace with the number of wounded people. Then the surgeon arrived, and with him the news that they were going to have to amputate half my leg.

I was admitted to Boston Medical Center for six months, which my employer's insurance only partially covered. In my nights of insomnia, with my eyes closed and unable to control my anxiety, I saw, one after another, scenes of robots collapsing, crashing down like the Twin Towers on 9/11. I thought a lot about the epileptic girl I had seen fall over. If I had gone to her aid, I would have escaped the explosion and its terrible consequences. I thought of Susana, of Ruth, of Cecilia, and of all the women I failed to care for when it came down to it. In the midst of a paranoid delirium, I told myself that each one of them had been an opportunity to save me from myself. I thought, too, of my mother and hoped she would never find out about my new circumstances. To elaborate now on the state of terror I found myself in would be immodest and above all unworthy of a man who for his whole life has venerated the rules of propriety. What I can say is that it was the fear of spending the rest of my days in a wheelchair that led me to acquire the most costly prosthesis, a kind of titanium column fitted with a revolving mechanism and capable of movements that a human leg cannot carry out. In the hospital I was offered psychiatric support. Instead of the commendable Dr. Menahovsky, I received a visit from a short, wide-hipped woman, who looked at me with pity. My alternative to antidepressants had gone up in smoke. I had no option but to ingest the substances she offered me.

I stayed in Boston for almost a year. In that time, the wound healed enough to be able to fit the prosthesis and then I began the long period of rehabilitation. Lacking a leg does not prevent it from stinging, burning, or bashing into things, sometimes unbearably painfully. In order to stop feeling it, the brain has to assimilate its absence and the patient must reestablish the mental map of the body. If other athletes had repelled me, I found the proximity of cripples terrifying. I found it exasperating that in the physical therapy sessions they would start sobbing or lamenting their bad luck. If I had had enough money, I would have paid for private sessions without thinking twice about it. Two people offered to look after me during my convalescence: my good friend Mario and the steadfast Ruth Perelman. It was she who took responsibility for finding an apartment on the ground floor of a modern building, situated a few blocks from the hospital. She also hired a woman to cook and clean. Ruth spent as much time by my side as her job and her children would allow. She brought me books, magazines, and Polish goodies, purchased in Kutsher's just before she left the city so they were as fresh as possible. I missed New York so much! Its streets, its parks, its restaurants, and its bookstores. Every object and treat that tasted of that city and that she brought to me in Boston was balm for my soul.

After the incident, I stopped fantasizing about the house in the woods and, above all, about the ideal women who, as I had it, was destined for me. I took it for granted that this dream would never now be realized. In the same way that, months earlier, I had understood Susana's place in my existence, I began now to glimpse the role Ruth had played in my life. Despite the scant credit I had granted her in the beginning, with our respective ups and downs and the odd estrangement, the bond between us was so strong that not even my history with Cecilia and her visit to New York had managed to break it. We were both aware of this strength and also that the time available to us was far from unlimited. Ruth was fifteen years my senior but better preserved. And in any case, women almost always live longer than men. According to my speculations, we might well have more or less the same amount of time left. One night, as we were speaking about this on the terrace of the apartment in Boston, she proposed, as she had once done in Hotel Lutetia in Paris, that I move in with her. She would adapt everything so I would be safe and comfortable there. She even offered to send her children to a Swiss finishing school for the first year so the two of us could get used to one another. It was not a new idea, she had already discussed it with them. This time I took her suggestion more seriously. As well as her attention, I was attracted by the elevator and the space. Despite my girlfriend's generosity, the incident severely depleted my retirement fund, which, over the years and with huge personal sacrifices, I had built up. The transitition from maturity—that age in which one still has great expectations, hopes, and dreams—to the start of decrepitude is surprisingly rapid, and in my case it was even more so. Before we know it, the body we trust in so much starts to betray us. Our wrinkles multiply like spiderwebs and the worst thing is that everyone, except ourselves, seems to accept this as something natural, logical, and irreversible. Resigning myself to the fact I would never run again and would have to put up with an endless series of new limitations was a test of my self-restraint. During my recovery I read and reread Seneca, and, when at last I had adapted to my titanium leg, I returned to New York not stronger, as I had dreamed when I first left, but rather accepting, in the most serene and dignified way possible, of what Mario insists on calling "our human condition."

CEMETERIES

Tom's funeral was more anodyne and discreet than any I had witnessed in Père-Lachaise. The Sicilian merrymaking was left behind at the hospital. Neither Valeria nor I were in the mood to organize anything and we decided to invite very few people. That morning, a frozen rain fell over the city, far too much of it for December. We left the ashes in the niche without any kind of ceremony. Afterwards, we sheltered in a café in Ménilmontant while we warmed up, she with a *double crème* and I with a *vin chaud*. Back at home, I stayed under the duvet for more than twenty-four hours, my mouth all dry due to the electric heater, but I could not muster the necessary energy to walk to the kitchen and drink water from the tap, the only water available in the apartment. A few days later, Tom's cousins came by in a removal van to take his things away. I have no idea what they did with them. Since I still had a key, I went in as soon as they had left the building to see the empty space. A masochistic gesture if you like, but also a necessary one. I picked up a couple of things they had left on the floor: a jumper with holes in it, some pajama bottoms I wore for months, a couple of magazines, and a stack of blank CDs. I went back to my apartment to stare at them, my behavior not unlike that of a scavenging animal in its lair.

After Tom's death I abandoned my thesis, abandoned all the paperwork for continuing my studies, and abandoned myself to resentment and sadness. I ate any old thing at any old time, and only when I remembered I needed to feed myself to keep on going. I went for several weeks without washing. When I left the house, I noticed with a certain amount of pleasure the aversion my appearance and smell caused in people, especially my neighbors. My body was the anchor tying me to a world in which Tom was no longer around, and neglecting it was a kind of vengeance. In such circumstances, the most prudent thing to do would have been to go back to Oaxaca; to return to my family home and let my grandmother cure me with cleansings and other remedies that exist for such things. But at the time I was beyond the point of making a reasonable decision. My only wish was to put an end to myself, and I could not do it. I had made a promise.

I did go out, but only to cross the boulevard and go to the *columbarium* by the niche where Tom's name was engraved. I could stand for hours in front of the gray stone, asking for some sort of sign. At other times, I wandered around the graves, listening out for the voices that, according to him, it was possible to hear among the tombstones. Anywhere felt more inviting to me than my own apartment. No matter the weather, I would spend hours in Père-Lachaise watching the people coming and going, observing their routines and their behavior. No longer from high up in my house, as I had done when I arrived in the building, but at ground level, halfway between the city and those who lay beneath it. When the guard walked past, ringing his little bell to say the place was closing, he would wink at me, wordlessly allowing me a few more minutes. He was a good sort, Lucien; very understanding. I learned the names of the other cleaning staff, too. These people constituted my new— and only—social circle, which included the down-and-outs who took shelter in open mausoleums or the ones with broken padlocks, and the grave diggers, two brothers called Creuzet, whom the *clochards* shouted at in amusement—"*Allez, creusez, les Creuzet!*"— while they carried out their work, as seriously as they could, wearing forced smiles. They too began to consider me an *habituée* it was possible to chat to or eat lunch with. I brought them bread, occasionally leftover pasta that, out of a kind of inertia but also in homage, I still sometimes made in the evenings. In spite of the cold, I did not like staying at home, where Tom's absence was more real than anywhere else. A couple of weeks after we had buried him, Madame Loeffler had placed a red-and-white sign in the building's window, announcing she was putting the apartment up for rent. Things happened at a speed I was unable to comprehend, like when you watch a film on fast forward. Just as quickly, one morning another removal van arrived with a couple of students who, in just one day, carried countless boxes up the stairs. They looked happy. They laughed and talked loudly to each other. At night they would fuck on the other side of my bedroom wall, stopping me from getting to sleep. I listened to them, imagining that it was us there and that my apartment was an abandoned house with a ghost living in it. Without realizing, on my visits to the *columbarium*, I began telling Tom about what was going on in that apartment which for me was still his. Sometimes sarcastically, in amazement, sometimes resentfully. At times I spoke to him about these kids tenderly, as if I were telling him what was happening with us and not to a pair of strangers. Then, to change the subject, I would describe my dreams or any other event in my hazy existence.

As I carefully observed the visitors to the cemetery, I realized it was not that unusual to address a dead person. In the same way many people talk to their pets as they walk them in the streets and some people talk to themselves, others converse with the deceased, almost always in silence but from time to time letting parts of this conversation that takes place in their mind slip out, and, if you are vigilant, it is possible to salvage a few phrases. Those who no longer take people's opinions into account, as in my case, do it aloud. I just had to see their faces to discover the toll loneliness had taken on them. Most of the time they were people in great pain or victims of someone else's cruelty and, although they too were cruel to others, they would go straight for the jugular of anyone who criticized or teased them; people so thirsty for affection that they sucked out like vampires any courtesy or kindness from whoever they came across. I imagined them going back to their houses at night, or to the homeless shelters, cooking any old thing and eating standing up, straight from the pan, while feeling sorry for themselves like someone for whom it has become second nature. They were all ages: from elderly folk who could barely get around to youngsters ravaged by drugs, by some work- or academic-related failure, or by an unrequited love. Any drop can lead to one of these prematurely filled glasses spilling over. Many of those attitudes that had shocked me so when I first arrived I now thought were entirely justified. I myself formed part of the hordes of neurotics and schizophrenics who frighten the tourists, but I could not care less. Although I was alone, my domain had increased considerably. No longer was I confined to thirty square meters in an ancient building smelling of damp. My domain was the streets of Paris, all its stairwells and hidey-holes. My companions were the marginal, the good-for-nothings, the *sans domicile fixe* and the rest of the pariahs.

INVOCATION

I want total silence to see if it is true that you have something to say to me, if you feel you did not interrupt the dialogue between us abruptly or if, on the contrary, you have disappeared forever, as I had feared. I do not know if dying was a project for you, a task, or something that happened to you. If, in the end, you found that purpose in life you spoke to me of in your final hours, or if something remained unresolved. What I do know is that you did not want to go, to draw the curtain here. I saw you fight against it all. Maybe you thought that you could stay in some other form, or that I would end up learning how to hear you, to recognize your voice among those of the dead. I have been waiting for your reply for weeks now, but the truth is I cannot hear a thing, not at home, not in the cemetery. You turned this love that was so alive, so present still, into an epitaph that was simultaneously short and intense, while I flail around in the world of the impossible because there is nothing I can do and this is what kills, like the unbearable need for someone who does not exist anymore, at least in the form they used to take. The living do not interest me. Nor do the dead. Watching scenes from everyday life without you is obsolete. You are the only thing that matters to me. But I think this has been the case for a long time now. And although at times I would like to shout, "How could you leave me on my own?" in my heart I know you did not want to leave.

In your case, the verb "to die" ought to be used as a transitive verb. You were died by the doctors and their ineptitude dressed up as wisdom. And I: did I choose to go with you, or did it just happen to me? I could have given up at any moment, I could have changed cities, fates, and yet the idea never once crossed my mind. Your existence made me happy. It was enough to hold your hand and smell you, to steal kisses from the oxygen mask. We thought we would have another ten years. We even believed in the possibility of a transplant. It all seems so brief now, and as small as a tiny toy circus there is barely enough time to play with. I feel like a fool surprised by the fickle will of a God without compassion. I have very few things to cling to right now, and among them is disenchantment. I would not like to lose it. There is something soothing about it, which is why I like it so much, this disenchantment I used to see in you without ever understanding it. I did not have time to give you everything I would have liked to. I did not finish—not by a long shot—getting to know you. I was not able to explain, for instance, that you were splitting me in two and that you were leaving an emotional cripple in this world, an incomplete, abandoned being who does not know what to do with herself. I did not tell you this— to avoid hurting you, but also out of pride. I did not scream the endless pain I was feeling and now I do not know what to do with it all. I have heard that suffering has medicinal properties. Should I allow it to spill out everywhere, like an acid that corrodes everything it touches? I have no idea if you can actually hear me. I cannot hear your voice. If there is no one stopping you, I beg you, please let me feel your presence. I want to believe that our conversation can continue, that it persists in my dreams or in some unconscious inner ear, that at some point there will be an explanation for all this.

*

In spite of my efforts, I never heard the voices Tom had promised me. Instead, I heard those of a multitude of beings condemned to live alone, longing for someone who had passed over into the other world. I met dozens of these beings, and others like them. I met Eleanor Rigby and Father McKenzie, sick people waiting for the day of their death as prisoners wait for the end of their sentence, and who, like Tom, had bought in advance the niche where their ashes would be deposited. I met people without hope, with whom I held long conversations I recalled nothing of a few minutes later, not because they were trivial, but because of the catatonic state I was in. I even witnessed one of them being buried. As soon as the cemetery closed its gates, I went back to my house to collapse onto sheets I never washed. I no longer missed the radio. In the mornings I would go out to buy bread or food of some kind, but I always ended up returning to Père-Lachaise as if it were a magnetic pole around which my existence gravitated. Later on I became interested in the stories of these people who walked among the tombs as I did, but especially in the dead and their life stories. I realized it was enough to walk up to a grave where someone had stopped to strike up a conversation about the deceased. For me to feel brave enough to do this, several circumstances had to come together. It was important, for example, that the person in question looked friendly and receptive, that the name written on the gravestone was evocative in some way, and that I was in the right mood.

"Did you know them?"

This was the key question that opened doors and thanks to which you could listen to a story, a secret, a morsel of humanity. As well as being divided into either niches or individual plots, the tombs had many categories: the touristy ones, like Oscar Wilde's or Jim Morrison's, always surrounded by Americans or Japanese, cameras, and smiling people; the ones of other talented though less respected artists; and finally, the ones I was interested in: graves of unknown people, professionals, housewives, businessmen, employees like Tom himself, with whose friends or relatives it was possible to talk for a few brief, luminous moments. I heard countless stories about children who longed for their parents or who bore them a slavish grudge, of lovers of all ages who would not resign themselves to living alone, of remorseful siblings, of loyal friends. I was also interrogated on several occasions as I stood next to Tom's niche. I too told our story to the delight of many a solitary soul. Receiving these tales, steeped in the pain of so many other people, was a kind of miraculous balm. Against all expectations, I managed, for a few minutes, sometimes even hours at a time, to forget the excruciating hollow I felt in the middle of my chest and, of course, to feel less alone. However, at night it was not them, the dead, or their visitors who peopled my dreams. My nightmares were recurring and almost always about the patients I had met in intensive care: the Indian teenage girl, Monsieur Kilanga, and all those I had seen struggle to the limits of their powers to remain in a world to which I felt less and less connected. The memory of those hopelessly ill patients made me feel guilty for not making the most of what they had all wished for and which I had in abundance: health and time. In the early hours of the morning, their faces would reproach me for my thoughtless, disillusioned, wasteful attitude towards my own life. Nonetheless, as soon as dawn broke, the specters who tormented me at night would vanish. With my head under the pillow and a pair of wax earplugs to block out the noise from my neighbors, I would sleep until 11:00 a.m. and then cross the boulevard outside to make my way into the cemetery once more.

One evening, as I got back to my apartment at around 6:30, I heard Rajeev's voice just as he was leaving a message on the answerphone. Excitedly, he was saying that their daughter had been born prematurely and was under observation, but that everything seemed to be O.K., and Haydée was really happy. He gave me the address of the clinic, in case I wanted to visit her. I did not pick up the phone. The next morning, however, I took the first shower I had had in more than a month, put on clean clothes, and tied up my now very long hair in a sort of bun. I tried to disguise the neglect of the last few weeks by putting on a rather over-the-top outfit, and I think the result was more than acceptable. I had not set foot in the métro since Tom's death. Luckily, the clinic was at the other end of town via a different line. I got out at Montparnasse and walked towards the hospital. After signing in at reception, I called the lift and went up to the fifth floor, where the nursery was: two rows of incubators, not unlike the aquariums in the Jardin des Plantes. The newborns moved as slowly as anemones beneath the water. It was a breeding center—there is no better way to describe the impression I got from the place. I asked which one was my friends' daughter and they pointed out a beautiful little body, dark as Rajeev, and wrapped in a pink blanket. As soon as I saw her, I began to cry. The nurse immediately assumed it was from happiness and, although I did not fully realize it then, I do not think she was wrong. I did not have the energy to explain, nor the necessary clarity. And so I decided to leave without going to the room where Haydée was resting after her caesarean. I left the clinic feeling disconcerted. The image of the little girl stayed with me all night long, like a soft, persistent little light.

A month and a half later, tired of calling my house without success, Haydée and Rajeev came to look for me in my apartment with their baby. As often happened, as I had left the house that morning I had left the door open without realizing. Haydée tells me that the smell was almost unbearable. They took advantage of the child being asleep and the weather being warm and decided to air the place. They waited an hour for me to come back, sitting by the living-room window. It was Rajeev who happened to spot me down on one of the paths leading to the *columbarium*, but he did not say a word. He asked his wife to wait for a moment and, without any explanation, went out to find me. I do not remember any of this. I do not remember how he intercepted me, or the words he used to convince me to come back home. The only image I have now is Haydée sitting on the sofa in the living room with her now wide-awake daughter on her lap. I also recall that when I saw her, I felt the same tenderness that had made me cry that day in the nursery. Without asking me anything, they filled a bag with my clothes and drove me to their place, not the apartment on rue de Lévis, where I had first lived when I arrived in Paris, but a slightly larger one, in the 15th arrondissement, a dull, *petit-bourgeois* neighborhood far from any cemetery. I stayed at my friends' house for more than three months. At first, I simply helped Haydée to look after her daughter and the house. I had no desire to go out into the street, but they still begged me every morning not to go back to Père-Lachaise. And so, when I informed Madame Loeffler that I was going to leave the apartment, it was Rajeev who took care of putting my things into boxes and moving and storing them in their spacious basement. Unlike the apartment on rue de Lévis, this one was bright and significantly more modern. It had a larger room where they would put the little girl as soon she stopped sleeping with them, and which, in the meantime, I used. To help with the rent and food, I transferred 80 percent of my grant into Haydée's bank account. Sathya was the only source of happiness in that period of my life—and perhaps the greatest to this date. Seeing her smile, pat the table, or crawl around on the carpet made my sojourn through this world a little bit more bearable.

RETURN

I went back to New York one Saturday afternoon. Mario had come to get me from Boston in a rented car and we made the journey in silence, while the CD player played *Kind of Blue*. He helped me take my things up the stairs and then started pacing in circles like an animal shut up in the apartment. He seemed nervous about leaving me alone. When at last he left, I sat down in the armchair in the living room to look over the mail. Most of it was unpaid bills and invoices. I spent the entire afternoon sorting it out. In among all the envelopes I found a letter from my favorite nephew, in which he told me his school results. He was an exemplary student. He also described his day-to-day life in detail, and at the end, just before signing off, begged me to come and visit him in Cuba. I folded the letter sadly. In spite of my circumstances, of which he was naturally totally ignorant, I regretted very much not being able to be at his side at an age when so much is being decided. I asked myself what right I had to grow old cut off in New York, while he, his entire youth ahead of him, grew up bereft of support. Then, when I listened to the messages on the answering machine, I recognized Ruth's voice welcoming me home. Gently, pleasantly, she insisted on inviting me to stay over that night. As in the best moments of our relationship, her girlish tone ended up convincing me. I picked up the receiver and dialed her apartment.

"I've just arrived," I told her. "Give me an hour to take a shower and unpack my suitcase. I'll be there for dinner."

Before getting into the shower I took off the prosthetic leg. I washed sitting on a plastic seat, with the aid of a walking stick. I sorrowfully admired my new leg's technical sophistication and recalled that some time back I had been thrown out of a restaurant for shouting that I wanted to be a robot. As I headed for Tribeca in a taxi, I thought about how hard it is for us human beings to maintain physical or psychological stability. I recalled the words of Juan Ramón Ribeyro, one of César Vallejo's most illustrious compatriots to whom Cecilia had introduced me: "Imperfect beings living in an imperfect world, we are condemned to find only crumbs of happiness." What is the alternative? Perhaps to accept our limits, our contradictions, our many needs; to try to be stronger than the weight of any guilt. To focus our talents on what we can do best, our minds on what we can best understand: one thing at a time. One life at a time. To live without losing, as much as is possible, the capacity to return to a center from where we can trust, hope, be happy right now in spite of it all, in spite of the pain and the certainty that life, essentially, is pain and impossibility. I continued thinking of this as I rode in the taxi. I arrived at Ruth's building and pressed the number of her apartment, surprised I still remembered it. Her voice came onto the intercom and I recognized that note of quivering excitement I had not heard for months. As soon as I opened the door, I was greeted by the smell of apple strudel, and the welcome feeling of someone returning home after a long journey.

A DAY IN THE COUNTRY

I decided to stay in Paris, partly to finish my studies, but mainly for Sathya. Making a huge effort to concentrate I finished my thesis and, once I got my diploma, began a doctorate, this time with a new supervisor. Recently, I have discovered that, as well as research, I am minded to write other sorts of things. In a stiff-backed red notebook I began to keep a kind of diary where I regularly note down the most important memories or scenes from my life that for some reason or other I am obsessed with. I like, for instance, to describe the people I have lived with and do not see anymore. I co-opt them as characters. Sometimes I mix them up, or invent plausible fates for them, benign or macabre. I do not know what value any of this has, as biography or literature, but what I can say is that I enjoy it and this is enough for me. Haydée reckons it is a good idea. According to her, I have a lot of experiences still to digest and I ought to make the most of being so introspective. Since I moved, and also since she got pregnant for the second time, I see her less and less, but this does not prevent us from enjoying intensely the time we do have together. On Saturday, for instance, I spent the morning with her and the little girl walking around Châtelet. We bought a couple of sandwiches and a salad and had an impromptu picnic in the gardens around the Tour Saint-Jacques. As her little girl crawled around next to us, we lay down to rest on the grass. Among the different subjects we talked about that day, Haydée asked me if I had heard from Claudio.

"He stopped writing to me a long time ago," I replied.

"He's probably still running, like Forrest Gump," she said, and we both laughed with a kind of mocking fondness.

Haydée's voice grew weaker as she was overcome by sleep. I was left in charge of Sathya. As I watched her crawl back and forth near the sandpit, I thought of the huge number of children who had never once interested me before. For a few months now, I have had the impression that I am seeing far more pregnant women on the street, starting with my best friend. Before we got to the tower, we took several turns with the buggy around place Joachim-du-Bellay, where a flock of kids was racing around like mad, precisely where the old Cimetière des Saints-Innocents used to be. I thought that, just as spring follows winter, making us forget its harshness year after year, so there will always be children running around and playing on top of our dead. And they, the children, were the ones who, while they would not consign our dead to oblivion, would best be able to renew our desire to live, despite the painful absence of our loved ones.

LITERATURE
is not the same thing as
PUBLISHING

Coffee House Press began as a small letterpress operation in 1972 and has grown into an internationally renowned nonprofit publisher of literary fiction, essay, poetry, and other work that doesn't fit neatly into genre categories.

Coffee House is both a publisher and an arts organization. Through our *Books in Action* program and publications, we've become interdisciplinary collaborators and incubators for new work and audience experiences. Our vision for the future is one where a publisher is a catalyst and connector.

FUNDER ACKNOWLEDGMENTS

Coffee House Press is an internationally renowned independent book publisher and arts nonprofit based in Minneapolis, MN; through its literary publications and *Books in Action* program, Coffee House acts as a catalyst and connector—between authors and readers, ideas and resources, creativity and community, inspiration and action.

Coffee House Press books are made possible through the generous support of grants and donations from corporations, state and federal grant programs, family foundations, and the many individuals who believe in the transformational power of literature. This activity is made possible by the voters of Minnesota through a Minnesota State Arts Board Operating Support grant, thanks to the legislative appropriation from the arts and cultural heritage fund. Coffee House also receives major operating support from the Amazon Literary Partnership, the Jerome Foundation, McKnight Foundation, Target Foundation, and the National Endowment for the Arts (NEA). To find out more about how NEA grants impact individuals and communities, visit www.arts.gov.

Coffee House Press receives additional support from the Elmer L. & Eleanor J. Andersen Foundation; the David & Mary Anderson Family Foundation; Bookmobile; the Buuck Family Foundation; Fredrikson & Byron, P.A.; Dorsey & Whitney LLP; the Fringe Foundation; Kenneth Koch Literary Estate; the Knight Foundation; the Matching Grant Program Fund of the Minneapolis Foundation; Mr. Pancks' Fund in memory of Graham Kimpton; the Schwab Charitable Fund; Schwegman, Lundberg & Woessner, P.A.; the U.S. Bank Foundation; and VSA Minnesota for the Metropolitan Regional Arts Council.

THE PUBLISHER'S CIRCLE OF COFFEE HOUSE PRESS

Publisher's Circle members make significant contributions to Coffee House Press's annual giving campaign. Understanding that a strong financial base is necessary for the press to meet the challenges and opportunities that arise each year, this group plays a crucial part in the success of Coffee House's mission.

Recent Publisher's Circle members include many anonymous donors, Suzanne Allen, Patricia A. Beithon, the E. Thomas Binger & Rebecca Rand Fund of the Minneapolis Foundation, Andrew Brantingham, Robert & Gail Buuck, Claire Casey, Louise Copeland, Jane Dalrymple-Hollo, Mary Ebert & Paul Stembler, Kaywin Feldman & Jim Lutz, Chris Fischbach & Katie Dublinski, Sally French, Jocelyn Hale & Glenn Miller, the Rehael Fund-Roger Hale/Nor Hall of the Minneapolis Foundation, Randy Hartten & Ron Lotz, Dylan Hicks & Nina Hale, William Hardacker, Randall Heath, Jeffrey Hom, Carl & Heidi Horsch, the Amy L. Hubbard & Geoffrey J. Kehoe Fund, Kenneth Kahn & Susan Dicker, Stephen & Isabel Keating, Kenneth Koch Literary Estate, Cinda Kornblum, Jennifer Kwon Dobbs & Stefan Liess, Lambert Family Foundation, Lenfestey Family Foundation, Sarah Lutman & Rob Rudolph, the Carol & Aaron Mack Charitable Fund of the Minneapolis Foundation, George & Olga Mack, Joshua Mack & Ron Warren, Gillian McCain, Malcolm S. McDermid & Katie Windle, Mary & Malcolm McDermid, Sjur Midness & Briar Andresen, Maureen Millea Smith & Daniel Smith, Peter Nelson & Jennifer Swenson, Enrique & Jennifer Olivarez, Alan Polsky, Marc Porter & James Hennessy, Robin Preble, Alexis Scott, Ruth Stricker Dayton, Jeffrey Sugerman & Sarah Schultz, Nan G. & Stephen C. Swid, Kenneth Thorp in memory of Allan Kornblum & Rochelle Ratner, Patricia Tilton, Joanne Von Blon, Stu Wilson & Melissa Barker, Warren D. Woessner & Iris C. Freeman, Margaret Wurtele, and Wayne P. Zink & Christopher Schout.

For more information about the Publisher's Circle and other ways to support Coffee House Press books, authors, and activities, please visit www.coffeehousepress.org/support or contact us at info@coffeehousepress.org.

RECENT LATIN AMERICAN TRANSLATIONS
FROM COFFEE HOUSE PRESS

Among Strange Victims
Daniel Saldaña París
Translated by Christina MacSweeney

Camanchaca
Diego Zuñíga
Translated by Megan McDowell

Comemadre
Roque Larraquy
Translated by Heather Cleary

Empty Set
Verónica Gerber Bicecci
Translated by Christina MacSweeney

Faces in the Crowd
Valeria Luiselli
Translated by Christina MacSweeney

The Story of My Teeth
Valeria Luiselli
Translated by Christina MacSweeney

ROSALIND HARVEY is an award-winning literary translator and a teaching fellow at the University of Warwick. She has worked on books by Guadalupe Nettel, Elvira Navarro, Enrique Vila-Matas, and Héctor Abad Faciolince, among others.

After the Winter was designed by
Bookmobile Design & Digital Publisher Services.
Text is set in Cycles Eleven.